Earth Legacy

ENLIGHTENMENT

LAURIE RYAN

www.laurieryanauthor.com

EARTH LEGACY SERIES

Survival
Enlightenment
Birthright

Earth Legacy
ENLIGHTENMENT

LAURIE RYAN

DEDICATION

To Alaina.
For being such an avid reader,
and for your brainstorming
and your unwavering support.

PROLOGUE

The girl walked into the large cave with sure steps but faltered when she saw destruction all around her. Some epic battle must have occurred there. She side-stepped boulders and rocks that were tossed around like playing stones and walked past gaping fissures in the walls to make her way to a circular stone table in the center of the cave. The man who'd told her about this place had said a single person caused this damage. That seemed unlikely. If it were true, magic must have been the ruin of this place. Strong magic, by the damage done.

Marta hadn't believed him. Still, she'd decided to see for herself. She ran her hands along the flat surface of the rock table. The stone altar, the lone structure that remained unscathed, thrummed as if calling to her. A golden light, the color of her hair, emanated from the altar's center, so weak it barely illuminated the cavern.

Bumps rippled across Marta's arms and she pulled

her long tresses over her shoulder, pressing them tight to her skin to calm the hairs on the back of her neck. She glanced around the cave and saw nothing, yet the sensation of being watched was overwhelming. Turning back to the light, she bit her lip. She'd never seen light like this. What was it? Could it be magic? Had this light given strength to whoever had destroyed this cave?

Deep longing filled her. She wanted that power. She'd always known her destiny extended beyond the life of a goatherd's daughter in a small village barely able to sustain itself. That belief had brought her to this cave. At eighteen, her family expected her to do her part, herding goats, cooking, cleaning. Endowed with a natural beauty and lithe form, Marta was not designed for menial labor and never would be.

She rubbed her trim waist and flat stomach. More than ready to step into her future, she reached toward the light.

"I suggest you not do that."

Marta leaped back. The voice, deep yet obviously female, came from nowhere, and everywhere. Inside her head, echoing off the walls of the cave. She turned in all directions, seeing no one until a shadow separated itself from the wall. A very tall shadow.

Gulping back a cry, she fought back the fear that screamed at her to run as the thing loomed over her. A cowled cape hid everything except golden eyes. Marta peered closer, unable to see any face. Darkness obscured everything except those shining orbs.

"You're the one with the power," she said, more to herself than to the apparition in front of her.

The giant floated around her, invading her space. Marta stood still and ramrod straight. She cowered before no one, even if the smell of decay made her want to gag.

"You like the idea of power."

Marta raised her chin. "I am destined for great things."

"You have much pride," the ethereal voice said as the apparition came to a stop in front of Marta.

Marta looked straight into the soulless eyes. "A deserved pride."

"Hmm. Too much, I think." The hooded head cocked to one side. "Still, you remind me of someone I once knew. And that pride may be of use."

"Who are you?"

The shape straightened and grew even taller, if that were possible. "I am Taegar. I am the *isa*, that which provides clarity to the world and bends it to my righteous path. I am *thurisaz*, creator of chaos, and *tiwaz*, ruler of all. I am the Dark circle."

A druid circle? Marta had heard the rumors. How the druids tried to help mankind when the magic first showed up, inevitably causing the Great Magic War that had almost destroyed Earth. That long-ago battle had led to the mundane, deficient life she'd been forced to live. She'd heard there were once great cities with lights that did not flicker and machines that carried you along so you didn't have to walk everywhere.

Marta wanted that life. She resented those who'd taken it away before she'd even had a say in the matter.

"Your kind destroyed my destiny," Marta said, contempt dripping from every word.

Suddenly, she was picked up by nothing but air and thrown across the cave. She thudded against the wall, her head smacking rock. Pain radiated through her body as she crumpled to the floor like a cloth doll.

"Be careful what you say and how you say it, pretty girl." The voice grew deafening, reverberating off the walls, crashing through Marta's head like thunder until she covered her ears. "Your words will cause you much pain if you do not censure them."

When the voice died away, Marta looked up to see that the druid stood beside the altar, looking into the dim light, mumbling to herself.

Maybe this wasn't such a good idea. Marta stood and wiped her hands on her dress, glancing back the way she'd entered.

"Do not try to leave. We are not done with our conversation." Taegar beckoned. "Come here."

An invisible force dragged Marta forward. Today had quickly gone from bad to worse. She needed to do something soon or she would not survive this encounter.

At the altar, the force dissipated with such speed that Marta barely stopped herself from falling. She'd about had it with this Taegar, playing with her like she was some toy. She glared at the caped figure. "I think it's time for me to leave."

"Not yet. I have a use for you."

"Well, I don't—"

Marta's ability to talk disappeared. She tried to speak, to scream, cough, anything. Nothing came out.

A thin, bony finger reached out and lifted Marta's chin until no choice remained except to stare into the golden eyes. "You will do as I wish, or you will die."

For the first time, probably in her whole existence, Marta knew deep, clenching fear. It permeated her, consumed her until her body shook with the need to flee, to run until she was so far away from this place no one could ever find her.

The hand, or whatever it was, lowered, pointing at her chest.

I'm going to die.

"You will not die," Taegar said.

Marta slumped against the altar.

"Not if you do exactly as I tell you."

Taegar opened her hand to reveal several small stones. Not ordinary stones. These had symbols on them. They were runes. Marta had seen them once before, when a self-proclaimed shaman tried to convert everyone by making them believe he was magical and able to conjure up a better life. All he'd really wanted was their food, and they'd run him out of town after only a few days.

Turning back to the altar, Taegar reached into the light, whispering words in a language Marta had never heard. At first, nothing happened. The whispering strengthened. The light sputtered as it fought the demands upon it. The ground shook. When everything stopped and the light disappeared, Marta gasped. One second, two seconds, more, then it roared to life, so bright it hurt her eyes.

Golden light shot from Taegar's hand into Marta's chest, weak at first, then gaining strength. Taegar's eyes flashed brighter. Power flowed into Marta. She grew warm, then hot, burning with a magic that screamed through her body, knowing without a doubt she could do anything now. She had the magic. She was supreme. And she would have anyone and anything she desired.

The light shooting into her dimmed, then faded completely as Taegar lowered her arm, releasing the magic back to the weak stream that came from the rock. Marta looked at her hands. A new tattoo marked her palm, an upward pointing arrow with a thorn on its stem.

She flexed and straightened her fingers, still tingling from head to toe. She felt the magic humming inside her. She'd never known such power. Her power. The life she deserved lay within her grasp.

Marta held her hand out toward the wall. She visualized a fireball and one shot from her fingertips, making her jump back. The cave wall in front of her exploded in a shower of rock.

Oh, yes, she planned to enjoy this gift a lot. Still, she'd learned the hard way that everything came with a price. Would great power require a great price? She glanced up at the figure who leaned against the altar.

"Yes, pretty girl, there is a price. This power is more than I've given anyone, but it will not last forever. There is a task you must do for me. If you accomplish it, I will make your powers permanent.

The light in the center of the altar was now almost invisible. She glanced at the wall, watched the dust settle to show the gaping hole in the rock. She'd done that with a simple thought. Who cared about the task? This reward was worth any price, so Marta turned back to Taegar.

"What do you need me to do?"

DECISIONS

CHAPTER ONE

Too much had changed in a few short years. It seemed unfathomable to Kaiden Darcy. He'd been twelve when Rianthe Royan stumbled into his arms and wormed her way deep under his skin. Then, he'd betrayed her and she'd run. Kaiden didn't blame her. He might have done the same thing in her boots.

Now she'd come home again, except nothing was the same. Half their home lay in ashed ruins, destroyed by a Dark druid who'd been hunting Rianthe. Kaiden was True-Named *thurisaz*, protector, yet his magic wasn't strong enough to save anyone. Torn between his impulse to protect Rianthe and his loyalty to the people who'd taken him in as a babe, it was no wonder he felt so conflicted. Add in the dark dreams he'd been having ever since the injury, and folks barely spoke to him these days.

Kaiden rubbed his shoulder and moved his arm to ease the ever-present ache. Roulf had said the poison would be slow to ebb. The funny little man had entered their lives almost as quickly as their mentor Bhren had left and had been a huge help. Time proved him right once again. More than five weeks had passed and Kaiden still couldn't fight like normal. Like he needed to.

Blowing out a breath, he watched it mist in the cool air. Patience didn't come easy for him, especially with his own performance. He was the designated protector of New Hope. He couldn't do that and keep Rianthe from harm unless he was healed and whole. Right now, even finding her seemed impossible. She'd disappeared yet again, which irked Kaiden to no end as he walked to the new Druid's Keep, the only two-story structure in New Hope.

He peeked inside.

"She's not here," Tevy said as he passed Kaiden in the doorway. Tevy, Rianthe's twelve-year-old brother, shared the living area with his sister.

"Where is she?"

Tevy laughed. "If you can't keep up with her, how do you expect me to?"

Kaiden scowled and swiped dark hair away from his face. Rianthe always said their friend Mokie had the magic of stealth, but she must be touched with some of that ability herself. When she wanted to, she disappeared faster than he could pull his sword free of its scabbard.

"Where are your wolves?"

"Gone to hunt." Tevy's face clouded over, unusual for the bright, happy youngling that spent much of his time making others smile. Tamping down the boy's perennial wish to be with the wolves was no easy task, for Rianthe, for him, or for anyone in New Hope. After their parents had been killed, Rianthe had staggered into

New Hope with her eight-year-old brother trailing behind and the newborn Tevy in her arms. The entire village had taken on raising the newborn. Kaiden was the same age then as Tevy was now. A lot had happened since then.

"Aren't you supposed to be at Studies?" Kaiden asked.

Tevy ducked his head.

"Better get over there now."

"Ahh, do I have to?"

"Yes." With a chuckle, Kaiden shooed the boy off to learn things. The sound of his own mirth seemed foreign to him these days and fell off too quickly. When had he last felt joy? The remnants of his smile disappeared. It had been a long time.

Shaking his head, Kaiden strode across New Hope's central commons to the dining house, the longest building in New Hope. Enough of it survived the fires that it was close to complete again. The kitchens sat at the far end. Because of the ovens, it happened to be the warmest place in New Hope, outside of the smithy. Most people spent their spare time there even without the worst of the snows yet upon them. The day's air had a definite chill to it, though, and the nights were downright cold.

Jonah, Kaiden's adopted father and the leader of their little village, stepped through as Kaiden reached for the door.

"Good morning, son." Jonah settled a light hand on Kaiden's good shoulder, but the vibration still set off a jolt of pain in his healing one.

Jonah frowned. "How's the injury?"

"Good days and bad."

"Give it time. It will heal. Didn't that man you met along the way, Roulf, tell you that?"

"Yes." Kaiden compressed his lips. He didn't like talking about his own shortcomings. He should be the strongest one in the village, not the weakest, or close to it.

"Raisa's been working with you?"

"Yes." Few could call upon the *awen* since the Great Magic War, and most of them lived in New Hope thanks to the druid Bhren, who'd gathered them there. New Hope was *wunjo*, filled with sympathetic people who only wanted to live in harmony with Earth. They'd been on the edge of success, too, until the village had been decimated by Deakon, Taegar's acolyte. The loss of Bhren in the fires had been a great blow to New Hope and to the future of Earth and humankind. He'd been the last of the Guardian druids and they tried hard to continue his fight. If they failed, there was no hope.

Soon, that battle would resume. Taegar, the Dark druid who'd almost destroyed them once already, had part of the talisman meant to bind Earth's *awen* to her for all time. Not the entire talisman, though. Rianthe held the runes that completed the set. Taegar would come for them. Everyone knew it. All dreaded it. At the moment, they were busy nursing their wounds.

Raisa, who'd raised Kaiden as her own son, possessed healing magic. That was her special talent. Even suppressed, as all their talents seemed to be since Earth's magic vanished, she could help.

"She's been trying to help," Kaiden told Jonah. "I'm not the best patient." Daily, she'd chased him down daily to sit with her so she could work to heal his wound more quickly. She'd admonished him to stay off the training fields, something that would never happen. "I wish my shoulder would heal faster." Time to change the subject. "Is Rianthe in there?" He pointed behind Jonah to the dining house.

Jonah shook his head. "I haven't seen her yet this morning."

Kaiden sighed, his frustration growing. "If you see her, please tell her I'm looking for her." Not that it would do any good. Rianthe avoided him whenever possible. They'd come a long way from the days when he'd been her closest confidant, from the nights when he'd held her to keep her safe. A long way.

Shaking his head, Kaiden realized he knew where she'd gone. He strode out of the main village. He passed the growing fields, now mostly fallowed for the winter. Further, he passed the Hallows, the remembrance fields where they'd held the *kenaz*, or death rites, too many times. Kaiden stopped for a moment as he always did, paying homage to those who'd given their lives to protect New Hope. So many stone markers. So much loss.

Relief flooded Kaiden when he found Rianthe at the place where he should have first looked, near where they'd spent many days making plans back before the world turned dark. Except she wasn't up on their plateau. She sat below it, at the lakeshore, staring out at the water. He frowned, unable to fathom her mood. He wanted to shake her for making him worry. He was her protector. He should remind her to respect that and to let him know when she left the village. Instead, he did what he always did these days. He remained back, away but close, ready but quiet, giving her the time she needed to think.

~~~

Rianthe Royan stared at the rocky promontory she knew better than any other place. Usually, it was an easy climb to the top of the craggy bluff. The early snowfall had melted, yet she could not scale it, weighed down by
~~~

the memories of a life she'd give almost anything to have again. Tainted memories now.

Turning her back on the rocks, she pulled her cloak tightly around her and settled against a pine tree in a grassy patch near the picturesque lake. Its waters always soothed her disquiet. Waters that should have been replenished by now, yet the lake seemed smaller than ever. Even the storms pelting the Rushmore Woods this fall had not raised the levels.

Lakes, trees, plants, everything seemed smaller, as if the world had closed in around them.

New Hope, her home, had survived harsh winters and arid summers before. This fall, since the burning, every negative nuance was worse. Now, dropping temperatures and ominous clouds forecast more snow.

They must survive it all. They had to.

Rianthe pulled her gloves off and glimpsed the signet ring on her forefinger. It still surprised her, seeing it there. The ring, one Bhren wore, had formed itself to the perfect size for her finger when he'd passed it to her.

She ran her hands over her hair. She'd kept it shorn for five years and had only stopped cutting it once she'd returned home. It was as long as her hand-length now, but a long way from the thick, dark lengths she'd spent so much time braiding as a child. Pushing her sleeve up, she smiled at the pictures of the Rushmore Woods that coiled around her arm. She'd added the tattoos to remind her of home during those years she'd been away.

Careful not to dig too deep, Rianthe parted the blades of grass in front of her. Brown lay beneath the reddish-green tips. Was this the normal color for this time of year or another change, another death blow to their environment? She should have paid more attention to

Uja's musings about soil and growth. Thoughts of Uja brought a piercing stab to her heart that still caught her off guard. When would she get used to her brother not being there to hug, to hold, to talk to?

Never.

Even gone, Uja helped them. His plan to start a second growing field further away had given them produce enough to sustain them while they regrouped. Still, not much remained, even with the bleak meals they'd eaten these past few weeks. New growth had recently been coaxed from seedlings in the warm, smudge pot stink of the growing hut. Hopefully, that, along with some hunting to nourish their need for protein, would get them through the winter.

Rianthe combed the grass, reveling in the freedom of not wearing gloves for once.

A new unease filled her of late. The sourness in the soil had not dissipated, but only she seemed to notice. It worried her. They stood on the precipice of danger. Taegar had been too quiet lately, waiting for who knew what. Her fury would return. Rianthe sensed it deep in her soul.

A pine cone smacked to the ground beside her, breaking in half as it hit, another portent of winter. Rianthe picked it up, surprised it was so dry after the recent storms. She glanced up at the tree. Did she see a hint of brown in the evergreen? Perusing the trees surrounding the lake, many had brown patches. Most were at the top while some rusted the middle. She didn't remember seeing this before, at least not to this degree. The early morning sun hung misty and shadowed in the sky, dimmer than she'd expect, even for this time of year.

A sorrowful sigh floated on the breeze, signaling

more change in the offing. Earth needed her. She was *sowilo*, the prophesied one expected to free Earth's magic and bring a better life to everyone. She'd been told this was her destiny so many times over the past few months it had become imprinted in her mind like the forest tattoo down her arm. Yet nothing from the past few years had helped her to understand her role in this life-and-death saga. If Earth possessed enough sentience to release power to heal itself as it had done before the Great Magic War, why didn't it give her a clearer sign of the way to help bring that magic back?

Even if Earth summoned her, she doubted she could answer the call. Rianthe tossed the pine cone to the ground beside her and watched it shatter into bits and pieces. She felt just as splintered. She didn't have the power everyone thought she should have. If she did, where was it hiding? She hadn't managed to save New Hope. So many had perished, including Uja, who'd given his life defending their home. He'd picked up a sword when all he really wanted to do was to make things grow. How could she help Earth when they needed her help right there in New Hope? They'd survived thus far, but winter was upon them and their struggles were just beginning. Everything inside her screamed this fight wasn't even close to finished.

She pulled the new leather pouch from around her neck. The day her father had given her the original bag was rooted deep in her memory. Both her parents had died that day. Rianthe had been left with two brothers to keep safe, one of which her mother had birthed only moments before her death.

Lighter now, the bag held only three runes. The remainder had been stolen and were most likely in the clutches of the golden-eyed Taegar. No rumblings had emanated from that one for a while. It worried Rianthe. What new torture did her nemesis plan for her? No. Not just her nemesis. Earth, and everyone who lived there was in danger of losing everything if Taegar could not be stopped and the magic brought back to its full, healing capability.

Rianthe shook the runes out into her hand. She'd been taught that an incomplete rune set was useless in foretelling.

The theory seemed worth testing and, one way or the other, she needed to know. Rianthe held the runes tight, chanting the words she knew so well. She turned her hand over, holding it a palm's breadth above the grass. If she held them and touched the soil, it might give her a clearer view. All she needed to do was reach down and touch Earth…

Her hand shook and she clutched it to her chest. She was not ready for that pain again. She'd been yanked into the *ehwaz*, the void between life and the dream world, too many times. Each instance, whether it be with Taegar or Earth, had almost killed her.

Someday, she might have no choice. Not this day.

Today, she had a village to see to. Bhren… Another stab of painful memory caught her unaware. The last of the Guardian druids had perished. Rianthe gazed at the ring again. The ring he'd given her on his deathbed. How he'd selected her, a twenty-three-year-old too full of fire and vinegar to settle down, was unfathomable. Yet he'd identified her as his successor in this village, where she'd lived in for most of her growing years.

Her life had seen so many changes. This lake would never again be the peaceful sanctuary of her youth. It was rare she even got a moment alone unless she was in the dratted tower Bhren had ordered rebuilt in the exact same spot as the original. Rianthe shook her head. That tower set her above everyone else and reminded her daily of her designation as the prophesied one. The one who would save them all. Except she hadn't been able to do one single thing to make their lives better so far.

What had Bhren seen that made him believe in her when she didn't even believe in herself? He'd been there when the magic was first revealed. Earth, fighting death from humankind's overuse of its resources, released magic to heal itself. Stories passed down through the years told how humanity tried to harness a power that enhanced the abilities of some but not others. Selfishness had caused a split in the druid circle formed to help man's evolution into this new way of living. The Guardian druids had wanted to help Earth and humankind live in harmony. Taegar had wanted to use the magic for her own selfish reasons. Then, and now. She'd defected to start the Dark circle, and now, she was the only druid left from the original group. None who remained could best her.

Except everyone thought Rianthe had that ability. Rianthe did not trust their belief. She didn't want to be the hope of the future. She just wanted to be left alone.

But she was not alone, this day or any other, despite her attempts to sneak away. He'd found her.

"Join me," she said quietly, knowing without having to turn around that he waited behind the nearby trees.

Dark-haired Kaiden, the boy-turned-man who used to be her best friend. Only one year older than her, his green eyes held a wealth of sorrow. A sorrow he worked very hard to hide. As his True-Naming had proclaimed, he'd become *thurisaz*. Protector of New Hope. And of her. He took that vocation very seriously, which meant he was rarely far from her side.

That constant presence had once been her deepest desire. Now, like the specs of pine cone remnants in her hand, little remained of what they'd been. And there was much to do before happier times could return or they could focus on each other.

Kaiden held his hand out, his tan much more pronounced than hers. In the few weeks since they'd come home, he'd worked tirelessly to help New Hope rebuild from the fire that had almost destroyed it. He put in longer hours than anyone else. Building, digging, whatever the need. Even with his injury, he pushed himself.

She reached up, the runes still cradled in her hand.

Kaiden grasped her hand. Skin-to-skin, with the runes between them, the strangest sensation spread through Rianthe. A warmth crept up her arm, a swirling blend of their energies that created something she didn't understand.

Kaiden's wide eyes matched hers.

Everything else faded. No cold breeze ruffled her short hair. No ripple lapped at the edge of the water. Nothing. There was only herself and Kaiden, connected at a deeper level than ever before. Gentle heat spread throughout her body, settling like a peaceful cocoon around her heart.

She saw Kaiden. Really saw him. Like the grains of sand in the dirt when she focused on the visions, she got a glimpse of the emotions he held at bay. The wonder at his own destiny, the confusion over where he'd come from, the overwhelming fear of something happening to…her.

Love. He loved—

Kaiden tore his hand from hers. "What the heck was that?" he asked, rubbing his hands together.

Rianthe didn't hear him at first, too awash in lingering emotions. She didn't move, didn't even blink, afraid it would all fade away. Kaiden, the man who hid everything, for whom duty overshadowed all else, was a wellspring of feelings. Awed at the privilege and power of this moment, she had trouble righting her world enough to even recognize he'd asked her a question.

"I—I don't know what that was," she answered him. "You felt that, right?"

"You mean seeing into that jumble of a brain you call a mind?" He tried to joke, but couldn't quite hide the same fear-tinged awe she felt.

Rianthe opened her hands, staring at the runes.

"Do you think they caused"—Kaiden gestured between them—"whatever this was?"

He rubbed his hands again, quick and hard, like trying to brush off something distasteful. Rianthe swallowed, trying to hide the hurt his reaction caused. For her, the sensations had not fully ebbed. She'd felt an infusion of, well, everything. She'd seen Kaiden, seen through him to his emotions, his strength, into his core. Even beyond, to Earth, to humanity. It was as if she'd gotten a glimpse into something larger than the world they lived in.

Something else hung in that space, too. A darkness, a thread of discontent in Kaiden, and an ache coming from somewhere deep within him that she'd not been able to see. Rianthe focused, trying to find the source of that elusive pain, but the last vestiges of their shared connection dissipated.

Surprised that it left such an empty chasm inside her, she reached out. She wanted so badly to reestablish the connection, but she didn't know how to build the bridge.

Kaiden took a step back, making it impossible for her to touch him. Rianthe squeezed her eyes shut against another sting of pain. He didn't want to touch her, or to know her in the way they'd just been privileged to share. This hurt on such a deep level it shocked her. They'd been close all those years ago. Maybe… Maybe too much had happened for them to go back.

She missed that more than she thought she could bear.

"You always have your gloves on." Kaiden's bemusement showed in the quiet tone of his voice. He leaned down, picked her gloves off the ground and handed them to her.

Rianthe opened her eyes. He was right. Ever since she'd been yanked into the *ehwaz* when she connected with Earth through contact with its soil, bringing visions with real-life consequences, Rianthe had worn gloves. She put the runes back inside the new bag her sister-in-law, Fraka, had made for her, then took her gloves. She was grateful for them, yet frustrated that she must wear them all the time. Would she now go through this with everyone and never be allowed contact with anything? Would Earth require that sacrifice, to never touch or be touched?

There was too much they didn't know about Earth's magic and how it worked. It had somehow been suppressed or all but destroyed in the Great Magic War. Bhren, who'd taught both Kaiden and herself, had died before finishing their instruction. Now, they floundered around like fledgling birds learning to fly.

"I wish Bhren were here," Kaiden said, as if reading her mind.

"Do you really think he'd give us answers?" The old druid had shown more interest in adding to the puzzle than in solving it.

Kaiden's laugh was more of a sharp bark. He nodded, but Rianthe knew he'd never completely agree with her. He'd been closer to Bhren than anyone. Bhren had saved him as an infant and Kaiden had spent his life showing the druid his gratitude.

"Do you… Do you worry about Taegar? Things have been quiet. I can't believe she would give up." Rianthe squeezed the gloves in her hand, wringing them tight.

"I worry."

Of course. Kaiden worried about everything.

"She isn't gone," he said.

"Agreed."

"So we must be vigilant."

Rianthe sighed. "Just once, it would be nice to let down our guard. To be here, now, content." She yearned for peace, not just with each other, but with the life and land around them. They fought so hard for every scrap of existence they had. When would they be able to rest?

Kaiden stared out over the lake, keeping his thoughts to himself. He'd always done that. Nowadays, that annoying habit seemed worse than ever. With every silence, a wedge drove deeper into their relationship and he pulled farther away.

"We'd better get back." He turned to her and held out a hand to indicate she should go first. This Kaiden, she was familiar with. Stoic, focused on duty, rarely smiling.

Rianthe missed the rare Kaiden she'd just glimpsed.

Somehow, someday, she wanted to bring out that side of him. To help the world see what she knew, that love and laughter lived inside him, along with everything good in this world.

For now, finding food and building more shelters to house the almost one hundred people who'd survived the fires was their priority. The monotony of their changed lives nagged at Rianthe. Today would be exactly like yesterday and tomorrow. At times, she balked at the never-ending chores of day-to-day survival. That was usually when she remembered how desperately dangerous the past few weeks had been, and that the danger would return. This was a brief respite in the struggle to free the magic to improve Earth and help humanity.

Somehow thrust to the forefront of the battle, she did not look forward to the next volley. So for now, to focus on food and shelter was enough. Tomorrow might be another story, but she'd figure that out then.

She turned to follow Kaiden, her hand brushing up against the tree as she passed. Rianthe gasped at the sudden flash of burning pain that filled her.

Kaiden was beside her in an instant. "What happened?"

She took deep breaths and rubbed her hands. "I don't know."

"Another vision?"

"Not really. More of a…a feeling. From Earth, I think. Pain. Intense, and…loss. It was only there for a moment."

"Did you touch the soil?"

She shook her head. "The tree."

"Without your gloves on." Kaiden yanked the gloves

from her and thrust them toward her one at a time, refusing to budge until she pulled them on.

"Do you have any idea what it meant?" he asked when they resumed walking.

"No." She truly didn't know, except for a strange worry that a little more of Earth's magic had just been stolen away. And that Earth had moved a little closer to the tipping point that would mean certain death — for Earth, humankind, and every living thing that eked out an existence there.

CHAPTER TWO

Kaiden paced outside the communal hut where most of the village slept these days. It was tiring, always having to search for Rianthe when it would take no time for her to tell him her plans. Was he so terrible to be around? And that—that thing that had happened between them. He pounded one fist into the other. What was that? Everything that defined Rianthe had been tossed at him like a fireball, all jumbled up, invading his psyche. It hurt to think that fast. Plus, he'd been stripped naked. She'd seen it all. The things he kept inside, buried deep, waiting for the day duty and protection weren't paramount. They had flown straight into her. The look in her eyes had told him she'd understood everything.

She wasn't supposed to see that. Not yet. Maybe not ever. How could he do what he needed to do if she knew of this weakness in him?

Kaiden tried to push the frustration and confusion away, to let it go. Not an easy thing to do. He doubted Rianthe would forget what she'd seen in him. Could either of them forget? He clenched his jaw, jittery and about to explode. He needed something to help slough off all of this, an outlet for all his bottled-up energy.

With a quick decision, Kaiden, who always wore his sword and scabbard these days, strode toward the training fields. He yanked off his shirt as he went, the cold no bother to his boiling need to release stress. A few people were practicing and Mokie stood off to the side, watching.

Kaiden pointed to the sword laying on the ground beside Mokie. "Want to spar?"

Mokie eyed him warily. "You going to take it easy on me?"

"Not my style."

"I know." Mokie sighed as he reached for his sword.

The familiar well of energy flowed into Kaiden. Every time he fought, practice or real, the sensation of power reminded him of who he was. He was *thurisaz*. Protector. He would kill whoever harmed those under his care. He would prevail. He would protect.

He would win.

Kaiden stalked his prey, watching for weaknesses, waiting for the first strike. When it came, he was ready. He'd always be ready. Sword to sword, he'd pit his strength against anyone.

Battling, even on the training fields, was the only thing these days that kept the darkness inside him at bay.

~~~

After Kaiden left her at the druid's tower that had become her home, Rianthe climbed the crude stairs to the
~~~

second floor destroyed by the fire and now almost completely enclosed and roofed. Standing in front of the unshuttered window, she watched New Hope begin its day and tried to figure out what to do next. Apparently, getting some much needed quiet time at the lake was not an option.

Fraka walked across the commons with Rianthe's newling nephew, Ujami, bundled to her chest. As on most mornings, she was likely headed to the fields to coax late growth out of the few viable vegetables covered and warmed by smudge pots. Tow-headed Tevy greeted Fraka as he headed in the opposite direction, probably to gather eggs, one of his daily chores. Rianthe wondered at the absence of his wolves. Most mornings the pack was with him.

Even at twelve-years-old, Tevy would rather be with those animals of his than with humans. Only a thin wall separated their bedrooms, and she heard him sneak off to the as-yet-unroofed barn each night soon after he wished her good sleep. Of course, Tevy's ability to mind-speak with the wolves made that understandable. They were as much family to him as she was.

We are all family, mind-spoke Taschia, the only female wolf among the pack of siblings, and Rianthe's friend.

Where are you? Rianthe asked. Unlike Tevy, she could not speak with all the wolves, only the sister-wolf she'd bonded with.

I hunt with my brothers.

Rianthe heard the smile in Taschia's voice. Nothing pleased her friend more than the hunt. *Good hunting, sister.*

Food is not here. We range far.

Tevy disappeared around a corner. Rianthe knew he missed his wolves when they hunted. Given the right encouragement, he'd probably race off with them. Not to hunt, but to share the experience. They were definitely close. Rianthe smiled as she ran her hand over wood being planed for a new table. All of New Hope had become Tevy's family after they'd arrived. The whole town took on the raising of him, especially during Rianthe's five-year absence. Tevy got pretty much whatever he wanted. While he wasn't the youngest anymore—Rianthe looked in the direction Fraka had gone with baby Ujami—Tevy's happy disposition was a rare bright spot in a town struggling to survive. Raising Tevy wasn't difficult except when he had to be torn away from those wolves for studies and chores. Then, it was another story completely.

Unsure of what to do, she watched as more people stirred. The sound of clanging swords from the training fields helped her decide. Rianthe deserted the shelves built for tomes yet to be written and ran down the stairs. She grabbed her sword, which had seen too much duty of late, and left the tower. The tower in which Kaiden had deftly ensconced Tevy rather than himself, muttering something flimsy about not disturbing her with his early hours.

Kaiden had taken the small outbuilding attached to the back of the tower for himself. Normally, it held wood and tools and such. He'd cleaned it out in record time in order to settle there. Close enough to protect, but not too close.

"Rianthe, a moment."

She stopped and waited as Jonah approached. He and Raisa were Fraka's parents, and they'd also taken in

Kaiden as a babe to raise as their own. After the druid Bhren's death, Jonah had become New Hope's leader by an unspoken but unanimous decision. Jonah's graying long hair, looped into a bun at the back of his head, was damp, and the sweat on his face proved he'd either been helping at the smithy or in the smoking shed. Judging from the smell when he stopped in front of her, the shed was the correct answer.

He wiped a hand across his brow. "I've been checking our store of meat."

Suppressing the desire to tell him she knew that, Rianthe nodded. "How are things?"

"Not good. We've enough for a week or thereabouts, but no more."

Since she'd returned, she thought they'd been hunting enough game to both feed the village and add to their stores. "Only a week's worth?"

Jonah nodded. "We've sent hunting parties out in each of the last two days. They've found nothing. It's as if the boars, everything has suddenly disappeared."

Rianthe frowned. Winters were not bad enough that animals ranged south, so there was usually plentiful game around the village. Back before everything changed, she and Kaiden used to go out by themselves. The intimacy of those quiet searches remained a fond memory for her. Going out with the parties these days wasn't the same. She'd dodged most of them since her return, but only because she'd thought New Hope was well-stocked.

"I planned to ask Kaiden to take a group out again tomorrow," Jonah said.

"I'm heading to the training fields. I'll ask him. And I'll join the hunters. I'm sorry, Jonah. I didn't realize we were in such straits."

"I know you've had other worries." Jonah placed a hand on her shoulder. The man's innate ability to read people, to know their troubles and problem-solve, seemed almost magical. Another of the reasons Bhren had brought him there. Everyone in the village had some latent magical ability, though it wasn't always apparent. Sometimes, it seemed as if Jonah looked right inside her. "Still having those nightmares?" he asked.

Though Rianthe squirmed under his gaze, she didn't want to talk about the ghastly dreams that crowded her nights, much less remember them. She nodded. "Not every night like before, but yes."

"Still working through them alone?"

Red heat suffused her face. Did the man know Kaiden joined her at night all those years ago? That he used to hold her as the nightly terrors invaded her mind? It had been too long. She missed that. Missed the Kaiden she'd known then. Now, instead of being with her, he settled for only being near enough to keep her safe.

Battle changed one's priorities, it seemed.

Jonah didn't need an answer. He knew. He squeezed her shoulder. "Give him time. A lot has happened."

Horrified at the sting of tears in her eyes, Rianthe shrugged off Jonah's hand and turned away. "I'll ask Kaiden about hunting tomorrow," she said.

"Appreciated," Jonah said, then headed off to whatever task lay next on his list.

Rianthe saw the growing fields off in the distance. Fraka wasn't the only one working this early in the morning. A few people had pulled the coverings back from the small section that still held some produce. They worked their way through the row, searching out anything usable, watering others in the hopes of coaxing a bit of growth from them, or refilling the smudge pots to warm them.

At the edge of the training fields, Rianthe stopped to watch Kaiden spar. He seemed almost healed from his wound, but she knew better. He hid the pain, hid the darkness. Physically, he tried to be the Kaiden who'd shown up in the Fringes looking for her five years after she'd disappeared, after he'd grown into manhood, fully vested in his job as protector. She remembered when she'd first met him. She'd only been ten years old when she and her brothers had arrived in New Hope, exhausted and half-starved from weeks of travel. Twelve-year-old Kaiden had championed the village's efforts to help them and had been her closest friend from then on. Well, except for that time she'd hated him. He'd betrayed her, hidden the truth of her True-Naming from her, something that was hard to forgive or forget.

Bhren had named her *elhaz*, animal handler, when she'd expected *thurisaz*, like Kaiden. Or even *sowilo*, the one sent to guide them to enlightenment. Kaiden had known what would happen. He let her walk into her coming-of-age ceremony blind. Because of that, she'd run away and returned too late to save even the animals when Taegar's acolyte set fire to New Hope in an attempt to find the bag of runes she carried. The runes meant to both release Earth's magic and bind it to the wielder of the talisman.

Now she was twenty-three, Kaiden only a year and a half older. They were both battle-tested. The last battle had almost killed him. Five weeks ago, he'd been close to death. Now, he trained, or worked to rebuild, for hours every day. Kaiden pushed himself too hard. She'd tried to tell him that, but there was no arguing with protector

Kaiden. Duty over everything. That was his motto. Thank goodness his sword arm hadn't been injured.

His shirtless body gleamed with sweat even with the morning chill. Squinting, she saw a sort of glow, an aura surrounding him. A sign of his magic-enhanced skills? Bhren had mentioned once that he'd become stronger after being named *thurisaz* at his True-Naming. She'd certainly had to work harder to keep up with him and rarely—okay, never—bested him. She had significant skills of her own, but that didn't help against Kaiden.

He must have been on the field for a while already, yet he still showed enough energy to attack Mokie, who was two years younger than Rianthe. Kaiden beat him back, strike after strike.More intense these days, Kaiden seemed solely centered on the fight. Some of the intensity came from battle-hardening, but lately, his passion showed the tinge of anger. Mokie was losing. He soon went to a knee, which signaled the end of their sparring. Rianthe stepped in.

"Care to continue?" she asked.

Kaiden barely broke stride, whipping his sword in her direction. Rianthe was ready. Back and forth across the field they fought, swords clashing, sweat flying. Rianthe grunted with the effort, proud of her ability to match his ferocity.

"Halt," she finally called, knowing Kaiden wouldn't stop until she did. They both bent over, hands on knees as they scraped for air to fill their lungs.

"I should make you say it," Kaiden said.

Rianthe grinned. Throughout their years of training, he'd made her call him Almighty Kaiden each time he bested her.

"Never."

Kaiden hefted his sword. "That is a challenge I will make you regret." A rare smile made his green eyes shine as he sheathed his sword. "But not today."

He wore a beard now. Not long or scruffy, like most of the men. He kept his fairly close to his skin. His dark beard and shaggy hair were a stark contrast to the lake green color of his eyes. She could stare into those eyes for an eternity if he'd let her. To have him stare back at her with the same emotions… Well, she needed to bury that desire deep since that wouldn't happen anytime soon. Kaiden had drawn the line. She'd sensed his feelings for her at the lake this morning, but he'd distanced himself again so quickly she seriously doubted whether she'd really felt that kindred emotion from him. Either way, he would not give in to it. Duty came first and foremost to Kaiden. Duty to Bhren, their druid teacher, may he rest in peace. Duty to this village, and duty to Earth. Nothing impeded that duty, not even love.

The only consolation was that Kaiden never noticed how the girls in the village stared at him. More than one had tried to catch him. Time and again he turned them away.

Good thing, too. Because if Kaiden didn't turn them away, Rianthe would. She ran her hands down the flat length of her sword. She might even enjoy it, considering the audacity of their attempts.

"Looks like that needs sharpening," Kaiden said, eyeing her sword. "Mine needs a better edge too. Want to visit the smithy?"

Rianthe nodded, sliding her sword back into its scabbard.

Walking through the village filled Rianthe with a fleeting contentment, so foreign to her now. The past few weeks had been rough. On the heels of the fire, winter approached, harsher than Rianthe ever remembered. But New Hope was resilient. Working together, they would survive.

"Good day, Rianthe and Kaiden," Fraka said, coming out of the kitchens with curly haired Raisa.

"Good day," they answered at the same time. Kaiden kissed his mother's cheek.

Rianthe took her nephew, Ujami, from Fraka's arms. The boy, a shy two–full-moons old, already reminded her of his father, Uja. Dear, sweet, gentle Uja. That pain of losing him still cut deep. To never see his smile again…

Ujami looked up at her, his big, dark brown eyes very much like her brother's. He grinned and reached out, finding Rianthe's nose almost by accident and making her laugh. It was hard to stay sad when such a good part of Uja lived in this little one. Rianthe hugged him tight.

"I still miss him so," Rianthe whispered into Ujami's neck.

Fraka placed a hand on her shoulder, sadness darkening her eyes. "We all do."

Rianthe nodded, working hard to set that melancholy aside. It accomplished nothing. "Have you had breakfast already?" Rianthe asked Fraka.

"Yes. We need to check on the new plant starts in the growing hut. You should see how good Ujami is with them," Fraka said, enthusiasm shining in her voice. "He can't do anything on a large scale, of course, but already each plant he touches grows better."

Rianthe hugged Ujami tighter, remembering the warning from Roulf, a druid apprentice who'd helped her and Kaiden in their quest to find the man who'd burned their home. He'd advised Rianthe about using magic, even though she hadn't been able to tap any power since that event. *Don't let the magic use you up,* he'd said.

"Maybe he shouldn't do too much," she whispered to Fraka, not wishing to usurp her sister-in-law's role as Ujami's mother.

"Oh, I don't let him," she said. "We spend a little time in the field, then the rest of the day is all about being a babe."

"That sounds perfect. And my nephew is clearly a happy newling." Rianthe returned Ujami's grin as his hand wrapped around her fingers and her heart yet again.

"There's porridge for breakfast," Raisa said.

Rianthe groaned inwardly. Food was food in this age of sparseness, but porridge had become an unwelcome daily staple.

"And eggs," Fraka said.

That got her attention. "Eggs?"

"Yes. The hens are finally laying again. It took a few days to gather enough for breakfast."

"Wow. Eggs." Rianthe's mouth watered.

"Enjoy," Fraka said, taking Ujami back with a laugh.

"We will." Rianthe waved as she headed for the dining house.

"Swords to the smithy, remember?" Kaiden laughed. "Then breakfast."

He didn't laugh often enough these days. The sound lightened Rianthe's heart.

"We could go later." She eyed the dining-house doorway, so much closer than Sam's metal-working hut.

"The eggs will be there when we get back." Kaiden put a hand to her back, directing her away from thoughts of food and her growling stomach. It felt so good, this camaraderie, that she might willingly forgo breakfast.

She joined him and they headed to turn in their swords, content to enjoy this moment.

"Jonah mentioned the meat stores are low," she said.

"Yes. I hunted with the group yesterday and we saw little sign of anything. We only caught some small game."

"Better than nothing, but it won't feed a village."

Kaiden shook his head. "No, it won't."

"Jonah suggested going out again tomorrow."

"We'd already planned to."

"Good. I'll join you."

His fleeting look of denial confused Rianthe. Kaiden had always loved hunting with her before.

"I'm not sure you should leave the village," he said, his words slow and deliberate.

Not leave the village? "What are you talking about? Why shouldn't I?"

"I can't protect you as well outside of New Hope."

"Oh, for the love of magic, you can't actually think to keep me holed up here forever."

"Not forever. Ri, we both almost lost our lives when we went after Deakon. I can't...I... Well, that just can't happen. Not to you. All right?"

"First, you are more aware than anyone else how capable I am of taking care of myself."

Rianthe huffed in anger at his slow and grudging nod. "Second, you can't keep me a prisoner."

"I can try," he said.

"You won't succeed." She glared at him, but he didn't back down one iota. Kaiden's patience and ability to wait her out had been the bane of her sword-training. She always moved before he did. Heck, the same might be true of their friendship. He was the most stubborn, infuriating man she'd ever met.

Rianthe stalked ahead of him.

"Hi, Sam," she said when she reached the forges.

"Good day." Sam was a great hulk of a man who looked able to bend cold metal with his bare hands, yet could also gently twist a filigree of metal thread into the most amazing art. Most of his work had been lost in the fire, reduced to a puddle of remembered beauty. He hadn't complained once. Instead, he'd gathered up all the pieces he could find and heated and formed them into cook pots or utensils, whatever was needed.

At the moment, he was bent over some metal he'd formed into a ladle. He raised his eyes from his work, looked back and forth between her and Kaiden, who'd caught up to her, and quickly refocused on his task.

Did they both look *that* angry? Rianthe glanced Kaiden's way. If her face looked anything like his, then she saw why the smithy didn't want any part of whatever was going on between them.

"May we leave our swords here for sharpening?"

"Sure, sure," he said, waving at them. Or waving them away. Rianthe couldn't quite tell which.

"Thank you," she said.

Kaiden's thank you quickly followed.

They stomped their way back toward the dining house. Rianthe tried to let their argument go. It wasn't easy. She took a couple deep breaths to calm herself. "Kaiden, you know I'm a good hunter."

"You are." His lips were a grim line.

"New Hope needs everyone's help. And that means I need to hunt." She hated that she sounded like she was begging. Gah!

Kaiden took a deep breath of his own before

nodding. "I don't like it, but you're right."

Could he be any more infuriating? With a patience unusual for her, Rianthe simply said thanks and changed the subject. "Did you know Tevy hasn't been going to Studies?"

"Yes."

"You did?"

"The whole village knows where Tevy spends his time." Kaiden smiled. "Tevy will probably never be a regular when it means being closed up in a room for lessons."

"He needs to learn, just like we did."

"I'm not as certain about that."

Rianthe stopped. "What do you mean? We have to pass the stories of our ancestors down or they'll be lost."

Kaiden was several paces beyond her when he finally turned and came back to her side. "They will be. There are a few students working with Anniah every day."

It still amazed Rianthe that silly Anniah had become their new Studies teacher. Turns out she'd been listening all those years they'd been taking instruction together.

"And don't forget Jonah's new missive that we write things down."

"We? Me, you mean." Jonah had expressly saddled her with that duty. Now, she was stuck in that tower room way too much putting ink to paper. She'd never been good at Studies and now she must write down everything she'd learned?

Kaiden scrubbed his beard with his hand. "Bhren set the rule that every child must attend Studies but a lot has happened since… Well, a lot has happened. I think we can stretch those rules."

Rianthe hadn't considered this. They were, for all intents and purposes, adapting since the fire and Bhren's demise. They'd reinvented survival, living like one big family in a couple of communal huts sectioned into compartments instead of individual homes. The homes were just now being rebuilt. Changes were made where needed. That was part of survival.

"Tevy will never sit in a classroom easily," she said.

Kaiden chuckled again. Twice in one day. Wow. "I agree."

"I don't want to let Tevy choose how to fill his time, though," she said. "He'll be out running with those wolves of his day and night."

"Again, agreed." Kaiden opened the door into the dining hut. "I suggest we find tasks for him. Chores around New Hope, herb-hunting in the woods."

It made sense. "I'll talk to Anniah, and then to Tevy," Rianthe said. "For now, I'm getting some of those eggs."

A while later, after some of the best eggs she'd ever remembered, Rianthe looked up to see a girl she didn't recognize standing in the doorway, maybe a year or two younger than herself. Rianthe stared, a sense of danger jangling through her head. Who was she?

The girl looked around and stopped when she saw Rianthe, her venomous gaze a slap that forced Rianthe to lean back on the bench, her hand reaching for her sword. Dram. She'd left it for sharpening. What she saw in the girl's face faded as quickly as it had shown up, replaced by a docile, doe-eyed beauty.

Rianthe kept her hand on her scabbard, wishing she had more than just her short knife. Danger lurked behind this girl's eyes. It had even seemed, for one quick moment, that their nondescript brown color had flared to bright gold.

Only once before had Rianthe seen that eye color. In the vision-warped face of the druid…Taegar.

CHAPTER THREE

Jonah and Kaiden jumped up and quickly moved toward the girl. She faltered, as if about to faint. They helped her to a seat at the table, next to Rianthe. Kaiden sat down across from her as Jonah beckoned for water and food. The frown on Kaiden's face proved he was as suspicious of the girl as Rianthe.

While Kathra, Mokie's mother and the woman who ran the kitchens, rushed to oblige, the group at the table stared at each other, worry readily showing on each face. New Hope welcomed strangers, or had until recently. Kaiden had been a stranger when he'd arrived, as a newling, as well as Rianthe and her brothers. And one other. The man who'd all but destroyed New Hope.

Only two full moons ago, Deakon, a stranger who'd ingratiated himself with the villagers years before, had turned on them, setting fire to their homes with balls of magic and killing over half of their friends, their family.

Because of that, everyone in New Hope remained rightfully suspicious of anyone new. Their town was off the beaten path, so not many made it this far.

"Where do you come from?" Jonah asked.

"My village is way west of here. There's nothing left. No food, and our well dried up."

Her voice, a broken whisper, didn't fool Rianthe one bit. She glanced at Kaiden. He was focused on the stranger, leaning closer when she spoke. Where was that suspicion she'd seen scant moments ago? He looked at this girl like she was the prophesied one.

Rianthe saw something different. Her hair had the look of someone who hadn't washed it in weeks, but only on the surface, as if she'd plastered it with mud this morning. Her skin glowed with a freshness that belied long travel. And she smelled of flowers, not the pitch and pine of someone who'd slept in the woods for days or weeks.

There was more to this stranger than could be seen. Rianthe was certain this girl had come there with a purpose only she knew, and that her motives would not bode well for New Hope.

"Everyone left," the girl continued in a honey-toned voice. "We were the last."

"We?" Jonah prompted.

"My brother and I. He—he perished." She hung her head, hair covering her eyes for a moment before she sat back up. "A misstep near the edge of a cliff." The break in her voice seemed real.

Kaiden appeared to be listening with rapt attention. He nodded more with each word she uttered.

His attention grated on Rianthe. She had to fight the strong urge to yank him away from the table. The man almost looked charmed. Rianthe was close to doing whatever she deemed necessary to break that spell.

"I've been wandering ever since. Looking for people, someone who might help me. I—" Again the crack in her voice. "I was so happy to find this place."

Wandering here? Nestled in the hills near the Rushmore Mountain, New Hope was difficult to find if you weren't looking for it. Bhren had purposely set them there, away from the main paths of travel. They were safer this way, or so they'd thought.

Mokie's mother set a mug of water, a bowl of porridge, and a plate with eggs and vegetables in front of the girl while she continued talking.

"First I found the lake. Then I smelled the food." The girl took a small bite. "I'm Marta, by the way." She smiled, her eyes never leaving Kaiden's.

Rianthe clenched her hands under the table, her sense of danger hitting high alert, except she didn't know if her concern was real or if the girl's attentiveness toward Kaiden had triggered it. Either way, her suspicion rose steeply, faster than an arrow could travel.

She glanced at Kaiden. Was he blushing? He didn't look at all uncomfortable under Marta's gaze. He sat forward on the bench across from the girl, a hint of a smile on his face. When he raked both hands through his hair, smoothing it, Rianthe almost threw her hands up in disgust. She turned narrowed eyes back to Marta. Sure, she had a certain prettiness to her, but it was all superficial. This had to be a setup. Why didn't Kaiden see that?

"I…I need a new home. A new place to belong," she said, her voice soft with a meek plea. Soft like a bobcat's disposition just before he clamps his jaws around your throat. "If you'd rather I didn't stay, then a day or two to recover my strength would be met with appreciation."

Was it all in Rianthe's mind or had Marta's voice changed as she spoke to Kaiden? Shyness gentled her face. She acted as if no one else sat there but the two of them.

Kaiden cleared his throat and looked at Jonah. "Seems fair to let her stay. We can't throw her on the mercy of the Rushmore Woods."

No! Distrust for this girl screamed at Rianthe. She opened her mouth but caught the quick shake of Jonah's head in her peripheral vision and clamped her mouth shut. She didn't know why, but Marta's appearance did not have good implications for New Hope. Rianthe's alarm now was much worse than the trickle of worry she'd had around Deakon. Yes, she and Jonah would talk later. For now, she bit her tongue hard to keep from voicing her concerns.

"We're recovering, ourselves, after a bad fire," Jonah said.

Did the girl's eyes flash brighter? It happened so fast, Rianthe couldn't be certain.

"I think we can find you a spot so you can recover," Jonah said, making it very clear this remained a temporary situation. "Kaiden, why don't you show Marta where she can sleep."

Kaiden rose without hesitation. Rianthe coiled her hands into tight fists, not be happy with this development. This girl played with Kaiden. Why didn't he see it?

Marta joined Kaiden, twining her arm through his and smiling up at him as they walked out of the dining house.

Jonah reminded everyone of their duties. Once

they'd left, he turned to Rianthe. "I get a very strong impression that this girl is not what she seems. What do you think?"

"I don't like this. I don't like her. Not one bit."

"Are you sure this doesn't have something to do with Kaiden? You two have been dancing around each other ever since you met as younglings."

Rianthe almost grunted in frustration. "Yes," she ground out. "Of course it has something to do with Kaiden. But it's more than that. Much more. Something is off about her. Her hair didn't look dirty through and through. Even the soil on her clothes looked almost planned. Also…" She hesitated to mention something she wasn't certain had actually happened, but Jonah needed to know. "I could have sworn her eyes changed color."

"That may not mean she's here for dire reasons. However, she does seem to be paying an unnatural amount of attention to my son." Jonah frowned. "Do you know anything specific?"

"No. I wish I did. Except…" Something elusive tapped at the edge of her memory. She just couldn't put her finger on it.

Jonah glanced at the door Kaiden and Marta had gone through. "Despite what has happened to us, if we choose not to help others, then we are no better than those that follow the darkness."

He was right, dram it. She hated it, but he was right.

"She's young," Jonah said. "Maybe it's just her age and lack of experience. She's latching onto the first friendly face she sees. Let's give her a couple days and see after that."

Jonah stood but didn't move until she nodded. Then he smiled. "Good. That's settled, then. I'd better get to my own duties, as had you, scribe."

Rianthe groaned. Jonah's break with tradition, assigning her to write down the stories taught in Studies, meant long hours in the tower room for Rianthe. He'd also requested that any useful information from her own experiences be added to the burned-out remains of Bhren's library. There were days when she wished Bhren had never taught her how to write.

After he left, Rianthe took her dishes to the kitchen, happy to see Tevy arm-deep in soapy water, helping the other children of New Hope clean the morning's dishes.

"Go to Studies today," she told him.

"Awww," Tevy said.

"Go to Studies. We will work on some alternatives, but you at least have to try."

Petulance was rare for Tevy and never lasted long. He grinned and flicked soapy water at her. "If I have to," he said as she jumped back, laughing.

~~~

Since they had only begun the rebuilding of individual huts, Kaiden brought Marta to a curtained alcove in the women's side of the longhouse.

"You can sleep here for now," he said.

"With all these other people? It will be so noisy." The sulk on her face should have made him laugh. That emotion would never touch Rianthe's face. Pouting wasn't in her blood. Kaiden didn't normally fall for this sort of ploy but there was something about this girl. She got under his skin somehow, and he didn't understand why or how.

Noon's appearance was hours away and Kaiden was exhausted already. He rubbed his face. There was so much work to do. So much required to ensure New
~~~

Hope's continued survival. He was overdue to help Ahren, their resident inventor, with the cistern the man wanted to build to capture and store rainwater so they wouldn't have to get water from the lake as often. He also needed to speak with Sam about processing more metals. They needed more weapons to defend their home. Maybe Ahren could help with that too.

"Come back to me, my handsome savior," Marta said. Kaiden looked around, confused. Somehow, they had moved from the longhouse and now stood in front of the little storage building where he slept, next to the druid's tower.

Marta peeked inside. "There's plenty of room here." She turned to Kaiden, reached up and set her hands on both sides of his neck. "I can stay here with you, right? You're so strong. After all these days of being scared that some animal might eat me, I need to feel safe."

Kaiden's head felt foggy, like his brain had grown sluggish. He didn't know how they'd gotten there or how she knew where he slept, and he barely understood Marta's question. Looking at her, he saw beguiling, soft brown eyes in a pretty face. Yes, there was something about her. He wanted to protect her, needed her safe. Nothing was more important…

Her hands trailed down the front of Kaiden's tunic, circled his waist, pulled him in tighter.

What was happening? Kaiden never got involved like this. He couldn't think straight. Why was that? He'd never worried about anyone's safety more than New Hope's or Rianthe's, yet he wanted, no, he needed this girl to be safe from harm.

Rianthe. Just the thought of her cleared the fog from his mind. Kaiden shook his head, trying to further tear the veil of confusion. He looked down, saw Marta hanging on to him, expecting him to give in to her wishes. He extricated himself from her grasp and stepped back. "I'm sorry, Marta. I'm not sure why you thought this might be possible, but I share my room with no one."

"What?" She looked as if he'd slapped her. A momentary rage colored her face before she got it under control. A soft pleading replaced the harsh tone of her question. "Please, Kaiden. I'm afraid."

"You will be safe enough with the other women around you. Come. I'll take you back to the women's sleeping house." He strode off without waiting for her. When he got back to the longhouse he'd originally shown her, he turned to find her following, albeit slowly.

"Do you need me to show you your alcove again?"

She sped up, whipped by him without a word, and disappeared inside.

Kaiden shook his head one more time to clear out the lingering cobwebs. As he headed for his meeting with Ahren, he tried to sort out what had happened. Had she put him under some sort of enchantment? He'd heard of that happening, though had no firsthand experience. Unfortunately, by the time he found the inventor, Kaiden had more questions than answers.

He didn't need that. He needed peace, not concern. Lately, it seemed like the only way he could exorcize his crushing worry was to fall into bed exhausted. Maybe, if he worked just a little harder today, if he made himself more tired than he already was, he might sleep without dark dreams.

~~~

Rianthe pushed open the door of the dining hut, her mind heavy with apprehension. She glanced up in time to
~~~

see Marta and Kaiden by his quarters outside the tower. Her heart flopped so hard, she clutched her chest, afraid it might stop beating. Had Kaiden invited that girl to share his quarters? He couldn't… He wouldn't. Not so close to her…

Kaiden turned and walked toward the longhouse. Marta stomped past Kaiden without saying a word and kept going. She disappeared inside without a backward glance.

The pain in Rianthe's heart eased as Kaiden stared after Marta with a scowl on his face. And, though she wouldn't admit it to anyone, a smile tugged at her lips.

CHAPTER FOUR

The new barn had been hastily erected, its haphazard thatch covering walls not quite tall enough to allow a person to stand. It kept what hay had survived the fire, and subsequent snow, dry and provided the perfect spot for a pack of wolves. Tevy took a deep breath. He loved the smell of hay, like musty sunshine.

Tevy had been happy when his friends returned, their bellies not as full as they'd like, but sated enough for now. Sarsa, mother-wolf, turned around and around in the hay, then settled into the hollow she'd created. She looked over her family before laying muzzle on paws and closing her eyes. The other wolves, Tevy's brothers, were not as sleepy. They wrestled and tussled and played, with Tevy right in the middle. "Tevy?" Rianthe asked, crouching to step through the low doorway. Tevy grunted, intent on getting Hark, the eldest of the sibling wolves, onto his back in a mock alpha struggle. But Hark slipped out of his grasp, jumped back, then pounced on Tevy, knocking him over and holding him down with two paws.

"Tevy?"

His sister sounded serious. With a final grunt and push, Tevy gave up the fight. Hark showed his teeth in a wide grin.

I win.

Only because of her, Tevy mind-spoke back.

I always win.

Tevy shook his head. Hark was right. The alpha wolf did always win. Would he ever have the strength, cunning, and senses of his brother-wolves? He yearned for that. With the wolves, he was home. They were as much his family as Rianthe was.

The tap on his shoulder brought him around. "What?"

"Seriously, Tevy, you spend too much time with these wolves. You don't even hear me when I call you," Rianthe said.

True. As his bond with his pack grew, he'd become more adept at tuning people out. Lately, he'd been worse than ever. He preferred to sleep outside or in the barn, didn't like enclosed places. And he had so many growing pains, like his body was trying to burst into adulthood all at once. Tevy ached all over.

"Are you all right?" his sister asked, brushing his blond hair back from his forehead.

"Sure." He ducked his head, uncertain of why he didn't want to talk about this.

"Really? You seem awfully quiet lately. Not your usual happy self." She nudged him in the arm, turning an ache into a true pain.

He forced a smile he didn't feel. "I'm fine. Really. What did you want?"

She stared at him. Tevy held her gaze, trying hard not to show his confusion. Finally, she gave up.

"Did you see the newcomer?"

"You mean that girl, Marta?" Tevy hadn't liked her from the moment he'd seen her walking straight through the center of New Hope with sure strides, then stooping and stuttering her steps the closer she got to the dining hut. That one had an aura of menace around her and he'd chosen to steer clear.

Rianthe nodded.

"I saw her. I don't like her."

"Neither do I. Did you get any sense as to why she came here? She said she 'found' us."

"That's hard to believe," Tevy said. "I don't know why she's here, but she's dangerous. I can feel it. I can't give you a reason, but I know it."

"Me, too. She bears watching."

"Yep."

Rianthe twisted her gloved hands, an unusual show of nervousness. There was more on her mind than New Hope's visitor.

"I'd like to try something and I need your help," she said after a long silence.

"What?"

"Something weird happened this morning."

Tevy frowned. He knew Rianthe worried a lot about the darkness closing in. Was their respite about to end? Would Taegar advance the fight, bringing it to their doorstep again? "What?"

Rianthe played with the edge of her gloves, not looking at Tevy. This indecision wasn't like his sister. It alarmed him. "You're safe here, you know," he said. "You can tell me anything."

"I know. I just…this is hard." Rianthe took a deep breath. "When Kaiden and I were at the lake this morning, he helped me stand." Rianthe kept staring at her gloved hands.

"And?"

"I wasn't wearing my gloves." She looked up at him then. "Something happened, Tevy. Something passed between us. I'm not sure what, but while we were touching, it was like we'd been joined somehow. Mentally. We were like one person."

It is the forever bond, Sarsa, the wolf-mother, mind-spoke.

Rianthe could only mind-speak through the wolf, Taschia. She didn't hear Sarsa's comment, which the mother-wolf warned was for Tevy's ears only. He smiled, liking the idea of Rianthe and Kaiden bonded. This was a good thing.

"Why are you smiling? I'm serious. It seems like I can't touch anything without having visions or…seeing into people's souls. I don't understand and it scares me. And…I, um, thought maybe if you and I tried…"

Tevy laughed. "I thought this was serious stuff. You had me worried."

"It *is* serious," Rianthe said.

"Not end-of-the-world serious, though." Tevy held out his hand. "Sure. Let's try."

It will not happen with you, Sarsa mind-spoke.

Why not? We're brother and sister, bonded just like I am to you.

The wolf-bond is different. You are meant for other things.

What did that mean? Tevy didn't have time to sort out Sarsa's comment. Rianthe was already pulling off her gloves. With a slight hesitation, she grasped Tevy's hand.

Nothing happened, just as Sarsa had said. Even Rianthe looked confused.

"Wait," she said, pulling the bag of runes from around her neck. "These were in my hand." Rianthe poured the three runes out of the bag, clutched them in her hand, then grabbed a hold of Tevy. Skin-to-rune-to-skin.

Again, nothing happened. They sat that way for a long time. Tevy tried to mind-speak with Rianthe. He'd been able to do it before, through the wolves. Now, nothing happened at all. Either her bonding with Kaiden had changed things, or something else had. But what?

Rianthe pulled her hand away and bagged the runes. "I don't understand this at all."

"Neither do I, Sister." There were a lot of questions that needed answering. Normally, Tevy got an inkling of how things might unfold. Now, though, only disquiet settled in his heart and mind. He didn't know how to proceed.

"Sis, can I ask you a question?"

"Anything," Rianthe said.

"You and me. And Uja. We all seemed to have something inside of us, something more than the others here. Do you understand why?"

Rianthe took a deep breath as Taschia settled on the hay beside her. "I've never really told you about your parentage, have I, little brother?"

He shook his head. He knew she'd brought him there as a newling. Once, when he'd been watching the village children with their parents, he'd asked her about theirs.

She'd told him they died, but not much else.

"I'm sorry. I should have. It's long past time. Except, this is something that can never be mentioned outside of New Hope. No stranger must know this, or it puts everyone, especially us, in great danger."

He'd pretty much already known that. Each omen, each flash of prescience had shown him the importance of keeping secrets because too many people turned information to their own purposes. Too easily, that information could leak to the Dark druid who wanted them all dead.

"Real danger, little brother. Promise you'll keep this information close?"

"You know I will."

"All right." Rianthe absently scratched at Taschia's ears, staring off into space. "Our parents died. I wasn't lying about that. Mother, Valena, died giving birth to you. Not because of you, though." She said the last part hastily as if trying to reassure him.

"We'd lived a quiet existence on the outskirts of a small town far away from here. We were content, even though we didn't socialize much or play with others. Our parents kept us apart, only going into town for supplies when needed. Uja—" Her voice still broke at the sound of their dear brother's name. "Uja and I played together, helped Mother make food, helped Father in the small growing field. We lived a simple life."

Tevy smiled. He liked that idea and easily pictured it. Very much akin to their lives there in New Hope. He wished he could have been part of it.

"Then one day, I was out in the field with Father. He stopped hoeing, cocked his head, then went white as winter wheat. He grabbed my hand, and we ran back to our little cabin. Inside, Mother had already packed light bags. The same panic shone in her eyes. She was newly pregnant with you. We left our home within the hour, leaving everything behind except a bit of food and some clothes."

Rianthe shuddered. "As we hurried away, I had the oddest feeling. A stark coldness fell over me." She shook her head. "I tried to ask Father, but he only shushed me and pushed us to move faster. For the next several months we ran, never in one place for more than a day or two, always shying away from people."

His sister grew tense as she told the story. Tevy almost told her to stop, but he needed to know the whole thing, so he remained quiet. Maybe it would explain his discontent.

"The night our parents died, we'd found an abandoned shack to ward off the chill. Father had even built a small fire to cook a warm dinner for a change. We never got to eat it. I heard a thrumming, first in my head, then all around us."

Taschia whined and settled her head on Rianthe's lap. She clutched the wolf's hair and continued. "It was Taegar. She'd hunted us down."

Taegar hunted them? "Why?"

"Because," Rianthe said. "Because our father was Damian Royan."

Tevy had never known his surname. He'd always been Tevy. It had never bothered him, until now. "So I'm Tevy Royan?"

"Yes. I'm sorry. I should have told you long before this."

Tevy Royan. The name had a ring to it, but also seemed foreign to him. Adding to his name did not change him or make him more or less important. He still felt like Tevy. "Why haven't you told me my name before this?"

"Because the Royan name has a special significance. You are the son of Damian and Valena Royan, both Guardian druids."

Pride welled up in Tevy. Pride and shock, even though he'd known something was different about him. He, Rianthe, and Uja all seemed to have talents the others didn't. There had to be a reason. Tevy thought back to the day Bhren died and it clicked. "That was what Bhren whispered to you before he died, wasn't it?"

"Yes. And, Tevy," Rianthe continued, grabbing his hand. "They weren't just Guardian druids. Damian Royan led the Guardian circle. That circle made this talisman." She pulled the bag out from under her tunic. "He was the one who led the druids against the Dark circle in the Great Magic War."

Bits and pieces fell into place for Tevy as his sister told him of their heritage. Why he'd never known his last name, why Rianthe held the runes that were supposed to save Earth, why Taegar hunted them and wanted the runes for her own purposes. "I understand things better now," he said, squeezing her hand before letting go. "Thank you."

"I should have told you a long time ago."

"I didn't need to know until now. You know I can sense things. I always knew you would explain when the time was right. Now, I understand why you are the prophesied one."

His sister shook her head, as she did each time that title arose. She didn't like the name and didn't think she lived up to it.

"You are, you know," Tevy said.

"Do you? Know, I mean."

"Not really. I get a feeling, that's all."

"You've always had an extraordinary ability to see what's coming."

"It's more like an impression. Like it's okay to be happy today, or that danger is nearby. Or that you will find a way to have faith in yourself." He smiled.

"You are wise beyond your years, little brother." She reached over and mussed up his blond hair. Tevy pulled away, but secretly, he loved this camaraderie.

"I only see what the world lets me see," he said. Except recently even that ability had evaded him. His world was pulling closer, his focus becoming more about him than the world around him. Only time would solve the riddle of his future. This had to unfold as it was supposed to and nothing he did would speed things up.

CHAPTER FIVE

After the confusing attempt to connect with Tevy, Rianthe helped in the growing fields for a while before giving in to the inevitable. She walked to the tower, a structure made of rock and mud that would eventually be covered with a thatched roof. The tower was impressive compared to the rest of the rebuilding. Rather emphatically, she'd told them not to do it, but Jonah had insisted that Bhren's wishes be followed. Brought together to help the one of whom the prophecy spoke, the weight of the villagers' faith lay heavily upon Rianthe's shoulders. If she was indeed the prophesied one, this was their way of showing honor to Bhren, who had guided them for many years, and to her, in whom they all placed much hope.

So she'd agreed, against her better judgment. Rianthe stoked the slow-burning fire in her small kiva, even though there was no roof to keep the heat in yet. That

Bhren had decreed the place be built did not force her to like living there. The building represented him, not her. Bhren the Guardian druid, mentor, and the man she'd both loved and hated. And now, though she was completely unprepared, both the tower and the position were hers. Bestowed upon her by Bhren, a prophecy, and the people of New Hope. Whether she liked it or not, Bhren had named her the newest Guardian druid before his death. New Hope had taken up the mantle of his beliefs. Kaiden, too, although he'd refused to live in the tower. Now they needed to figure out what it meant.

At a makeshift table beneath a window, Rianthe rolled out crude paper, usable, though not as thin or smooth as in the ancient books she'd seen. Ahren, New Hope's resident wild-haired inventor, had an uncanny knack for innovation. Only ten years older than she, the man was wise beyond his years when it came to creating something new.

He'd built ovens with intricate clay piping behind them that heated water for baths while cooking food. He'd devised a grid-like webbing which made thatched roofs sturdier and easier to build.

He'd also found a way to make paper and writing instruments, which gave Rianthe the ability to record their ancestors' tales as Jonah requested. Rianthe toyed with the dipping pen in distaste. Some of his inventions were more popular than others. At least, for her.

She stared at the blank paper, not sure where to begin. Jonah had only assigned her this task a few days ago. She'd been reluctant to start, afraid she'd be stuck in this dratted tower for hours each day. He'd asked her to record Studies lessons, what she'd gleaned from her time with Bhren, as well as her own experiences. Rianthe wasn't too excited about reliving any of that.

Opting to start at the beginning, she penned the first phrase ever taught in Studies—the One Prophecy.

Shattered by darkness the magic vanished.
It lays in wait for one who's banished.
Hidden power will blossom anew.
Only by passing the darkness through.

She continued with the second verse, only recently learned from Roulf, a hermit who'd once been a student of the Guardian druids.

The runic key ignites the fire,
That coupled with the conduit's power,
Must send the magic to the white height
Defeating darkness, restoring light.

Bhren, and now Roulf, applied this prophecy to her, even though she'd shown less ability at magic than anyone else in this village. Jonah always knew what people thought, sometimes before they did. Raisa's healing powers were unmatched. Ahren dreamed of things to make their lives easier, then Rhand, their carpenter, shaped the wood to build what Ahren designed. Even Kathra, Mokie's mother, had shown a strong ability to infuse atypical spices into foods that were mundane and tasteless without her flavorings.

Brought together in New Hope to assist the prophesied one bring the magic back to the light, all these good people had rallied around her.

And she hadn't produced anything to fuel their hope. She'd drawn upon her magic only once, to defeat Deakon and save herself and Kaiden from certain death. The power had disappeared right after and never returned. Plus, it left her so depleted she would not have been able to fight had the need arisen.

Powerless. That's what she was. And one of these days, the village would recognize it.

Rianthe set the pen in the well of dark liquid with a plunk that splashed ink onto the page and her table. Swabbing it up, she managed to spread the ink all over her hands. Rubbing only made it worse, frustrating her further. As good as Ahren was at his inventions, the dark blobs now coloring her hands might easily be permanent.

Gah! Rianthe stood and walked away, leaving the mess to dry on its own. Putting her roofless room behind her, she walked downstairs and out into the hazy noon sunshine, rare these winter days.

She peeked in the door of the dining house, the most complete structure they had for now, and the warmest. True to Fraka's earlier words, it was playtime for Ujami. Rianthe heard his coos. From where she stood, she saw him laying on a blanket spread out in front of the ovens. Fraka and two village women laughed with him, clapping their hands. Ujami startled at the noise, then stuck his fingers in his mouth. When he pulled them out, he bunched all his fingers to stare at them, then broke into a wide smile, slapping them together.

He'd found his hands.

Rianthe clapped her own together, grateful to observe a small piece of all the things Ujami would learn over the next months and years. Life without Uja wasn't the same, but getting to watch his son grow up helped ease Rianthe's sorrow.

Kaiden sat with Tevy at a table. Apparently, he'd gotten out of Studies early. She'd have to talk to Anniah and see why. The two had their heads bent over something they were carving. Must be another one of the wooden toys Tevy liked. It warmed Rianthe's heart to see Kaiden making time to spend with Tevy. He did this almost every day.

Rianthe's smile died when she noticed that Marta leaned against the kitchen wall, watching Kaiden and Tevy, with her long, golden, perfectly wavy hair. Tugging at her own much shorter hair, Rianthe, for the first time in years, missed being able to twirl it around her finger or have Kaiden do that. He used to do it all the time back when they were friends. It would be a couple more months before her hair reached her shoulders. She tucked it behind her ears, a frequent motion for her these days. Maybe growing it out hadn't been a good idea.

Marta looked up at Rianthe and smiled, but it missed her eyes and seemed filled with malice. Evil rolled off of this stranger in waves. Rianthe had no basis for her fears about Marta other than a knack for sensing danger that had saved her many times while she'd wandered alone in the Fringes, a lawless expanse northeast of the Rushmore Woods. Jonah, aware of her concerns, still advised a wait and watch posture, though it grated at Rianthe to do so.

Marta's smile transformed into a glare. Her eyes flashed a bright golden fire, then faded to their usual lackluster brown.

Rianthe shivered as if Deakon's ghost had just tapped her on the shoulder. With every ounce of her soul, she did not want this Marta girl there. She could only be vigilant and wait for the girl to slip up. Rianthe would protect her family and friends to the best of her ability. No one would get past her to harm them. Never again.

CHAPTER SIX

The next morning, Kaiden walked to the edge of town to meet the day's hunting party. He'd been awake half the night, trying to determine which path to follow. Game had been too scarce these last few days. Scarce? More like nonexistent. Recent hunts to the west and north, both routes usually the better choices, fetched nothing. Today they'd go east, toward the Rushmore Mountain. When he and Rianthe used to hunt in that direction, they'd been successful.

He missed those days. They were full of responsibility and duty, but there had also been times when he could let that go and just be himself. Mostly with Rianthe, and he missed that. He couldn't talk to her these days, not like he used to. He couldn't talk to anyone.

"Hello, Kaiden." Marta stepped out from the shadows and twined her arm with his. "Where might you be going so early in the morning?" The foggy breath of cold air prefaced her words, like tendrils of gray cloud that reached out to him.

Kaiden extricated his arm, wary around the woman. She'd obviously set her sights on him, something he would never reciprocate. His heart's focus lay elsewhere, even if he couldn't say so out loud. "Hunting."

Undaunted, Marta ran her hand up and down the sleeve of his shirt. When she looked up at him, her smile was…dazzling. She didn't look ordinary at all. In fact, he'd say she was the most beautiful woman he'd ever met. An aura surrounded her, like a fog he wanted to walk into, become one with. Kaiden pulled at the neck of his tunic; warmth spread through him, a heat that made his blood boil and his heart race. Was he getting feverish?

"Must you go hunting?" The words came as if from a great distance, tugging at him. "Wouldn't you rather spend the day with me?"

Yes. Hunting could wait until tomorrow. Nothing mattered, nothing except being there, with Marta, liberating the heat within him. He turned away from the others and let Marta lead him away.

"Kaiden!"

Rianthe's voice reverberated through him like the strings of an out of tune lute, jarring the sense back into him, clearing the fog. What just happened? Kaiden looked around, shaking his head. Where was he going?

"What are you doing, Kaiden?" Rianthe strode to his side, radiating fury as she scowled at the girl beside him.

Marta tightened her hold on Kaiden. "We're going on a picnic."

"In winter? No. You're not," Rianthe said. She yanked Kaiden several feet away from the woman.

"Marta?" He remembered how beautiful he'd thought her to be. Now, frowning, she looked more sinister, more…menacing.

The two women glared at each other. Rianthe looked ready to take Marta on with her clenched fists and fighting stance. Kaiden shook his head again, clearing any remaining haze from his brain. He'd need to mull this over later because Rianthe looked ready to blow.

He turned to Marta. "I don't remember agreeing to any picnic, but it doesn't matter. Today we must hunt."

"Yes," Rianthe said through tight lips. "We must. Everyone's waiting."

Marta stepped forward and reached up to kiss Kaiden on the cheek. "Another time, my warrior," she said. She gave Rianthe a pointed glance before turning and strolling off, hips swaying.

"What in the name of the Guardian druids were you doing with her, Kaiden?"

In all honesty, Kaiden did not understand what he'd been doing. It was as if he'd been under some sort of spell or something. Still, Rianthe did not make his decisions for him. "What I was doing is my business," he said, setting off to join the waiting men.

Rianthe didn't keep up. Kaiden looked back to see her rooted in the same spot he'd left her, mouth agape. He grinned as he turned back in the direction he'd been headed, happy she'd been reminded she did not run his life. Even if she did.

Still, this morning's events bore some further thought. Twice now, around Marta, he'd lost time and even his own will to choose. Was this some sort of Dark magic? If so, it wasn't good that he, True-Named protector, could be beguiled like that. Kaiden made a mental note to have a talk with Jonah later. The need to understand Marta's reasons for being here had just reached the top of his to-do list.

"Come on," he said to Mokie, Rhand, and the others. "Today we hunt over by the Rushmore Mountain."

Kaiden led the way, setting a fast pace. He knew the group would follow him, but his ingrained need to protect Rianthe made him seek her out. She followed at the back of the pack, watching him with a look of complete bewilderment on her face.

Kaiden turned to the path ahead, grinning again. Everything that weighed him down lifted a bit and his smile widened. He hadn't felt in control like this for a long time. He liked it.

~~~

After several hours with no game in sight, they took a rest. Rianthe yanked her gloves off. She slapped them against the downed log where she sat. Could this day get any worse?

First, Kaiden and that woman. That alone was enough to turn her day sour. He'd looked almost blissful as he stared at Marta. Never once had Kaiden looked at her that way.

Not one time. Rianthe slapped her gloves against the log a second time. What was that girl doing to him?

Even worse, the forest that had always sustained them seemed devoid of game. No boars, not even a rabbit. Her skill in the one field where she excelled—hunting—seemed to have failed her, and New Hope. Nothing she did worked. Worthless, that's what she was. A fraud. She should leave New Hope, let them find another person to solve their problems. She certainly didn't seem to be the right choice. Rianthe threw her
~~~

gloves down on the log, then watched them slip off and hit the dirt.

Argh! Rianthe wanted to run off somewhere and scream until her voice went hoarse. Even the mountains seemed sympathetic to their plight. As they'd passed the Rushmore, she'd looked up at the carved profiles and noticed that one man's face almost looked as if it were weeping.

New Hope's need for food approached desperation. Rianthe was sick of watching everything turn sour, unable to do anything. She stared at her gloves, wondering. Maybe she could do something. If she wished hard enough, thought hard enough, the magic might come to her, show her where to find game to feed them all.

Rianthe glanced at Kaiden, wondering if she should let him know what she was about to do. Having sunk back into a dark mood of his own, hopefully recognizing Marta's true spirit, Rianthe decided to proceed without him.

Her gloves lay on the dry ground. With no rain or snow the last couple days, today's hunt had been a cold but dry trek. Settling down next to her gloves, Rianthe looked at the dirt, tried to see through it like she had in Bhren's tower all those months ago. Grains of soil, the same yet different. Grays and browns and reds. She focused on the animals who provided sustenance for New Hope, then reached down, both hands splaying out across the dirt, pleading for the magic to guide her.

Where are the animals?

Skin-to-Earth, no portent about animals came. Instead, a numbing fear permeated her. Rianthe clenched her hands, trying to pull away, to protect herself from the emotional hit of contact with Earth's soil. Something held her tight. So much pain. A thousand embers coursed through her, burning nerves and sinew. Something suppressed was trying to reach through the agony for the surface. Rianthe expected to see something jump up through the soil, but nothing moved.

She ground her teeth to keep from crying out as the whine of pain, coming from the bowels of Earth, throbbed in her ears. And then nothing. Except for two desperate, barely audible words.

Help. Come.

Suddenly freed, Rianthe yanked her hands back, taking slow, deep breaths to calm her racing heart. In the past, these visions were of Taegar, the Dark druid that worked to subvert the world's magic and keep it to herself. This hadn't been Taegar. Instead, this plea came from something softer, gentler. Weaker. She'd felt it before, but did not recognize it. Who needed her help?

Rianthe clutched her head in her hands, tired of these mysteries. She needed to talk to someone. To Kaiden. She looked up at the very moment he glanced at her.

Something in her look must have alarmed him because he jumped up and headed her way. When the ground beneath him moved, Kaiden froze. They all did. The shaking rolled through, lasting only seconds. Before they'd steadied, the brush behind Kaiden erupted and three large boars charged into their small clearing. One charged straight for her. Rianthe side-stepped and whipped her sword out, dealing a swift death blow before the animal could do her any harm.

Kaiden took down the second one and two of the other hunters grappled with the third, killing it.

Rianthe dropped to a knee, dragging in great gulps of air, trying to understand what just happened. She'd never in her life felt the ground move like that. Then, immediately following the quaking, a desolate hunt had turned plentiful.

Kaiden stood straight, turning in every direction, sword at the ready. Ever watchful. "What was that?"

Everyone shook their heads except Rianthe.

"This will probably sound crazy," she said, pulling her gloves on as she stood. "I think Earth helped us. Earth sent us this food." Her voice strengthened, along with her belief. "Earth wants us to survive."

"You're talking like Earth can think."

"More like an instinct for survival." Everything she'd seen coalesced into one thought. Earth was dying and calling out to her, and had used precious resources to help them so she could help Earth in return.

Their world cried for help. The prophecy already said that, but everyone kept waiting for the prophesied one. The fog cleared from Rianthe's thoughts all at once and it became perfectly clear. It didn't matter if she believed she was or wasn't this prophesied one as Bhren had said. It only mattered that right now, she was being asked to help Earth and humankind.

She needed to step up.

To accept the challenge.

And she would, only… She didn't know what to do next.

CHAPTER SEVEN

Everyone in New Hope knew their meat stores were low, so a big cheer went up when the hunting party strode into camp with game tied to poles. They would use every part of the boars for food, for cooking oil, fire-starter, even window coverings and blankets.

Rianthe handed her end of a pole over to Rhand, glad to be done with that weight. Plus, she needed to get away for a while and reason out the next step. The one thing she'd avoided, those visions, had become the only things that might give her answers. About to head for the dreaded druid's tower to see if what remained of Bhren's books offered any guidance, a loud and gruff voice stopped her.

"I hear this is the place where a druid lives," a mountainous voice boomed.

At the strange voice, a murmur of apprehension grew as people froze, searching out the sound, poking their heads around corners and through partially rebuilt doorways. From her vantage point, Rianthe could not yet see the man behind the voice, but unlike the others, she grinned. She knew this voice.

She raced out into the commons, turning around and around. "Where are you, old man?" She saw nothing until the air shimmered beside her and a great bear of a man appeared.

"I am right here, child."

Kaiden rushed in from the outskirts of town, sword drawn, determined to meet this new foe if the crazed look on his face gave any indication. When he reached them, recognition had to override the adrenaline that coursed through him. Rianthe saw him struggle to tamp down his reaction to what he must have believed to be an imminent attack.

The behemoth beside her glanced at Kaiden, then at the group that stood a distance away, weapons of their own in hand. He leaned into Rianthe. "Is it safe?"

"Yes," she said with a laugh. "For now, it's safe."

He shimmered, and a tiny person who barely reached Rianthe's shoulders replaced the big man who'd greeted her.

Several people gasped.

Rianthe leaned down to hug him. "It's good to see you, Roulf."

He patted her back. "It's good to see you as well, child."

"It's all right," Kaiden said, waving to everyone, drawing them in. "Join us."

They lowered their swords and sticks and surrounded Kaiden, Rianthe, and their guest until it seemed like the entire village was there.

"This is Roulf," Rianthe said.

"Ohhh," the large group exclaimed as one. They clapped their hands together, and some slapped Roulf on the back.

"Thank you."

"You're the one."

"How can we ever repay you?"

Different voices all. They knew Roulf, not by sight, but by story. Rianthe and Kaiden had made certain everyone in New Hope knew Roulf was a friend. They'd told them how crucial Roulf's help had been in the fight against Deakon, and with Kaiden's injuries in the aftermath. Everyone loved all the fruit he'd sent to New Hope. It was helping them get through these trying times and would continue to do so for some time to come, thanks to the underground cold room they'd dug. Under the direction of Fraka, seeds had been saved in the hopes of proliferating new trees when the weather improved.

Because of his generosity and helpfulness, Roulf would always be welcome.

He accepted New Hope's gratitude, although it surprised Rianthe to see him turning deep shades of crimson. He was not used to accolades.

In fact… Rianthe's smile dimmed. Roulf lived the life of a hermit, hiding from the world. What worry brought him out of his self-imposed solitude? Why had he come?

Roulf pulled her toward him as if sensing her concern. "Later, child. There are many ears here, not all of them friendly." He glanced at Marta, who stood back from the group, watching.

"Agreed," Rianthe said. She sent a silent thank you to Roulf for recognizing the need for concern.

At dinner that night, Kaiden sat beside Rianthe, giving her hope that Marta hadn't gotten her claws too far into him. Speaking of the darkness herself, Marta sidled past and sat on the other side of Kaiden, giving him all her attention. Rianthe sniffed. She wanted to call Marta out but now wasn't the time. At least Kaiden stiffened when she sat down. Again, hope flared within her that Kaiden saw through the girl's guise.

Tevy jumped in beside Roulf on the other side of the table. Her brother had already become enamored with the little man who barely stood taller than he did. Jonah rounded out the group as they dug into the stew and baby field greens seasoned with a late berry dressing that tasted amazing.

"Supper is, once again, wonderful," Jonah told Kathra as she walked by. Mokie's mother's coaxed savory tastes from meager offerings. Were her abilities enhanced by magic? Everyone thought so and was grateful for it.

She smiled, dipping her head. "I thank you for your kind words." Kathra, always formal, much like Rianthe's own brother Uja had been. Rianthe swallowed against the pain.

Since most everyone at the table seemed to sense the need for caution in their speech around Marta, supper topics remained general and superficial.

"So, Tevy," Rianthe said. "How were Studies today?"

Tevy ducked his head. "Um…"

So, he'd dodged lessons again.

Roulf settled an arm around his shoulders. "Not every child is meant for a classroom."

"Gah! Is everyone against me on this?" Rianthe

asked.

Kaiden chuckled and Jonah shrugged.

"Anniah has agreed to work with Tevy one-on-one," Jonah offered.

Rianthe stared at Tevy. Dark circles marred the skin beneath his eyes. These days, her normally ebullient little brother seemed more pensive than joyful. A change might help him.

Resigned, Rianthe threw up her hands. "All right. I give up. No more sitting in Studies for you, Tevy."

"Whoopee!" he hollered, and she was glad she'd brought the smile back to his face.

Roulf whooped with him.

"But—" Rianthe mock-glared at Tevy, unwilling to spoil the boy completely. "Anniah sets the schedule. And if I hear you are not studying with her, you'll be right back in the group Studies."

"All right." Tevy tried to look humbled, an empty attempt since he couldn't quite wipe the grin off his face.

"Also, you will have more chores. You cannot spend your entire day romping around with that wolf pack of yours."

"I'll do whatever you want me to, Ri. I promise."

"Just don't let him gather eggs anymore," Jonah said. "Those wolves of his scared the hens so bad, they didn't lay eggs for days."

Everyone chuckled at that. Except Marta, who watched with an almost overzealous interest. Rianthe didn't like that the woman sat there, part of their group. Danger emanated from her in ripples that Rianthe feared wouldn't fade anytime soon. Since she had zero facts to back that up, she must continue this wait and watch mode. Glancing at Jonah, the frown on his face reminded her she wasn't the only worried one. Jonah's patience and desire to understand a situation before deciding on an action didn't usually grate as much as it did right now. He should send the girl packing.

At that moment, the bottom fell out from beneath them. The ground dipped, table and benches following a scant second later. A loud crack preceded a deep rumble that rolled with Earth's movement.

Everyone in the room froze until a piece of thatch fell to the ground.

"Duck!" Kaiden hollered.

They all dove. Roulf grabbed Tevy and disappeared under the table. Marta clutched at Kaiden but he shoved her away, down, and under the table. He then reached for Rianthe, pulling her down with him.

Screams.

Clattering dishes hitting the ground.

The deep rumble of Earth in turmoil continued. The sounds, the shaking, it kept going on and on. Peering between the bench and the table, Rianthe saw pieces of the roof falling everywhere.

Boom!

Something hit the table above them.

Rianthe jerked, her head connecting with the underside of the table. "Ouch!"

"I think it was a support beam for the roof," Kaiden said, pulling her in tighter.

Thank goodness Rhand built tables to last. They'd even survived the fires. For once, Rianthe didn't mind Kaiden's protective instincts. With Earth's screams pounding in her ears, mingled with the shrieks of her friends and her family, she watched all of New Hope's hard work crash down around them. On and on the chaos continued. She clutched at the bag with three small runes around her neck, begging Earth, the druid spirits, anyone or anything possible, to give her the power to stop this.

Could she stop this? There was no time to think. She needed to connect with the ground. Rianthe yanked off her gloves and put a hand to the dirt floor without hesitation.

She focused on the shaking, tried to see through the debris, into the heart of Earth. Her hand tingled, then infused her body with a restless energy. Everything around her, the noise, the chaos, faded. It was only her and Earth as she begged it to stop. A hand settled on her bare arm, the familiar touch of Kaiden. Warmth, both new and known, grew within her, spreading out as she reached toward Earth with her mind and heart. Glancing at Kaiden, she saw fierce concentration on his face as he gave her his strength, and let her direct his power as she chose. Beads of sweat formed across his forehead. Another hand, more warmth. Roulf. And Tevy's hand added even more. She felt them all, in her head, in her heart, in her quest to dig into the soil and stop this quaking.

Her strength flared. She sent it deep into Earth's core, shoring up its own power to stop the destruction.

You're killing us. Please, please stop, Rianthe mind-spoke.

Trying. Help. Come. The words were so faint, Rianthe wasn't sure she even heard them. But it hit her like a vision. Pain, so much pain. And an overwhelming sadness. Earth was dying.

I will help, she said. *I am helping.* Over and over she mouthed the words, sending the warmth, the power from the four of them deep into the crust, trying to stabilize the soil their world sat upon.

After what seemed like an eternity, Earth's movement lessened. Rianthe sensed the effort it took to stop the quaking. Earth had not set this off to gain her aid. Earth did not want this. Indeed, the world fought against it. And it had taken their combined energies to make a difference.

Unlike its sudden entrance, the shaking ebbed slowly. It seemed to roll on forever, lessening, lessening, until it finally grew quiet and all Rianthe heard were the whimpers of those around her.

Kaiden and Tevy let go and slid away from her mind. Roulf held on for a moment longer, his warmth easing her almost complete exhaustion. He squeezed her shoulder, waited until she nodded, then released her.

Kaiden climbed from under the table and reached a hand out to help Rianthe. She clambered out and sank onto a bench. The devastation was almost total. The roof, poles, beams, thatch, all lay in ruins on the ground, and two of the walls had collapsed.

"Help!"

Kaiden beat everyone to the source of the cry. He and the others tossed debris aside and lifted the collapsed table out of the way. Anniah and Mokie climbed out.

"We're all right," Mokie said. "We're all right."

"Just scared, that's all," Anniah added, her voice shaking almost as much as the ground had done seconds ago.

Rianthe bent over, hands on knees, trying to catch her breath and will her tiredness away. She looked around the room. It appeared everyone only had scrapes, and probably bruises. Sam the smithy held his arm tight to his side. Raisa was there, helping him to a bench.

Drawing slow, deep breaths, Rianthe tried to calm her panic, an effort that failed when she noticed who was missing. "Where's Fraka?" She raced around, frantic. "Ujami! Fraka! Where are you?"

"She's not here," Anniah said. "Ujami fussed, so Fraka went to put him to bed early."

CHAPTER EIGHT

Rianthe barely heard Anniah's words. She rushed out of the ruined dining house, speeding toward the small hut where Fraka and baby Ujami lived. "Fraka!" Rianthe cried as she neared. Their home lay in ruins, nothing more than a pile of torn and fallen debris. Rianthe's heart stopped. If she lost them, after everything else, she wouldn't be able to stand it.

The faint cry of a babe reached her. Encouraged, Rianthe tore at the crushed building. Kaiden joined her, digging deep and throwing anything he picked up behind them. It seemed to take forever to get beneath all the quake-tossed layers. The faster Rianthe tried to dig, the slower it seemed she was going.

Forever passed before they got to Fraka. She'd taken refuge under her bed; the frame had held most of the rubble at bay. Fraka pushed Ujami out first. Rianthe picked him up while Kaiden grabbed Fraka's hands to pull her out.

"We— We—" Fraka's breath came in quick spurts. She took the screaming Ujami back, trying to calm him even when she couldn't calm herself. "We hid under the bed. I didn't know what else to do."

"You did right," Rianthe said, hugging both her and the babe. Their hearts raced as fast as hers. "You did just fine," she said. "Are you hurt?" Rianthe felt along Ujami's arms and legs.

"No," Fraka gasped. "I don't think so."

They were both okay. They had to be. New Hope couldn't take another loss. Neither could Rianthe. By now, Ujami had quieted, so Rianthe helped the unsteady Fraka and they joined the rest of the people gathered in the village commons.

In an all-too-familiar scenario, the first need was to account for everyone and deal with injuries. They spent the next couple hours checking every part of New Hope, from the perimeter to the center. Thankfully, they found everyone and injuries were minor. Still, their *berkano*, Raisa, would be busy for a while. Rianthe watched the healer as she moved from person to person.

The process of assessing the damage to the buildings took much longer, made more difficult as dusk faded to the dark of night. Most people huddled around the fire pit used for kettle cooking, more willing to chance a cold night outside than have one more thing fall on them.

Rianthe knew her face looked as grimy and dejected as everybody else's, and her shoulders were even more slumped than theirs. Not only had she failed to save New Hope from harm, she'd been no help at all until the others lent her their strength. She hugged herself, bowing under the weight of her guilt. She had tried to draw on the magic, yet even with help, it seemed she had failed. Again.

There'd been something. A warmth had spread through her when the others touched her. A burgeoning magic? If that was true, she should have been able to stop that quake much sooner.

Several people stared at her with forlorn looks. Others with…accusation? She couldn't fault them. According to everything they'd been told, she should have been able to stop this.

Dram! Rianthe hit the log beside her, startling those nearby.

"Sorry," she mumbled. And she was sorry. For so much. "Just frustrated."

"We all are," Raisa said, coming up behind her. She squeezed Rianthe's shoulder. "Jonah would like to talk to you."

"Why?" Rianthe stood. "So he can yell at me for not saving New Hope again?"

Using one finger, Raisa turned Rianthe's head her way. "There are plans to make. Jonah wants you involved. Feeling sorry for yourself will not help."

"You're right." Rianthe took a deep breath. Even knowing the truth in those words, her footfalls were as heavy as her mood as she walked to the shambles that remained of the dining house. Her stomach seemed ready to shake itself empty, just as Earth had tried to do. An unusual, deeper chill had settled around New Hope, seeping into her bones. She shivered.

Inside, where they'd eaten a scant hour earlier, Jonah, Kaiden, and Roulf sat at a cleared table. Glow pots cast an eerie light on the destruction around them.

"Come, Rianthe," Jonah beckoned. "We need to

talk."

She sat next to Kaiden on the bench. Warmth still radiated from him, surrounding her like a cocoon. She didn't understand why, but it felt good.

"It's been a long day," Jonah said.

They all nodded glumly as he continued.

"Most structures have one or more walls caved in. No roofs are intact that we've seen so far, other than the partial one here and one over the men's sleeping quarters. This dining house is a wreck"—he waved his hands around—"but it looks like the ovens aren't damaged. That's a blessing."

"I went out to the growing fields and the remembrance fields before full dark descended," Kaiden said. "They both look fine. The crop coverings are all right for the most part, and I saw no damaged crops or downed trees."

"Good news," Jonah said. "A bright spot in a dark day."

Tevy wandered in and sat next to Rianthe. She hugged him tight.

Jonah gave her a quick nod. Family was all they had right now.

"So tonight," Jonah said, "we'll make do. Tomorrow, we'll begin to clear the debris and rebuild."

"Again," Rianthe said, tasting the bitterness of the word on her tongue.

"Yes." Jonah fixed her with a stare. "Again."

"Could that girl, Marta, have done this?" Tevy, astute as ever, piped in.

"She's disappeared, hasn't she? It makes sense," Mokie said, joining them at the table.

"As much as I'd like to lay this blame at that girl's

feet"—Rianthe glanced at Kaiden, whose eyes were shuttered and vague—"I find it hard to believe she has enough magic to do this. This would take more than we, as a community, could accomplish." Rianthe shook her head. "I don't think this was her doing."

It could have been Taegar's. Except, when Rianthe had tapped into her magic as she reached for the depths of Earth, she'd sensed nothing of the Dark druid's taint. "It wasn't Taegar, either," she said. "I think… I think it was Earth."

"I'm inclined to agree," Jonah said. "So tomorrow…well, we have decisions to make. Earth sent us a message today we all understood. It can no longer help us. We are alone in our struggle to survive, something that will become harder and harder." His voice was monotone, his dejection complete.

"Earth is dying," Rianthe said.

"And it will get worse from here," Jonah answered. "Much worse."

For a long time, they all sat quietly, mired in their own thoughts. No one knew the next step, Rianthe realized. No one knew how to fix this.

Kaiden broke the silence. "What can we do?" He was always happier with a list of tasks to accomplish. It probably kept him from thinking too much.

Jonah glanced at Rianthe. "Roulf has been telling me an interesting story."

So tired she could barely put two cohesive thoughts together, Rianthe stared at them.

"He mentioned your visions."

That woke her up. "You've known about them," she said. "Everyone here knows."

"Yes. But I hear this recent one was different."

Earth had spoken to her directly, so, yes, this one was different. Rianthe clasped her hands together on the table.

Roulf leaned to cover her hands with his. "Those of us in contact with you heard the plea, child."

Help me. Come.

"Did Earth do this to us on purpose?" Jonah asked, the hint of anger apparent in his voice.

"No." Rianthe's response was immediate and certain as she pulled her hands from beneath Roulf's. "This was not Earth knocking our heads together." Rianthe tried to wrap her own mind around what she needed to convey. "Something has suppressed the *awen*. Earth can't access it. It can't heal itself any longer. Earth is dying. We know that now more than ever. If it had meant to harm us, it would have destroyed our crops. It would have disrespected our dead. It didn't do that, and no one died today. Unlike before." Her voice grew quiet. "I believe Earth was trying to free itself, like some sort of final thrust to loosen the *awen*, which tells me there is no more time. If we don't help now, we will all suffer the same fate as Earth."

"Then we help," Kaiden said.

Tasks again. Was that all life meant to him? Tasks and duty?

"How?" she said.

"You are in contact with Earth," Jonah said.

Roulf nodded as Rianthe shook her head.

"Maybe," she said. "But I've learned nothing."

"That's not true," Roulf protested.

"Nothing I understand."

"Bhren believed you are the prophesied one. We do, too. It's become apparent that now is the time," Jonah said. He inclined his head, maybe in apology, as he sealed her fate. "You're the only hope we have left."

"I don't know what to do," she said, panic rising like bile in her throat. "I've tried. I'm not even sure the magic was there for me during that quake. I couldn't help. I'm so sick of everyone saying I'm their savior. I can't manifest one iota of power." Rianthe covered her face. "If I could help New Hope, help Earth, I would. I'm not the prophesied one. I can't be. Because, if I am, we are truly doomed."

She stood, unable to look at them, to witness the despair on their faces. She'd failed them. To see that reflected back to her…it was too much. "I'm sorry," she said, gulping in great gobs of air. "I'm so, so sorry!"

With that final apology, Rianthe whirled and fled the room. She didn't stop until she reached the remembrance fields and sank to the ground beside Uja's marker.

"Uja. Dear Uja. I wish I could have saved you. But they're wrong. I am not who they think I am."

Rianthe pulled off her gloves and ran her hand along her brother's marker. He'd died trying to save New Hope, a truth forever etched in her mind and heart. Sweet Uja, who'd always ditched weapons practice to work with his plants. Yet, when swords were needed, he'd picked one up.

If she'd been there, she might have saved him. That was a guilt she'd carry the rest of her life. And now, more guilt settled on her shoulders, the weight heavy. She hadn't been able to help the very home Uja had died trying to protect. Would she never live up to everyone's belief in her?

Rianthe toyed with the grass at the base of Uja's stone. She'd always thought the grass grew greener there than anywhere else. Maybe that was her own pride in all that Uja had accomplished in his too short life.

I wish you were here to guide me, Brother. I don't know what to do. Letting instinct nudge her, Rianthe splayed both hands out on the grass, sinking down, touching Earth, bringing the vision on, and praying for guidance.

This time, it wasn't an immediate change. She wasn't tossed into the maelstrom of the struggle between Earth, humanity, and Taegar. This was more of a gentle, weeping plea. The world around her faded, replaced by a cave filled with sparkling bits of gems in the rock, defining the small area.

Rianthe's breath caught, and she clutched at the bag that hung around her neck. Taegar's cave? If so, she was a fool to have entered the vision without someone there to break her away from it. Taegar had almost killed Rianthe on more than one occasion during her visions.

Yet this didn't look like the same cave. It was smaller. And…Rianthe squinted. There was no altar. There was, however, an outpouring of light from the center of the ground that shined whiter than the light in Taegar's cave. The light glowed brighter still, then, out of that light, scenes grew.

Scenes of a world teeming with people and machines. Forests disappeared as mankind spread out, the air grew thin, and there was less and less fertile ground for crops.

She learned of Earth's growing sadness at these crimes against the lands, nutrients and minerals used until there were no more. She saw the burst of energy as Earth belched *awen*, the magic from its core. Everything brightened and the healing began. Mankind was happy.

So was Earth. Everything would be all right.

She saw how mankind reacted to this new power, some with awe and good intentions, some with longing and greed. War had sprung from these two diverse ideals.

And she saw the *awen*, a great whiteness of light, descend deep into Earth, back from whence it came, rainfall tears of sadness closing the opening through which it had erupted.

The last vision was of her, walking through the forest, resolute in her destination.

Come.

Rianthe slipped from the vision, but not before sensing a hint of anger and desperation. A very familiar anger.

Taegar.

Shaking her head, Rianthe closed her eyes. When she opened them, the remembrance fields once again surrounded her. This vision had differed from any other. Earth had guided her through a history lesson, then sent her a plea.

Come.

Rianthe faced north, an overwhelming need building inside her to journey in that direction. But now? How could she leave New Hope with so much to do? They were back in full survival mode and needed roofs to keep the rain out, and walls to keep them warm and safe through winter.

Too much needed doing.

"Ri?"

She startled at Kaiden's voice. Unusual for her. She always knew when someone, especially Kaiden, was close.

~~~
~~~

Kaiden settled on the ground beside her, running his hand along Uja's marker like he'd done a thousand times before. "I thought I'd find you here." When he'd first seen her, he'd known right away that she'd entered a vision. Gut-wrenching fear and anger had immobilized him. She'd promised never to touch Earth, to have one of these visions, without him there. It was too dangerous. She'd almost died before.

He'd wanted to rush to her side, pull her hands from the soil that held her enthralled. As he strode forward, he saw how different she looked this time. Serene. Her hands spread among the blades of grass and her shoulders relaxed, her look focused, not afraid.

So he'd stopped. Waited. Watched.

When she'd come out of the trance, he'd given her time to orient back to this place, then made his presence known. Now, he touched her hair. It pleased him that she'd chosen to let it grow. Sitting just past ear length, it was as soft as he remembered it. "You had a vision?"

Rianthe nodded, still staring off into the distance.

"You said you wouldn't do that without me here."

"I know. This was…different."

"How?"

"I was in a cave—"

He tensed. "Taegar's cave?"

Relief filled him when she shook her head and looked at him. He saw the truth of what she said in her eyes.

"Not like Taegar's at all, really. There was no danger. A stream of light emanated from the ground. Different. Stronger."

"What did you see?"

Rianthe paused. "I think Earth was guiding me,

telling me to go to this cave. I'm not sure why, or even where it is." She looked off, to the north, as her words faded.

Fear gripped him. The last time she'd said she must leave, it had about killed him. Nothing in this world would keep him from her side if she left New Hope again. He had to be at her side. He had to protect her. His life, his heart depended on keeping her safe. Kaiden took a deep breath and tried to still the panic within him. "When do we leave?" he asked.

She stared at Uja's memorial marker for such a long time, Kaiden thought she planned to refuse him. He would follow her if that was the case. After an interminable amount of time, she nodded. Relief flooded Kaiden, making him weak in the knees.

"Good," he said, hearing the gruff emotion in his voice. He cleared his throat. "We should tell the others." He held out his hand to help her up.

Rianthe reached out, then froze. When she reached for her gloves, Kaiden understood. He wasn't sure what had happened the last time they'd been hand-to-hand, and until he knew more, she was right to put on her gloves. Still, he longed for the day when they didn't have to be so concerned. When they could be free of all this dire responsibility and free to see if they could find their friendship again. And hopefully more.

He shook his head. That kind of thinking got him nowhere. Life was what it was and too many people counted on them to solve the riddle of Earth's missing *awen*. All of humanity counted on them, though most did not understand that.

With her gloves on, Rianthe accepted his hand. They walked back in silence, each deep in their own thoughts.

In the dining hall, some of the men worked to shore up the roof at one end, using fallen thatch. That would work well enough for some to sleep there that night. Jonah and Roulf still talked quietly. Raisa had joined them, but Tevy had disappeared, probably to snuggle up with his wolves. It was late and they all needed sleep.

"…haven't seen her since shortly after the shaking stopped," Raisa said.

"Seen who?" Rianthe asked.

"Marta," Jonah said. "She seems to have disappeared."

Kaiden saw Rianthe glance at him. Probably looking for his reaction. Marta was… an enigma. He did not like her. He knew that. She was wiry and cunning. Yet every time he got near her, those feelings changed. As a protector, it would take a strong magic to supress his nature and subvert him. More and more, Kaiden believed the girl had extraordinary abilities and used them on him, but for what purpose? Gah, there were too many questions, and no answers, at least not any they understood. Maybe this journey with Rianthe would help.

"Marta was uninjured right after the earthquake," Kaiden said.

Rianthe stiffened beside him.

"I haven't seen her since."

Jonah nodded. "I did too. So where is she now?"

The question sat in front of them all like a pile of rocks weighing them down. Finally, Jonah shook his head. "This is getting us nowhere. Roulf and I have been talking."

"Kaiden and I have too," Rianthe said.

Roulf stared at her. "You have somewhere you need to go."

Rianthe nodded.

"Another vision?"

Another nod. "This one seemed different. Quieter, more desperate. It was Earth, calling me to find another cave. I'm not sure why."

Roulf clapped his hands together. "A journey. I haven't been on one in some time. I will accompany you, child."

"As will I," Kaiden added. No one, not even Roulf, would usurp his right to protect Rianthe. If they did, it wouldn't be for long. His shoulder still bothered him, but even that would not keep him from going with her.

Rianthe toyed with her gloves.

"What are you not telling us?" Kaiden asked.

"There was something, at the very end of my vision. An anger renewing itself. It didn't feel like Earth."

"Taegar?"

Rianthe shrugged. "Maybe. Whatever short lull we've been allowed...well, it might be coming to an end."

"Seems to me," Jonah said with a sigh, "it already has."

Kaiden looked around, hating that he'd be leaving once again while New Hope worked to pull itself back together.

"At any rate, we have no choice," Jonah said. "Rianthe must go, and you, Kaiden, must keep her safe."

Exactly what he planned to do. "All right then. We leave at first light."

"And we will repair and rebuild while you are gone," Jonah said. "I'm about as tired as I've ever been. I think we all need to get some sleep."

They stood. Jonah clapped Kaiden and Rianthe on

the shoulders, but Raisa pulled them each into healing hugs. "I know you will leave early in the morning, so I'll say my goodbyes now. Come back soon, safe, and without injury," she said, giving them a *berkano's* blessing.

The druid's tower still stood, though no one knew yet if it was safe to use. Kaiden and Rianthe walked together to what used to be the men's sleeping hut. The village had split up into two large groups to get everyone under a roof for the night. A cold, light mist fell, making every person grateful for the men's work on the two partial roofs. When they got to the hut, Rianthe sank to the ground against a wall, exhaustion evident in her limp hands, her drooping eyes, and her complete lack of concern over where she would sleep. Every time she used her power, and Kaiden believed she had called upon it tonight and saved them from a worse fate, it wore her out. It scared him how much the magic took out of her. If she had to dredge up more, how would she survive it?

Kaiden settled next to her, worried about her, about New Hope, and about Earth. He had no idea how to help. Dram. He wanted to make things right for the people he loved. So far, he hadn't been able to affect a thing.

He missed Ri. Missed the closeness they'd shared. Their conversations were stilted, their reactions to each other's comments were inflammatory, and, ever since that touching thing, they avoided contact like the plague.

Yet there they were, seated next to each other. Not touching. Not talking. Rianthe shivered in the cold until Kaiden nudged her gently. When she leaned into him, he put his arm around her. Just for tonight. Like old times. This was all he could do to help.

Rianthe sighed and curled against him, already more

asleep than awake.

It felt so nice. It scared him, how good this was. Tomorrow, they'd head off once again into the unknown. What would they find?

"Where is Tevy?" Rianthe asked through a yawn.

"I don't know. Can you reach out to Taschia?"

Several still seconds passed before Rianthe answered him.

"He's with the wolves. Safe and warm and sleeping, Taschia says."

"Then he's in good hands. Sleep, Ri. We both need to," he said. Tomorrow, a new reality would toss them different struggles, he was certain. For tonight, right now, he had a momentary peace, keeping her safe and warm. Kaiden leaned his head on hers and made a conscious effort to forget everything for just this little while.

~~~

Taegar stared at the runes spread out on the altar in front of her. Multiple attempts to free the magic brought only failure. The runes should work. They were the talisman she'd searched for all these years. They must be. Everything pointed to their authenticity. The girl, whoever she was, had kept them close. Then the boy had gotten them somehow, and he'd fought with everything he had to keep from losing them.

Light emanated from the center of the altar, *awen* streaming from Earth's core. Much fainter now, it grew weaker with each passing day. Such a pure, exquisite, golden perfection, and a power that should rightfully be hers. All the years of struggle, of searching for the talisman to bind Earth's magic to her for all time. She must not lose now. Too many years she'd waited for the day the power would answer only to her and she could
~~~

exact vengeance upon a world that had turned against her.

It hadn't always been that way. In the time of the awakening, she'd been one of the most beautiful and powerful druids. The world had idolized her. Then, the shroud got ripped away to reveal that it was the power they wanted, not her. Those who'd turned against her were the first victims. Even that had not sated a fury that still burned deep within. Humankind would submit to her great power. Earth would submit.

Taegar picked up the runes, reaching with them into the light. Weak as it was, the power thrummed through her. This was what she wanted. What she needed. To be one with the power. To *be* the power. This was everything.

The light flared, almost as if recognizing a connection to the runes. Brightness filled Taegar with energy, yet it quickly dimmed. No grand release. No marriage between her and the magic for all time.

Nothing.

Her fingers crackled as she tightened them around the runes, yanking them out of the light. The urge to destroy something vibrated within her. Someone must pay for this delay in the realization of her destiny.

A burst of activity pulled her attention away from the light. Shaking, somewhere in the distance. She sensed it came from the east. Was this a renewed effort to take back her rightful power? A new battle was brewing. One she would win. No one could equal her, especially once the talisman bound her to Earth's magic for all time.

No one.

The girl in the visions could not best her. Neither would that boy. They must perish. Taegar turned back to look at the weak light, unfurled her skinless fingers to gaze at the runes. A few were missing, and the last person who'd held them had been that boy. She'd sent the girl out to find him, to show him the power of darkness.

To bring him to her.

It had better be soon.

CHAPTER NINE

Morning came too soon for Rianthe. Not yet ready to say goodbye again to the friends and family of New Hope, she went looking for Tevy, while Roulf and Kaiden stocked knapsacks for the journey. She needed to tell her brother she'd be leaving and why.

Peeking inside the destroyed barn, neither wolf nor blond child was to be found. She walked all around the central areas of New Hope. No Tevy. Rianthe went to the remembrance fields, then to the growing fields. Still no Tevy.

Back in the village, Rianthe found Fraka and Raisa cleaning up in what remained of the dining house. Roulf, Kaiden, and Mokie were there too.

Trying to soothe her nerves, Rianthe smoothed her hand over Ujami's fuzzy hair as he snuggled in the wrap Fraka used to carry him. Something seemed off. "Have any of you seen Tevy?"

Fraka shook her head, frowning. "I haven't seen him all morning. Isn't he with his wolf friends?"

It wasn't unusual for him to head into the woods with the wolves, but Tevy always told someone. That was the rule and he'd never broken it.

Panic lodged in her throat like an aborted swallow. She tried to tamp it down, but until she found her brother… She had to find him.

All of a sudden, the room filled with howls as Tevy's wolves raced in, agitation plain to see in their worried gait and soulful yelps.

"What's going on?" Kaiden asked.

Taschia? Rianthe mind-spoke to her friend.

They cannot sense our brother. Taschia cocked her head. *I cannot sense him either.*

Fear congealed in Rianthe's stomach like a heavy rock that pulled her down, making it difficult to even move. The wolves always heard Tevy. The only reason that connection would be severed was distance or… No! She sprinted out into the open air, screaming as her heart stuck in her throat, stealing her breath.

"The wolves can't sense Tevy and I can't find him. Tevy! Tevy!" Over and over she called, with others joining as her search widened. Rianthe collapsed, unable to fathom this turn of events. *Where is he?* "Tevy!" she screamed again, pounding the ground.

"Take your gloves off, Ri," Kaiden said, his voice as urgent and hoarse as hers.

Rianthe yanked her gloves off, spreading her hands along the dirt, begging the *ehwaz* to show her Tevy. At first, she only saw a dark void.

Tevy! Rianthe reached out to him, but couldn't see him, couldn't find him. There was nothing but darkness.

Then, a pinprick of light appeared in the distance. The light grew, changed, turned golden as it expanded, separating into the evil, golden eyes she knew well. No words were spoken. The eyes just watched her, then...

The vision disappeared, even though Rianthe still touched the ground.

"No!" she said, falling back. "No. No. No."

Taschia nudged her hand and Rianthe sat up, burying her head in the wolf's fur as she held her tight. "I didn't protect him. He's gone. I'm so sorry." *I've failed again.*

With tears streaming down her face, she looked around at the village.

Tevy was gone. And she knew exactly who had him.

"Taegar has Tevy," she croaked out, burying her head in Taschia's fur. How had this happened? Was he still alive? She couldn't bear it if—

I do not sense his death, Taschia mind-spoke.

That did little to reassure Rianthe. He might be all right at this moment, but anything could happen to him. Especially in Taegar's clutches.

My brothers and I agree. We must find our lost brother. We will scent him.

Rianthe lifted her head. "You're right."

"Right about what?" Kaiden said.

You didn't let Kaiden hear? Rianthe asked Taschia.

This was not his conversation.

Rianthe jumped up. "Where's my pack? I'm going after Tevy."

A crowd barred her way, stopping her in her tracks, all talking at the same time.

"Wait a minute," Jonah said. "Let's figure this out together."

"Rianthe, you must go where Earth is directing you,"

Roulf said.

"Not without me, you aren't." Kaiden glanced at Taschia with a scowl, realizing the wolf had withheld a conversation from him.

Rianthe held up her hands. "There's nothing you can say to keep me from going after Tevy."

Earth rumbled, sending them all tumbling to the ground. It lasted a fraction of the time of last night's quake, but it got their attention. Everyone clung to each other, white-knuckled and with terror-widened eyes. They turned almost as one unit. Toward her. Needing her to do the right thing. To save them.

She needed to save Tevy. She couldn't desert him.

Roulf settled a gentle hand on her shoulder. "You must follow Earth's directive, child." His voice, soft with sadness, carried emotion that told her he knew what this sacrifice meant.

Jonah nodded. "You must go. Too much is at stake here. I'm sorry, Rianthe."

How could they ask her to make this sacrifice? Tevy was the only family she had left. Rianthe looked at all the faces, saw their fear mingled with years of hardship, of the struggle to survive until the One Prophecy could be fulfilled. Hope that dwindled with each event that tore their lives apart and caused them to rebuild.

Rianthe shook her head. "Don't ask me to do this, Jonah. Please. I'm begging you."

Jonah hung his head but didn't give her the answer she needed. He didn't tell her not to go after her brother. Nor did he say that, even if she found him, there was no saving his life if Earth died. He didn't have to.

She turned to Kaiden, seeing the turmoil on his face, the war going on within.

"I will find Tevy," he finally said.

Roulf squeezed her shoulder. "And you must go on a journey, child."

No. It should be her. Tevy was her baby brother. The only one she had left. She'd raised him from the time he'd left their mother's womb. She couldn't trust this to anyone else. Yet Kaiden, who normally would not let her go anywhere without him, had offered to separate from her to find Tevy. Kaiden had set aside her protection for Tevy's. That alone weighted her choice. If she was to be denied Tevy's rescue herself, Kaiden was the only one she trusted with her brother's life.

Rianthe stepped in front of him, looked deep into his eyes. "If I do this… If I go north, you'll go with the wolves? You'll find him?"

Kaiden nodded and swallowed hard. This was not easy for him. He loved Tevy as much as she did, but he'd sworn to protect her.

"Promise me," she said, grasping his tunic in her fist and pulling him closer. Kaiden had never made a promise he hadn't kept. "Promise me you'll find him and bring him home safe."

Kaiden's nostrils flared. It was a promise he had little control over, but she asked it just the same. She needed it.

"If you promise not to let your emotions send you off on some stupid, life-threatening vengeance side trip…"

"I have no idea what I'll find or what I'll have to do," Rianthe said.

"And I have no idea what I'll find or what I'll be called upon to do," he countered.

Rianthe gritted her teeth. "Fine."

"Say it."

"I promise."

Infinitesimal relief touched Kaiden's eyes. He tugged a tuft of her lengthening hair, almost bringing her to tears with this gentle reminder of their past. "Then I promise, too," he said.

"Good," Roulf said, reaching up to clap them both on the shoulder. "Taschia and I will journey with Rianthe."

Jonah joined them. "I know this is not what either of you wants, but it is the best solution to an impossible situation."

It was a horrible solution. And the only one available.

In a short time, they'd all pulled their packs and supplies together and met back at the commons, ready to depart.

Taschia moved beside Rianthe. *I go with you. My mother stays here to make sure those who stay behind know what happens.*

"Keep her safe, Taschia," Kaiden said.

So he can hear you now? Rianthe asked.

There was a need. My brothers go with Kaiden.

That reassured Rianthe. She wanted to find Tevy with a desperation beyond anything she'd known, but she needed Kaiden to be safe too.

"Which way will you head?" she asked him.

"The wolves say southwest."

"The same direction we went after Deakon."

Kaiden nodded, not saying what they both probably knew. Southwest was the most likely location of Taegar's lair. "And you're headed north."

"Yes." Rianthe turned in that direction.

"The vision told you that, right?"

"It was more of a feeling, that north is where some

answers lie."

Kaiden tugged on Rianthe's cloak, and she turned toward him. "Remember your promise, Ri."

Rianthe gulped back tears and punched Kaiden in the shoulder. "Don't get dead."

He chuckled. "I'll try not to." When he looked at her, myriad emotions touched his eyes. Worry, resolve, fear, and…love?

Rianthe knew those same emotions. She set her hand over Kaiden's heart, felt its beat quicken even through the glove, her own matching it. "Find him, Kaiden. Please."

He covered her hand with his. "I intend to. Be safe."

"I intend to," she mirrored, a smile tugging at her lips. "We can keep in touch via the wolves for as long as possible. Taschia had been unable to speak to her brothers or Tevy while we were in the Fringes, so there are limits to the wolves' telepathic ability."

Nothing remained to be said. Rianthe waved to everyone and, with a last glance at Kaiden, she, Roulf, and Taschia headed north.

DISCOVERY

CHAPTER TEN

Kaiden stood rooted in place, watching Rianthe walk through the trees and out of his sight, off to an unknown and probably dangerous future. Letting her go a second time proved to be the hardest thing he'd ever done. His nerve endings screamed to run after her. His worst nightmare, playing out in real life all over again. She was leaving, and he was powerless to stop her. Worse, this time he'd agreed she must go.

He slapped his chest, trying to stop his heart from jumping out of his skin. Would life never give them a moment's peace? He knew it had to be this way. If she'd gone with him to find her brother, their lives and the lives of all humanity might suffer beyond any cost he could imagine. Her trust humbled him. Nothing meant more to Rianthe than Tevy. This knowledge fueled his strength, but it didn't lessen his pain.

"She can take care of herself," Jonah said beside

him.

"I know that. Still…"

"It's hard to watch her go."

"Again."

Jonah nodded. "Destiny, Roulf, and her own instincts must guide her now. She also has Taschia. They will protect her."

Not as well as I would. Kaiden shouldered his own pack and resettled his scabbard belt around his waist. "The sooner I get going, the sooner I can find Tevy and join her."

"The wolves are anxious. They want to track."

Kaiden clasped Jonah's shoulder in their way of saying goodbye. "We will be careful."

"And so will we, son. Be mindful. The weather is not what it should be for this late fall season."

Kaiden nodded. "It's worse."

Both of them worried over the shifting weather patterns. Each season seemed worse than the last, but if they couldn't free the suppressed magic, they wouldn't have to worry about the weather or anything else, because nothing would survive the onslaught to come.

"I'll be back as soon as possible, with Tevy," Kaiden told Jonah, who nodded.

With one more look at the trees that had swallowed Rianthe, Kaiden turned toward his own journey. "Let's track," he said to the wolves. *Can you hear me?* he mind-spoke to Hark, the oldest of Taschia's brethren and the pack alpha. He'd only hear them if they allowed him to.

Yes. We seek now?

"We seek now," Kaiden said. He crashed into the forest, not worried about stealth. The only thing that mattered, the only focus that remained was to find Tevy and bring him home safe. Tevy, who loved to carve wooden toys. Who imprinted dried skins with pictures from memory. Who loved his wolves as much, if not more, than he loved people.

He sensed the wolves spreading out among the trees, searching for Tevy's scent. Kaiden ran with them, hoping against all hope that their extraordinary noses would give them a promising direction in which to search. He couldn't match their fast pace for long, but he didn't need to while they were close enough to mind-speak.

We will not get too far ahead.

Good.

Kaiden slowed his pace to conserve his energy. The wolves could go without rest for longer than he could. He needed to be ready for a long haul. Who knew how far away Tevy was by now? Had Taegar herself come for him? They'd not heard any inkling of her leaving the cave, so something must have changed. The thought made Kaiden worry about Rianthe's partial set of runes. The rest of the set was in Taegar's possession and may have already enhanced her powers. If that were so, defeating her would be more difficult than ever.

Marta might have somehow been party to Tevy's disappearance. Something was off about her.

It galled him that sweet Tevy had been stolen on his watch. And, for one of the few times in his life, Kaiden was afraid. Tendrils of unease wrapped themselves around him, squeezing him like a python. Everything had changed, amped up, and gotten much worse. He was in a maelstrom of danger and couldn't seem to claw his way out.

Kaiden scolded himself. This was not helping. He needed to focus on what he could affect, not things outside his control. Reaching out with his mind, he checked on the wolves. Even out of his sight, Kaiden knew they had not yet found the scent. It worried Kaiden that they weren't able to mind-speak with Tevy. They'd have to find him to solve that riddle.

They searched their way past the Rushmore Mountain without a single clue to help them. Kaiden prayed hard that their direction was true.

After about four hours, one of the wolves howled. Kaiden honed in on their whereabouts.

We scent our brother, Hark, the oldest, mind-spoke.

I'm coming, Kaiden answered.

We follow the scent. You follow us.

Wait. Kaiden raced to join them, but he arrived too late. The wolves were gone. When he saw the carved wooden wolf lying on its side on the ground, he knew he'd found the place where they'd picked up Tevy's scent. Kaiden retrieved the toy and rubbed the dirt off with his thumb. They'd spent hours, he and Tevy, carving the wolf to the exact specifications Tevy had wanted. If anything happened to the boy, Kaiden didn't know what he'd do. He clutched the toy wolf, looking around.

Which direction? Kaiden reached out for Hark, Marin, Joek, or Grog. Any wolf who heard him. Hark's missive that they must hurry was a bare whisper in Kaiden's mind. They were moving out of range, so Kaiden resorted to his own skills to track the wolves and prayed they were on the right path. He dropped to search the ground He inspected the paw prints, so many it looked like they'd jumped all over the place in their excitement. After searching for several minutes, he found a trail of deeper tracks, as if they'd dug in to kick off their run. The tracks headed east, which surprised him. When they'd gone after Deakon, who they'd thought was returning to Taegar, the trail had led southwest.

Several more hours into his trek, Kaiden focused on two things. The tracks in front of him, and the wisp of remaining contact he had with the wolves. He'd always done well on journeys by narrowing his concentration. It kept him from thinking too much and kept him aware of the immediate. Which was why it surprised him when he caught movement, very close to him, out of the corner of his eye.

"Kaiden."

He leaped back, yanking his sword out as he turned. He'd heard that whisper before, but out there in the woods, hours away from New Hope, it took a second for him to determine who'd called his name.

"Come out where I can see you, Marta," he said. "Slowly. No fast moves."

Marta stepped out from behind a bush right next to him.

"That's close enough," Kaiden said, holding his sword in front of him as a deterrent. He didn't understand how the woman got so close. She scrambled his brains like morning eggs and until he could figure out how to fight that, he'd best keep her at arm's length. How had he not known she was near? At the very least, the wolves should have warned him.

"How did you get here?"

"I followed you."

"Except you disappeared right after the earthquake. How did you even know I left?"

She took a step toward him and Kaiden raised his sword again, unsure of when he'd lowered it.

"I saw how you protected that woman after the

ground moved." She pouted, matching the plaintive sound of her voice. "I couldn't stand it, knowing she was important to you. So I left. I waited outside the village for a chance to…talk to you. When you and the wolves left, I followed until I had the chance to make myself known."

"I don't tolerate subterfuge." Kaiden checked the area to make certain she was alone. When he turned back, Marta had moved closer yet again. "Stop. You stay right there." Kaiden tried to move back a step, but nothing happened. His feet wouldn't shift.

"It's all right, Kaiden," Marta purred. "It will be all right. You can put your sword down."

Somehow, she'd shifted to his side and he'd sheathed his weapon. When had she moved? Kaiden tried to rip the fog away from his brain. It wouldn't budge.

Tevy. I have to find Tevy. He couldn't seem to put two thoughts together. Hadn't Marta disappeared? After the earthquake. Yes. So why was she there? Had she helped kidnap Tevy?

"Where is he?" Kaiden demanded, his tongue thick. He shook her none too gently and, for a moment, Marta's eyes appeared almost golden in her ire. Something shoved him to the ground. Marta?

"Do not touch me like that again," she spat, then visibly worked to get her emotions under control.

"Where's Tevy?" Kaiden yelled, getting back to his feet.

"The boy, right?"

Her voice soothed him, calmed him down.

"I don't know," Marta said, the angelic smile back on her face.

"You have him. I know you do." Kaiden whipped his head from side to side, searching for any clue as to

Tevy's whereabouts.

Marta's hand lay on his arm again. How had he let that happen? He shook her hand off, trying to clear the shadows from his mind. He stepped back, putting distance between them.

"How could I harm that cute little boy? Besides, I'm here with you. I'm alone. There's no way I took him."

He recognized the sense in her words, although they came to him through a thickness that didn't set right. She'd had no time to take the boy.

"No, there hasn't been time," Marta purred, as if reading his mind. "Someone else must have taken him."

Someone else. Yes. Taegar. Taegar had taken Tevy. Exactly as Rianthe said. Rianthe. Warmth infused Kaiden when he thought of her. His thinking cleared until Marta tugged on his arm and spoke again.

"Yes, Kaiden. Someone else must have taken him."

Kaiden nodded. "Tevy wouldn't leave on his own. Not without telling his sister."

Marta's eyes narrowed at the mention of Rianthe. "Yes…the sister." She took a long breath. "I may know of a place."

"What? Where?"

"It's not a place I've been to. It's dangerous there."

"I'm not afraid of danger. What is this place?"

"A town. There's a mine there."

"A mine? What's there to mine these days?"

"I'm not sure I remember. Some sort of soil. Hummer? No, humate. That's what they called the stuff. Apparently, it's a type of, uh, fertilizer. That's it. Something that helps plants grow."

Kaiden had never heard of such a thing. Just the possibility gave him a glimmer of hope. There would be a great need for something like that. If some greedy person got control of the mine…

"I've heard children work in that mine. Children sold to them, enslaved."

Sold. Just like him. Though Kaiden retained no memory of his arrival in New Hope as a newling, the story Bhren had told him left a deep ache in his heart. A man, wandering in with a babe in his arms, sold him to Bhren for a few days' food and water. He'd left as quickly as he'd appeared, never uttering a word about whether Kaiden was his son. Kaiden had been unwanted and that grated on him. He'd worked hard to overcome that unworthiness as he'd grown up in New Hope. No matter how hard he tried, it nicked him like a knife. Always irritating. Always reminding him he had no roots.

It was unforgivable that any children were sold, ever. He could not tolerate it. Kaiden's heart constricted at the thought of young Tevy working a pickax in the mine for nothing more than a bite of food.

"Children are being sold into slavery, Kaiden. Did you hear me?"

The lilt of Marta's voice called Kaiden back.

"Maybe Tevy is there," she continued. "Maybe he's been forced to work in the mine. Most children do not last long under those conditions."

Working in the mine must be horrific. Heavy dust swelling in their lungs, and probably no water to soothe dry throats. His hands clenched and unclenched as rage filled him. No child should have to endure that. "We have to go there and rescue those children. And Tevy. We have to find Tevy."

"We will." Marta soothed. "We will."

He started off in the direction she'd indicated. "How

far is this town?"

Marta stepped in line beside him. "Not far. Maybe three days walk? I'll show you."

"You'll not only show me. Tell me everything you know about this place."

Something wasn't right. Kaiden knew that he wasn't thinking this through and had missed something vital. He'd been listening for something, hadn't he? Shaking his head, he tried to un-muddle his brain, to no avail. He'd need his wits about him, traveling with Marta. Whatever her plan might be, he seemed to figure into it. He needed time to determine why she wanted him to follow her. And time to find Tevy. Her information gave him the best lead he had. If he could help other children at the same time, wasn't he obligated to?

Once he started on this path, he'd need to see it through. It was a lead he must follow, but only time would tell him if he'd chosen the right path.

He motioned for Marta to lead, heading south after an idea that he wasn't truly certain was the right one.

CHAPTER ELEVEN

Something wasn't right. Rianthe couldn't put a finger on it, but it felt like she'd lost something… inside. Like a part of her had split off and disappeared. Was it because she and Tevy were so far from each other? Or that he'd… No. She wouldn't think of that. Tevy was alive and well. Somewhere. He had to be.

She, Roulf, and Taschia walked for several hours in a direction dictated by her instincts alone. Being blind to their destination made Rianthe anxious. Even more worrisome, a darkness lay ahead she didn't understand. It grew in her mind with each mile they traversed. And now, that omen vibrated through her body like the strings on Jonah's lute. The path ahead seemed to widen into a clearing. Whatever had set her on edge was just ahead. She could feel it. She signaled for Taschia and Roulf to stand behind her.

Foreboding weighed down Rianthe's legs, making

every step an effort. Sword ready, she forced herself to walk beyond the trees, ready for whatever danger waited there, her heart pounding like hard rain.

The clearing was empty. Rianthe looked around, confused. Where was the danger? She saw nothing, smelled nothing, heard nothing. Lowering her sword, Rianthe wasn't sure what to do next. Something had triggered her warrior instinct, but what?

Two newling oak trees, only a foot or two taller than her, stood guard over the clearing. Moss and brush covered the ground. No one had been there in quite some time. Realization snaked through her, strengthening when she saw the burned-out hulk that had once been a crude dwelling. Droplets of memory gathered into a familiar nightmare.

Her sword clanked to the ground. Rianthe barely heard it as she sank down beside it.

"Noooo." Grief surrounded her, invaded her, burned her every nerve ending until she thought she would explode from pain. "Not here. No. No. No. No."

Rianthe curled into herself, trying to keep the memories at bay. Everything from that night played over in her mind, a vivid, bone-chilling loop of horror.

Gentle fingers squeezed her shoulder and Roulf quietly asked one simple question. "What?"

"This is where…" Rianthe gulped great bits of air. "This is where—my parents died."

"I didn't know," Roulf said, his voice quivering with sorrow.

Some part of Rianthe heard Roulf's voice, but she didn't listen. All she could perceive was the place, being back in this hell, her nightmares turned into reality. Anguish filled her. Sorrow for how things had changed that day.

Taschia licked her on the cheek. *I feel your pain, sister.*

Rianthe clutched her friend. She held on too tight, but the wolf didn't whine. Roulf sat on Rianthe's other side and placed an arm around her shoulders. "I'm so sorry."

Words would not form. Rianthe nodded, gulping deep breaths of air to calm herself. The ache would not diminish. Rianthe tapped her chest with her fist, paying homage to a pain that was never very far away.

After too long a time, she pushed herself up. Roulf and Taschia gave her time to think, to feel, for the pain to ebb.

Rianthe walked into the charred remains of the building. Nothing but a stubby, blackened, partial wall remained. Rianthe cocked her head to stare at the nearby oak newling. It was strange how life reasserted itself after death had destroyed it. She walked to the spot where her mother had given birth to Tevy, the only good thing to come out of a day that had shattered everything she held dear.

She turned as if looking out the window at the scene that played out on that dreadful day. She could almost see the gray shadows. One of them had been the traitor, Deakon. She knew that now. And one, taller than the rest, had been Taegar, a name Rianthe hadn't known then. The wraith had leaned over Rianthe's father, trying to force Damian Royan to tell her where the talisman lay hidden.

Rianthe clutched the bag at her throat that held three of the runes from her father's original gift. The others had been stolen and handed over to Taegar.

Everyone had been surprised when nothing dire

happened after Rianthe lost the runes to Taegar. That alone gave her a seed of hope. Maybe all the runes must be together for the magic to take hold.

With heavy steps, Rianthe walked to the second young oak tree. This one grew in the very spot her father had fought so valiantly to buy his family time to escape. The spot where he'd given his life to keep his secret— that he'd carried the talisman and had given it to his offspring.

She placed her hand on the oak and it shivered. Had it reacted to her touch? Rianthe slipped off her glove and placed her hand against the rough bark, already cracked with growth.

Daughter.

Rianthe yanked her hand back. What was that? She turned to look at Roulf and Taschia, who sat where she'd left them. "Did you say something?"

"No." Roulf shook his head. "Did you?"

"I thought, when I touched the tree... " Rianthe looked the young tree over. A few years old at best, it must have sprouted shortly after she'd last been there.

Could this tree have grown from the ashes of her father? Rianthe twisted to stare at the other oak newling. And that tree from the ashes of her mother? There was only one way to know.

Rianthe squatted in front of the tree, settling a shaky hand on its bark. "Father?"

Waiting. For you.

Tears streamed down her face as sensations of love enfolded her. She didn't wipe the tears away. She placed both arms around the tree, embracing it like the ghost of a remembered past. "I didn't know."

Not much time. Memories fading. Soon I will know

nothing except to reach for the sun and drink the rain as the seasons unfold.

Overcome with emotion, Rianthe gazed at the other tree. She couldn't reach both at the same time and did not want to lose this tenuous connection. "Mother? Can she—?"

Your mother did not have the strength. I've barely managed. Had you arrived any later…

Rianthe's grief equaled her emotion on that terrible day. To never talk to her mother again… Rianthe leaned into the tree as her tears darkened the bark. "I've missed you so much."

And I, you. Listen now, before it is too late. There is a cave.

The voice was her father's, and yet not her father's. It had changed, grown deeper, with a croak in it. Enough remained that she wanted to listen to it for as long as possible. It didn't matter what he said. What mattered was this tender thread of contact. She couldn't lose him. Not again.

Daughter. Listen. There is no time.

What had he said? A cave. He'd said something about a cave. "Earth sent me a vision of it. Small, with a light stream, somewhere north of here."

Yes. That is where your mother and I were taking you. You must go there.

"I don't know where it is."

Trust your senses. They will guide you. It is two or three days walk from here. Distance grows…faint for me…

The thoughts trailed off. "Father! Don't leave me. Please."

The oak straightened, then sighed as it settled back. *I*

am almost gone. Know this, Daughter. You are loved. You have always been loved. I am sorry to put this burden on you, but you are the only one.

"The only one?" she whispered.

The prophesied one.

"But I don't have magical ability." Not much, at any rate.

It will come when you need it. There is a book, in the cave.

If trees could gasp, this one did.

All our thoughts... All our love... I'm sorry...

"No! Don't leave, Father. Please, don't leave me!" Rianthe clutched the tree, scraping her cheek against the rough bark, begging him to come back.

The only answer she got was the wind whistling through branches devoid of leaves.

She didn't know how long she sat there. When Roulf touched her shoulder, Rianthe let go of the tree. She rubbed her cheek, sore from the bark's indentation and scratchy from dried tears. As she hugged Roulf, her sadness slowly lifted. She'd lost her father all over again, but this rare opportunity, this chance to talk to him one more time, was a gift that gave her more joy than she'd known for a long time. The ache in her chest lessened and she smiled. "I spoke to my father." She heard the wonder in her voice. "This tree"—she patted the oak—"grew from his ashes. That one grew from my mother's."

"From the ashes," Roulf mumbled. "Oak trees have always been the sacred symbol of the Guardian druids. Look at your signet ring."

Rianthe glanced down and ran her finger over the proud oak engraved upon her silver ring. "Did you know this was possible? For a druid to inhabit a tree?"

He shook his head. "There's so much I don't know."

"My father told me of a cave, the one I saw in my vision. He said there is a book there that will help." Rianthe pulled on her gloves and brushed the dirt from her pants. "He said it's maybe two or three days north of here and I should let my instincts guide me."

"Did he say anything else?"

She glanced sadly at the tree. "We didn't have much time. He'd nearly lost sentience, on his way to becoming the hardy oak, on his way to his new life."

Roulf nodded. "This is good, child. Yes, this is very good." He patted the tree, bending his head for a long moment. "I knew your father. He was a good man, a great druid."

Crossing to the other tree, Rianthe pulled off a glove and lay her hand on its bark. Yes, her father had said she couldn't talk to her mother, but she still needed to try. No words came, yet the sensation of love, of being embraced, swirled through her. She chose to see it as her mother's final message. She knew her nightmares of that day would no longer return. Her parents, in one final gasp of support, had helped her see the truth of that day. They'd given their lives to save Earth. She would always miss them, but they were at peace now, and that went a long way toward easing her sorrow.

You are surrounded by love, Taschia mind-spoke.

Rianthe nodded. Her parents had done everything possible to make certain of that. Now, it was her turn to carry the torch. She turned to Roulf and Taschia. "I'm ready."

"All right, then," Roulf said, handing her the sword she'd dropped. "Where are your instincts telling us to go?"

As she sheathed her weapon, Rianthe glanced for one last time around the clearing that had changed her life, a place that now renewed her hope. She turned and headed north, her purpose resolute, her two good friends at her side.

CHAPTER TWELVE

"Who is that girl?" Marta said.

Kaiden startled at the sound of her voice, lost in his own thoughts. Thoughts bordered by darkness, with no way out, no solution in sight. Like the dreams he'd been having. Dark voids churning with dread. Worry was his constant companion. Where was Tevy? Was Rianthe safe?

They'd been traveling for hours in a silence broken only by the occasional scuffle of small animals foraging for food as the world morphed into the starkness of winter. He'd remained silent because Marta confused him. Or maybe it was more that confusion swallowed him up when she was near? He couldn't tell, so he'd made a point of traveling single file, close enough to protect her, but far enough behind her to keep his head clear.

Except that hadn't worked. He saw no simple path through whatever darkness lay ahead of him. And he still thought he'd forgotten something.

"Who is that girl?" Marta asked again.

"What girl?" Kaiden didn't want to talk, and he sure didn't want to answer any questions. Ignoring her wasn't an option though, because she was taking him to Tevy. No. That might not be true. She was taking him to a place where children were sold as slaves. Hopefully, Tevy was there.

"That girl who hangs all over you back in that village? What did you call her? Ri?"

Kaiden squinted. He didn't like Marta using that nickname. Only those who knew Rianthe called her that. Her friends. Her family. Him. Not some stranger they barely knew.

"Rianthe. Her name is Rianthe."

"Rianthe, then." The name, on Marta's tongue, sounded sharp-edged and discordant. "What is she to you?"

She's the reason for everything I do. "A friend."

"Seems like more than a friend, the way she treats you."

He didn't want to talk to her about this, but seeing his relationship with Rianthe from someone else's eyes was irresistible. They'd been distant for so long, he didn't know if they'd ever break through to find what they'd once had "What do you mean?" he asked.

Marta's voice softened, beguiling him. "Just that she kind of runs you. She tells you what to do and when to do it."

"We work together." Occasionally, though, the tasks she tossed his way like orders grated on him. Bull-headed and focused on doing things how she thought best, Rianthe rarely allowed much discussion.

Marta shrugged. "Seems to me, it's kind of her way or no way. Not like you and me. We're working together to find your friend."

Were they? Kaiden wasn't even certain how he'd ended up heading in this direction. Marta had convinced him that this was the right way to go to find Tevy, but he'd had no choice. He'd needed help. Had he been alone? Wasn't someone searching with him? Gah! It galled Kaiden that he didn't remember. A blanket had been thrown over his mind and he'd found no way to yank it off.

Marta stood beside him now. "I heard that you saved her years earlier, that she was almost dead when you found her."

The first real smile in a couple days touched Kaiden's face. That had been a pivotal day. It decided his future, even though he hadn't known it at the time.

"Where did she come from?"

Kaiden's smile disappeared. No way would he answer. Only a select few knew about Rianthe's parentage and one person had already died keeping that secret.

"Fine. Don't tell me," Marta huffed. "But if you work together so well, why aren't you better *friends*? Seems like there's a lot of tension between you two."

"We had…a parting of the ways. For a while." Kaiden spoke slowly, reluctantly, as if the words were dragged from his mind.

"She left you, didn't she?"

Any lingering peace at the memory of how he'd met Rianthe got ripped away by the question, reminding him of the gaping wound in his heart that had never quite healed. He scowled, remembering how he'd pushed her away. Their relationship had never been the same since.

"Why did she do that?" Marta cooed. "You're a strong man. A good protector. You'd keep her safer than anyone else. Why would she toss you aside?"

Beside him now, Marta tugged at Kaiden's cloak. The darkness drove deeper inside him. The seed of discontent grew. Rianthe had tossed him aside. She never even gave him a chance to explain.

"She always does that, doesn't she?" Marta said. "Makes decisions, doesn't include you in them, like you're not good enough to be included."

Yes.

"And you endure the brunt of her actions. Poor Kaiden," she soothed. "Always protecting, never included. Never part of the family. You're the outsider looking in, aren't you?"

He always felt that way. No matter how inclusive New Hope tried to be, he wasn't born there. He wasn't one of them.

Kai-den. The faint voice in his head came from far away. But from where? From whom?

Family. Search. Tevy.

Tevy. Yes, Tevy. He must find Tevy. Where had that voice come from? Kaiden concentrated. He listened for the voice but heard nothing more. Why couldn't he figure this out? Kaiden raked a hand through his hair, struggling to keep his equilibrium.

Marta. She'd somehow clouded his mind again. How could he do what he needed to with her here? Yet, she'd offered him the only clue to finding Tevy. It seemed he'd need to work with her. He must remain wary and keep her at a distance. He must not fall prey to her wiles. Too much was at stake.

"Enough talk." Kaiden pointed behind him. "Single file."

Marta hesitated. For a second, her face changed, appearing sharper, more haggard.

No. It couldn't be.

Was something messing with his vision? Because Kaiden swore he'd seen a hint of golden light in her eyes.

~~~

Rianthe almost missed the sign. Roulf, supportive as always, had followed her instincts for days without complaint or question, as had Taschia.

I trust you. I follow you, her wolf-sister said. Rianthe wasn't sure she deserved that amount of trust. What if she didn't find the cave?

"You'll find what you need to find when you need to find it, child," Roulf reminded her as they'd sat around the fire the night before.

She'd never been as certain as him. In fact, her own doubts had probably compounded the difficulty in finding the cave. The elusive hint from the barely sentient spirit of her father as to their direction did little to ease her worry.

This day, they'd been walking in circles. When she woke, Rianthe had been filled with the overwhelming and urgent conviction that they were near the cave. They'd eaten a hasty breakfast, broken camp, and started out before the sun had fully risen.

Several hours had passed without a sign. Frustration boiled in Rianthe like she was a pot forgotten on the fire. It didn't help that she couldn't stop thinking about Kaiden. Something was amiss. He hadn't found Tevy yet, either. Of that, she was almost certain.

She sat on a log and tapped her gloves against her
~~~

knee, trying to sort out her jumbled emotions. She breathed deeply as her sorrow and doubt slowly dimmed. As determination grew within her.

Go north, Daughter. Find the cave. You can help Earth. Mankind. Yourself. Those you love.

Rianthe focused on the hopeful words, laid her hand on the log and reached out with her mind, trying to see the landscape through a druid's eye.

At first, nothing changed. She stared at the nearest pine tree, saw the dry, browning needles, the rough bark, and the fissures between that cried for nutrients. Rianthe panned the area. Striations in the rock mountain, oranges, tans and whites, all mixed into a canvas of life. As she'd done with the tree, she looked closer at the colors and crevices in the rock. They followed a rough pattern, like an upside-down "U" that seemed unusual. Rianthe focused on the lines, trying to see deeper.

She cocked her head. What was that? A faint light? She focused harder, looked deeper, and suddenly saw through the rock, into a cavern that lay beyond.

Rianthe's head snapped back. She yanked her hand from the log's bark. Had she actually just looked through solid rock? Or had that been a vision?

"What did you see?" Roulf asked.

"A…a cave." She pointed in front of her. "Behind that rock face."

"Excellent. Then we have arrived." Roulf smiled his ingratiating smile that said Rianthe had done something good. The timbre of his voice indicated he'd never doubted her.

"I guess," she said. "But that doesn't get us inside. It looks like solid rock. There's no entrance."

"That you can see. Yet."

Rianthe yanked her gloves on and sprinted over to the mountain of rock. She ran her hand along its crevices. "There's no latch or catch that I can find."

Roulf shook his head. "There wouldn't be. This is a magically sealed entrance. I can sense it now."

"Then how do we get inside?"

"You must answer that question yourself. Your parents hid this place so only you could find it. The riddle that gains us entrance is yours alone to solve."

Riddles. She needed answers and all she ever got were riddles. Just once, couldn't the world hand her some answers? Rianthe wanted to throw up her hands, curl up on her bedroll, and let the world fall apart around her. She'd never been good at puzzles. Glaring at the rock, she almost walked away from it.

Behind her, she knew Roulf and Taschia stood patient and silent, waiting for her to act. Rianthe couldn't turn away. And to figure this out, she was on her own.

She'd found no handle or latch in the line that defined the doorway. She ran her hands over the rock face. Nothing there either. She closed her eyes and reached for the light inside the cave. Focused on it. She removed her gloves and set both hands against the rock.

Open.

Nothing happened. Of course, it wouldn't be that easy. She dug deeper, into the pit of her stomach, focused harder, tried to pull the light to the door to open it.

Earth shuddered, but nothing happened.

I am Rianthe Royan. You must open for me.

Still nothing.

Rianthe sank against the rock. Nothing worked. She didn't have the strength to do this. Everyone's faith in her was so horribly misplaced.

If she failed, everyone else would fail too. She knew that. New Hope, the lake, that special spot she only shared with Kaiden, all would disappear, swallowed up by a darkness no one could stop. Humanity would cease to exist, or worse, morph into acolytes of darkness, bound to serve Taegar and her Dark circle forever.

Earth would die. No more flowers. No birds. No rainfall to smell like fresh new beginnings after long days of sunshine.

Earth, Bhren, New Hope…they'd all decided she was the only thing standing between them and death. Rianthe cried against the rock, her tears darkening the rusted orange. Something deep within the rock sighed. She pushed again, sensing the despondency, the weakening. She pushed harder and stiffened in shock when her hands disappeared into the stone. Something vibrated deep in the core of Earth. *Let me help you,* she begged. *You brought me here for a reason. Please, let me in. Help me to help you.*

Uncertain if it was magic she'd wielded or something else, Rianthe pushed with mind and body. Her arms followed her hands into the rock. She tried to pull them back, but they stuck hard. She could only move further in.

The vibration grew.

"You can do this, child," Roulf said from behind her.

Rianthe barely heared. Her face almost touched the rock now. All she had to do was dip her head and she'd be inside. Just a little faith. In herself. In Earth. In everything she'd been taught and told. How was she supposed to do this? She wouldn't be able to breathe. Fear froze her, pulled her back. Now, it took more effort to pull back than to push forward.

She no longer had a choice. Rianthe swallowed her fear, or tried to. *Earth, protect me.* Pulling back as far as she could, she closed her eyes and plunged ahead.

Expecting to crack her head open on the hard surface, Rianthe instead felt herself falling, falling, falling.

Oomph! She hit the ground hard. Her hands dug in, her palms raking across the dirt. The *ehwaz* vision stabbed her like ice rain.

Golden eyes glared at her. Hands devoid of skin snaked out from beneath a caped arm, red fire shooting directly at Rianthe.

"Where is he?"

The voice, Taegar's voice, consumed Rianthe with needles of pain. She clutched her head, screaming, trying to push the pain away, but it kept on coming and coming.

"Where is he?"

Who? She mouthed the word as agony washed over and through her. She couldn't move, couldn't speak.

"The boy. The one with the runes."

No! With tremendous effort, Rianthe shut down her brain, forced it to not think of him. Sweat dripped down her face, whether in real life or the vision, she wasn't certain. She must not say his name. Must not give him away. She tried to picture anything else. The cave. Taegar's cave. Looking around, she saw rock broken and strewn all over, like some great battle had occurred there since she'd last taken on the leader of the Dark circle.

"I will have the talisman. Whoever you are, whoever he is, you cannot hide it from me."

Fear roared through Rianthe. Fingers dug at her mind, trying to pry the information from her.

So much pain.

"Give me what I seek and oblivion will be your reward. No pain. Just happiness."

That sounded so good. It would be easy to simply let go. Forget it all...

No! She must protect him. Must help.

Rianthe roared her defiance, stood and pushed back against the pain. It lessened. She pushed back more. It dulled further.

Taking deep, gulping breaths, Rianthe stood. Held out her hand and pushed the pain back toward Taegar.

Golden eyes widened in surprise. "You have some power, little one. Power such as I haven't seen since... Well, it is no matter." Taegar redoubled her efforts. Red light spat from her, widened, grew until everything glowed red.

Rianthe reeled from the renewed effort. Losing her concentration for a split second, Rianthe found herself thrown back against the cave wall.

Taegar's eyes gleamed. "You cannot win. Give me what I want."

No! Power welled up within Rianthe, blossoming, filling her. She straightened as the power grew in her. In this moment, she believed in herself. She knew she would win this day.

Taegar's sinister radiance stopped just short of Rianthe's outstretched hands.

"You will learn nothing from me," Rianthe cried. "You will never get them. Ever. I will defeat you." Rianthe widened her hands, forming an arc, then a circle, creating a white, protective shield. She moved forward, toward Taegar, the shield compressing the magic back into itself as it went.

Though fear ripped through her, Rianthe closed in

on her nemesis. Taegar's strength held Rianthe back. She could go no further.

"It seems, little one, that we are at an impasse."

She was right. Sweat trickled down Rianthe's face with the effort it took to hold her place.

"I have other ways of finding what I desire," Taegar continued. "Now is not our time to battle, I think."

Rianthe breathed for the first time in what seemed like forever.

"Know this," Taegar said. "I will have the rest of those runes. When I possess them all, I will come for you. And I will destroy you."

A shiver ran down Rianthe's back. "You can try."

Taegar's magic faded as quickly as it had flared.

Devoid of magic to battle, Rianthe's shield disappeared. She fell to the ground.

Gasping for air and struggling to find enough energy to even sit up, Rianthe looked around. She expected to see the war-torn cave where she'd just had an epic magic battle. She expected to see remnants of Taegar's red power. She thought she'd found Taegar's hiding place.

Nothing looked like what she'd seen. Where chaos had been, order resided. Crystals in the walls were lit by a stream of light emanating, not from an altar, but from the ground itself. The glow was white, not yellow or red and full of barely suppressed fury. This was a place of calm, whereas Taegar's cavern had overflowed with agitation, anger, and fear.

Rianthe got to her feet, hands on knees, forcing herself to find the strength. She looked at the wall she'd fallen through. It still looked like rock. Yet she'd found a way through.

She stumbled to that wall, knowing what she had to

do. Somehow, that battle had opened a deep-seated knowledge she'd not known she carried. Rianthe splayed both hands against the granite and whispered words unfamiliar to her, both in language and designation. The wall shimmered, then disappeared.

Taschia rushed in, Roulf right behind the wolf. Taschia yipped and danced around, searching for what danger had beset Rianthe.

"It's gone," she said. "She's gone." She laid a hand on Taschia's back as Roulf grasped her other hand and helped her to sit. "Child, we heard you yelling. What happened? Are you all right?"

"I… I battled Taegar."

"Here?"

"No. At least, I don't think so. I think it was in a vision."

Roulf sat beside her, handing her a water bag from which Rianthe sipped gratefully.

"The *ehwaz,* the place where thoughts are actions and actions can kill. These visions are real struggles within the magic that surrounds our world," Roulf said. "Tell me, if you can. What happened?"

Rianthe nodded and spoke in between sips, grateful that Roulf was gentler than Bhren with his demands to know everything.

At the end of her tale, Roulf stood and paced, digesting the information. "She seems," he finally said, "to have gained strength."

Having been on the receiving end of Taegar's magic, Rianthe agreed. She fingered the bag around her neck. "She has all but three of the runes. Do you think they've helped her magic grow?"

"I fear it is so."

"Yet these three runes have not helped me in the least."

"You don't know that. You just described how you found more power this time than you knew you possessed."

"Yes, but the need was greater. Whatever I have inside me could have been responding to that."

"We won't get any answers this way," Roulf said. "Let us gather our strength—your strength, at any rate—and examine this place. Damian Royan brought us here for a reason. Maybe we will find the answers we seek."

Rianthe stood on shaky legs. She'd recovered more quickly than she had the last time she'd tapped into the power. Maybe her magic was getting better. Stronger. With a silent plea that this be true, she followed Roulf as he wandered about the cavern.

CHAPTER THIRTEEN

Darkness surrounded Tevy. He curled into a tight ball against a dank wall covered in mud and vegetation, unable to push away the misery that grew inside him. Fear, clawing at him like sharp talons, held him captive as much as the pain. He wanted to go home. To stop the hurt. To see Ri. His sister's hugs, embarrassing before, would help if he could just get to her. He ached to feel the comfort and safety of her arms around him.

Tevy moaned as another spasm of pain wracked his body. What was happening to him? His entire body was molten agony. He couldn't stand it.

His howl roared out into the night sky, its hollow echo a reminder of how alone he was. Never in his life had he felt so lonely. There had always been someone around. Rianthe, Uja, the wolves. He missed them all so much.

Restless unease had grown in him until he'd had to leave home, to run, get away and find some peace. Except he'd found none of those things on this journey. Instead, he was more miserable than if he'd stayed at home.

There must be someone, somewhere, who could help him. Tevy searched the surrounding woods. Tree after tree swayed in the cold breeze, but nothing moved.

Tevy howled again. Over and over, he tried to scream the pain away. When would it stop? Tears wet his cheeks. He couldn't stop the misery that snarled through him.

Rianthe. Help me.

The plea went unanswered. He hadn't sensed her in hours and didn't know what that meant. He hadn't sensed his wolf pack, either. He'd purposely shut them out when he'd left New Hope. Something deep inside had told him this must be a solitary journey. Now he was paying for that decision. He lay there, alone in the night. In agonizing pain. And there was no one to help him understand why.

Or to heal him, like Raisa might be able to. Maybe he should go back to New Hope.

Tevy tried to stand. Pain shot through him, as if bones were crunching and shifting. He fell back to the ground, screaming again, awash in an agony he could not define. Time passed without notice. He managed to curl once again into a ball, waiting for the end.

~~~

Darkness had descended hours ago. Rianthe stood at the entrance to the cave, looking out at the trees and the stars overhead. A rare clear night. Good hunting for
~~~

Taschia, who had not yet returned.

I have fed. I come.

Frustration welled up in Rianthe like the geysers she'd heard about in stories, natural hot springs that blew deep waters sky high. Would nothing ever be easy? Her parents, and the druid circle of which they'd been a part, had placed the hope of everyone's future in puzzles, and in her ability to solve them. She'd failed miserably so far, and tonight's test seemed no different. Rianthe and Roulf had searched the entire cave, finding two tunnels and five antechambers. Now, in darkness, there was no thought of quitting no matter how weary they were.

Iridescence from the ground light hitting crystals in the walls allowed them to see, so glows weren't necessary. For all their exploration, they'd found nothing except that central stream of light coming from the ground. No evidence that any human had set foot in there before today. Nothing at all. Why had Earth, and her father, directed Rianthe there?

She ran her ungloved hands along the wall, feeling the cold, rough stone, hoping for more help from Earth. Nothing happened when she touched the rock. Considering her backup plan—to find the answer in a vision—Rianthe shivered. No, she wasn't ready for that again. Not this soon. Her energy still lagged from the last go-round with Taegar. She'd need more time before any attempt to reenter the *ehwaz*.

"Anything?" Roulf asked, his voice a quiet echo in the emptiness.

Rianthe shook her head. "There has to be something here."

Roulf sat and took a drink from his water bag, muttering something about being too old for this. Then he closed his eyes for a few moments. When he opened them, he looked around the cave once again. "I sense an energy."

"What sort of energy?"

"Like something hides from us," he said.

"That's logical. Look at how we fell into this place." Rianthe rubbed her sore elbows.

Roulf chuckled. "You mean, *you* fell into."

Rianthe circled the cavern, stopping when she got back to Roulf. "We've found five empty alcoves." She pointed to the small openings for each of them. Equidistant, except for the area near where she and Roulf rested. Nothing showed there but hard wall. Rianthe ran her hands over the rock again, but this time, not randomly. She methodically checked the wall, inching along, closing her eyes to better feel the anomalies in the rock.

There. A uniformity she'd missed before. A circle. Rianthe ran her finger over the design. Three circular indentations with three lines emanating out below them. Too smooth and too regular to be natural. "Roulf, this isn't Earth-made," she said, and he was beside her in a second, running his own hands over the carving.

"You're right."

Barely able to contain her excitement, Rianthe told Roulf she'd seen this symbol before. "This same design is etched in the rock wall of the druid's tower back home. Or had been until the fire destroyed it. There must be a connection between this symbol and the Guardian druids, Roulf."

"I don't remember ever seeing that symbol before. Maybe it was designed after I left. Try it, child." Anticipation laced his voice, the cadence of a man revived.

Rianthe stuck her finger in the center circle, but nothing happened. Together they checked the rest of the wall. "Why won't it open?" Rianthe said, hitting the rock. She returned to the indentation. "This has to be it."

Roulf nodded. "It must be magically enhanced."

Taschia returned and sniffed along the ground below the sign. *Air flows.*

Rianthe studied the indentation. Her finger fit easily, but the hole wasn't much larger than her thumb. Her thumb! Could it be that easy? Rianthe placed her thumb inside the indentation and held it there.

No movement or grinding of rock. The cave grew quiet enough that she heard their breathing, heard the low hum of magic from the light flowing from the ground and the scurry of some small creature on the far side of the cave.

She pressed harder. Still nothing. What more did she need to do? If this doorway was hidden by magic, then magic must be what would gain them entry.

Rianthe leaned in, laid against the wall, her free hand moving along the rock. She tried to see into it, down to the core of its existence. Striations of light and dark, veins of shiny gold and diamond crystals. She grew warm, and the rock wall warmed with her. Rianthe focused on the rock, reached out with her mind for what was beyond it. Shallow vibrations answered her. Then the wall shimmered and slowly disappeared.

Determined not to fall in this time, Rianthe stepped back, surprised at what she saw. Where a solid wall had been, a smallish opening now greeted them.

Roulf patted her back. "Well done, child. Well done."

Taschia yipped her agreement.

Rianthe nodded. "I guess this is what we came for." Squaring her shoulders, she squatted and stepped inside.

The antechamber was the largest alcove they'd found, yet for all its size, it held only one item. In the center, a pedestal stood with a book upon it.

Rianthe and Roulf moved to the book, using a glow to see. An oak tree carved on the front cover told them it was a druid's tome.

Roulf tried to open the cover with no luck. He put his thumb in the divot on the front. Still, the pages did not give up their secrets. He stepped back to give Rianthe a turn. When she placed her thumb in the divot, the same thrumming coursed through her as with the wall. The book sighed, then opened by itself to the first page.

It looked to be a letter. Rianthe's eyes dipped to the bottom of the page.

Lovingly, and with hope for all, your father and mother.

Tears stung her eyes as Rianthe ran her hands over pages her father and mother had touched. This was their book, their writings. Awe settled on her like a warm blanket. Her parents had left a gift only she could open.

Taschia leaned against her. *You are happy.*

For this moment, yes. Rianthe picked up her new treasure, then almost dropped it as the sensation hit her. Pain. Agony. Torment.

Rianthe. Help me.

"Tevy!" Rianthe whirled, almost expecting to see him writhing on the ground behind her.

"What happened?" Roulf asked.

Taschia's whine joined Rianthe's, who reached out with her mind for her brother, but heard nothing more than a slight moan, felt only a tendril of pain.

"Tevy's in danger. I have to go to him." Rianthe thrust the book into her pack and yanked it on, reaching for her water bag.

"You only just found what we have been looking for. You can't leave yet."

She tossed off the hand he'd used to waylay her. "I *have* to go find Tevy. He's in pain, Roulf. A great deal of pain."

Roulf gazed out the cave entrance into the darkness of night before turning back to Rianthe. "I know this is difficult, but we have to trust Kaiden. He will find Tevy. You have a different road to follow." Roulf patted the knapsack on her back. "You must find out what's inside this book."

"I can do that anywhere." Like she could even focus on this book right now. Tevy needed her.

"Think, child. You were brought here for a reason. This hiding place was chosen for only you to find."

Rianthe paused. She'd only once seen a cave with a stream of light inside it, and never in person. Only in her visions. Roulf may well be right, but that was no longer her focus. She had to get to Tevy.

She yanked her gloves on. "How can you ask me to make this choice?"

"Because we have no choice. Earth has no choice." Sadness furrowed his brow.

Rianthe knew he didn't want to ask this of her. He was as torn as she was.

"I will come back after..." She couldn't finish the thought. The possibilities terrified her. "You can come with me or stay here, but I will save Tevy. Taschia?"

I come with you.

Nodding, Rianthe strode out the cave entrance and walked away from that particular responsibility.

Or tried to. Each step she took became a huge effort. The pack on her back grew heavier, dragging her down. Her feet seemed stuck in quicksand. Sweat trickled down the side of her face as she struggled through each footfall.

After several futile attempts to leave, Rianthe crumbled to the ground only a few yards from the cave entrance. She turned furious eyes on Roulf. "Did you do this? Did you make it impossible for me to leave?"

"No, child. That is beyond my ability," Roulf said. "The choice is not mine to make."

"What choice? I have no choice. Apparently, I must stay here and my brother must suffer. Gah!" Rianthe pounded the dirt. Earth, it seemed, had made her choice for her. If she couldn't save Tevy, what good was saving anything else?

"Trust in Kaiden. He'll find the boy," Roulf said quietly.

Tears streamed down her face as she looked up at him. "He's all the family I have left, and I can't stand that he's hurting. I don't even know what's happened to him."

Nor do I, Taschia mind-spoke, settling beside Rianthe.

"None of us do," Roulf said. He paced from tree line to cave entrance, muttering under his breath. "I do not know the answer to this dilemma."

Rianthe sat there, morose and forlorn, sifting dirt through her gloved fingers. She must stay, but Tevy needed her. He wouldn't have called for her if the need wasn't dire. Tevy, whom she'd helped bring into this world. Whom she'd kept warm in her arms for weeks as they'd searched for New Hope and Bhren. Whom she'd nursed through every ache and pain since. How could she not help him now?

Her euphoria at finding the book had evaporated. Every time she moved forward, something yanked her back. It was all so futile. How were they supposed to accomplish anything, save anyone?

Staring at the dirt in her hand, Rianthe threw it to the ground in disgust. Fine. If she couldn't go forward, she'd focus on the present. Tevy. She yanked her gloves off and plunged both hands into the soil, her thoughts focused on her baby brother.

Instead of seeing Tevy, as she'd hoped, Kaiden's face waited for her. He sat against a wall, maybe of rock. The darkness made it difficult to tell.

Darkness wasn't the only thing surrounding him. Confusion swirled around him like a tsunami.

Kaiden?

He looked up, his eyes unfocused and filled with sorrow and angst. "Do you hate me that much?" he asked.

"Hate you? What are you talking about?" He wasn't the only one confused now.

"You never let me in, Ri. Never. You hold me at arm's length and make choices without consulting me."

He wants to have a relationship chat now? She'd wanted to have this conversation for years. Now, she couldn't. Other things were more important.

"I am supposed to keep you safe and you won't let me."

The resignation in Kaiden's eyes chilled Rianthe to the bone, and there was little time to sort this all out. That would have to wait until Tevy was safe. "Where are you, Kaiden? Is Tevy with you?"

"I've failed everything I've ever attempted."

Kaiden had fallen deep into tormented thoughts she could only guess at, and Rianthe didn't know how to break him free.

Tears filled his eyes. "I'm sorry, Ri. I'm so sorry."

Sorry about what? Fear gripped Rianthe. Had he tried to help Tevy and been unsuccessful? She wished she could touch him, pull his concentration away from whatever cesspool he was mired in. Rianthe reached for his cheek but her hand went right through.

"Kaiden, focus. Please. I'm begging you. Have you seen Tevy? Are you with Taegar? Is Tevy there?"

Kaiden shook his head. "Taegar does not have Tevy."

"Then who does?"

He shook his head again, returning to his earlier mumbling. What had happened to him that he'd turned so dark and morose? What had Taegar done to him?

"Kaiden, get out of there. Come, find me. We'll look for Tevy together."

Empty pain filled his eyes as he shook his head.

"Kaiden, please."

He held out his hand as if to touch her, then dropped it. "I'm no good for you, Ri."

She caught a small wave of his hand, then the vision darkened and he disappeared.

Rianthe was back in front of the cave that held her prisoner. And now, she had more questions than when she'd driven her hands into the soil. Many more questions. And many more worries.

CHAPTER FOURTEEN

Kaiden crouched low and peered over the top of the promontory. The sun had broken morning's plane hours ago, but the small canyon below that held Minor Town still lay in shadow. Bigger than New Hope, it bustled with activity in comparison to home. Tucked back in the hills like it was, only one road led in and out. Travelers must choose to find this place. It didn't happen by accident. Old, half-crumbled buildings had been repaired with tree poles and brush. There were two long buildings, similar to the longhouses they'd constructed, and lost, in New Hope. Single dwellings were spread throughout the area.

On the north side, nearest Kaiden, a barricade blocked the entry road, which was guarded by at least four men. Business was brisk, if the small line of wagons waiting for to enter was any sign.

Some way behind the barricade sat a two-story

building that looked well-maintained and lived-in. Until now, the only two-story building he'd ever seen still in one piece was the druid's tower. He'd thought only crumpled ruins remained of any others.

On the far side of the canyon, there was a large opening in the rocky hills that must be the mine entrance. Was Tevy down there, right now? Being whipped if he didn't work hard enough? Kaiden's hands clenched at the thought.

He glanced the other way. Entering via the road was out of the question. The valley walls consisted of steep rocky slopes mostly devoid of cover. He wasn't sure he'd get down unseen. It sure would be nice to have another one of those stealth rocks like Roulf had given him when they'd fought Deakon.

Except they'd lost the runes, even with Roulf's helpful trinket. Kaiden frowned. Lately, it seemed like everything he tried to protect disappeared or got lost. He was True-Named protector, yet he hadn't kept anything or anyone safe. Not the runes, not New Hope, not even Rianthe or Tevy.

Kaiden tried to shrug off the melancholy and guilt that suffocated him. He needed to stop this pity thing and focus. Tevy. That's what this was about. Finding Tevy.

A series of crevices further along the canyon wall looked interconnected. If he could make his way over to them, maybe they'd give him some shelter as he climbed down to the town.

Kaiden pulled back from the ledge and sat, brushing grime from hands that hadn't seen a good washing for days. Marta, who looked as fresh today as she had three days ago, even though he'd pushed them hard and there'd been no lake or stream to wash in, sat quietly watching him, waiting. For what, he had no clue.

"You're sure the only guards are at the barricade, and in the mine during the day?"

"I told you that already," she said, biting off each word in irritation. "From what I know, more guards wander town during the night. During the day, most of them are in the mine watching the workers."

"Slaves, you mean."

She cocked her head in answer.

"And, if we can get into town, we'll blend in?"

She shrugged. "This town has the biggest trade store around, so it crawls with travelers. I can't believe you don't know about this place."

"Never heard of it." He wasn't about to tell her that, until he'd gone in search of Rianthe, he hadn't traveled further away from New Hope than it took to hunt. "What about overnight travelers?"

"There's a place men can bunk. It's not much, from what I remember. I don't think they allow you to stay for any more than one night. And it will cost you."

"Cost?"

"Food."

Kaiden nodded. Food was about the only thing traded these days. Food, tools, and cloth or hides for clothing and warmth.

"All right. We'll climb down via some crevices I saw, but not until tonight." He thought they could use the additional cover of darkness.

"Nightfall won't work. I told you. They close the town up tight and no one gets in. There are guards everywhere."

This kept getting worse. "Fine. We'll time it for dusk, and hopefully slip in unnoticed."

"Can't we stay here and go in during the day tomorrow?" Marta asked, moving next to him. "I've enjoyed sleeping beside you these nights."

Being late fall, the nights grew chilly in these hills and they'd been forced to sleep in close proximity. Kaiden hadn't liked it, but it was the only option. His dreams had been dark and filled with mysterious voices the past few days. Whispers of the abuses from his past and the mistakes he'd made. He'd be happy when he had Tevy safe with him. Maybe then he could put those nightmarish dreams, and all this angst, behind him.

"Isn't there a place for women here?"

"Yes. It's also the local brothel." The disgust in her voice made it clear that such a place was beneath her.

"I'm sure you can make do for a night." Kaiden glanced upward. "We've got a few hours before we can start, so I suggest we rest."

Marta's eyes lit up, and she snuggled tighter to Kaiden, forcing him to disentangle himself from her limbs. "It's warm enough for you to rest by yourself."

"But not nearly as much fun," she said with a pout.

Something tugged at Kaiden, pulling him to join her. He fought the urge, though it took some focus to do so. "You rest," he said, moving away. "I'll keep watch."

Unhappy, but unable to do anything about it, Marta turned to her side and drifted off to sleep.

Kaiden stared at her back. She wasn't Rianthe and didn't even come close. He needed to remember that. It seemed the only thing that yanked the veil off whatever enchantment Marta tried on him.

Where is she when you need her?

The unbidden thought stuck in Kaiden's craw. Rianthe was doing what she had to do.

She should be here.

No, he argued with himself. She should be exactly where she is.

Always something more important than you, isn't there?

Yes. He couldn't deny it. That was how it had to be.

Her selfish needs always come first.

No. The needs of Earth and humanity come first.

And you. Always last. Never getting what feeds your own soul.

Kaiden nodded to himself. That was how it had to be. It was hard though. Really hard sometimes. And getting tougher. When would this all end?

Even then, happiness will elude you.

This was his lot in life, to have his own desires tossed aside, always for the sake of protecting others.

You will always be alone.

He would always be alone.

Except for the one who's here. With you. Now.

Kaiden looked across at Marta, who lay curled up beneath a shrub trying to stay warm. What kind of magic was she using? And why had he ever agreed to let her travel with him? Except that, if it meant getting Tevy back, he'd do almost anything.

He sent up silent prayers he'd find Tevy and rescue him. Lately, everything he'd undertaken had gone awry. This must go well. Rianthe would never forgive him if he didn't bring Tevy safely back to New Hope. He wouldn't forgive himself.

Marta had told him what she'd heard about the self-proclaimed sheriff of Minor Town. He set his own laws and didn't care about anyone but himself, sounding a lot like the man who'd tossed Kaiden away. A man without principle or conscience. Kaiden had been a newling when he'd been sold. He didn't remember the event, yet he could envision it. A man, bargaining with the life of an innocent babe. His life. It hurt like a festering sliver deep in his soul that he'd been discarded so easily.

He hoped the fates would be with him tomorrow and he'd be able to stop this sheriff from ever buying or enslaving another child. Kaiden's knuckles grew white as he gripped his sheathed sword. He had a few questions for this man.

~~~

Rianthe didn't like the sensation that thrummed through her. A constant tingle set her on edge, like getting a bit too close to a lightning strike. Was it related to the light flow in the cave? Probably. Magic, or so Roulf said. Earth's *awen*. She'd seen the same thing in Taegar's cave in her visions.

She sat outside the cave entrance, trying to ignore the surge of longing from the cave that both called to her and repelled her. Shaking her head, she tried to clear her mind for what she needed to do next. They'd slept under the stars last night. She couldn't have slept inside if she'd wanted to. At least out there, the tingling lessened.

Rising and stretching, Taschia whined her agreement. *I hunt,* she mind-spoke.

Be safe.

Always.

Rianthe smiled as she watched her friend lope off. Then she stared at the book in her lap, running her hands over the oak tree carved into the cover in intricate detail. Her parents' book.

They'd found it yesterday, but she'd been reticent to open it again, to read what her parents had written. Roulf
~~~

had told her the choice lay with her, even as she knew there was no choice involved. Learning from Bhren that her parents were both Guardian druids had been an eye-opener. Rianthe didn't feel ready for more surprises.

Still, this was the reason they'd sought out this cave. To find things out. This was the destiny she'd been born to fulfill and all that was left was for her to accept it. Rianthe looked up, let the midday sunshine warm her face before she slid her hands to the side of the cover and opened the book.

Dearest Rianth,

It had been a long time since she'd seen this spelling, the way her parents named her. Over five years since her True-Naming had changed her life forever.

We deeply regret we cannot be there to help you on this journey. Please know that you and Uja have been the greatest joys in our lives. Even the unborn babe is well-loved. And, we sense, it will take all of you to help our crippled Earth to heal.

Rianthe ran her finger over Uja's name, despair bringing tears to her eyes. She would never get over the loss of her beloved brother. Neither would all of humanity, if his magic was needed to heal Earth. Magic that had died with him. She wiped at her tears and kept reading.

The magic lies buried deep within Earth, protected from adversaries by the talisman you carry. That same talisman is also the key to unlocking Earth's awen.

More than anything, she wished she could talk to her father. She needed advice. His advice. If the runes were meant to save humankind, then she must get them back from Taegar. But how?

Only you can manifest the runes. Only you can heal

Earth. But you are not ready. We pray you have time to prepare. Inside these pages lie some of the history of our world, both good and bad. And some exercises, ways to help bring out your magic, to help you understand it better.

We wish more than anything that we were there to guide you. We are so sorry that this burden is upon your shoulders. You do not deserve this. Nor does your brother, nor the babe. It is not fair.

But it is necessary. If you remember nothing else, remember to trust yourself. You are our daughter and, as such, Earth's awen is with you. Believe in yourself. Talk to your brothers. Talk to Bhren. Let them help you through this.

You are the hope of the future, Rianth, but know that, above all else, you are loved.

Lovingly, and with hope for all, your father and mother.

Tears welled up in Rianthe's eyes as her parents' love flowed around her like an ethereal hug, cocooning her against the unknown. She missed them so much and wished more than anything that they were there to help her, to guide her on this journey. The fleeting sense of well-being and protection their missive had given her fled in the face of what they had set her up to do. She hadn't asked for this burden. She'd been born into it.

Rianthe slammed the book closed. Get help, they said. But everyone who might help her was either dead or had disappeared.

Sounds from inside the cave reminded her she wasn't alone. Roulf moved around, searching for any more information or assistance the cave might impart.

So this was all they had. One girl who could not tap

into this *awen* like everyone said she should be able to do, and one little man who'd probably forgotten more than he remembered.

New Hope, no—Earth—was in so much trouble.

CHAPTER FIFTEEN

So far, so good, Kaiden thought. They'd slipped into town via the hillside crevices as dusk settled into night. Marta, still whining that he should have stayed the night in the hills with her, pointed to the bunkhouse, then stomped off to find her own place to sleep.

A look around seemed more important to Kaiden than sleep. He worked his way toward one of the two long-buildings that were closest to the mine entrance. No one seemed to be around, so he slipped inside, then stopped in surprise at what he saw. Wide platforms were built four rows high with ladders every few feet. From what he saw, the platforms held sleeping mats. Lots of them. Room enough for three hundred people to sleep.

Just how many children were forced to work there?

Kaiden didn't have time to ponder. Noise from

outside suggested people were headed this way. Barely in time, he slid in behind the pulled back skin that was the lone door.

Children filed in and climbed up to the sleeping mats. Boys, girls, younger, older. Grimy from mine work, their ribs were too visible to be healthy. These children were half-starved. Weren't they fed? How did they work when they could hardly move? Kaiden had never really believed Marta until this moment. If the people living there had conscripted this many children, this was worse than anything she'd told him.

This was his worst nightmare.

He watched each child shuffle in, all the while searching for Tevy, both hopeful he'd find the boy and afraid of the same thing. Tevy had disappeared almost a week ago now. How much mistreatment had he been subjected to in that time?

When the last child to enter did not look like Tevy, Kaiden's shoulders bowed with disappointment. He wasn't there. And if Tevy wasn't in Minor Town, where had he been taken? The entire trip had been a wild-goose chase.

The last boy to enter stumbled and fell, catching one guard's attention.

"Get up, you maggot," he screamed. He brought down his stick once, twice, three times on the boy who had no strength left to do anything but crawl away.

Kaiden roared into protector mode and slipped out from his hiding spot, ready to shred the guard with the man's own stick for what he'd done to the boy. Movement outside the door stilled Kaiden before he showed himself. Another guard stood just outside. Clenching his fists to hold tight to his rage, Kaiden slipped back behind the skin.

"C'mon, Lefty. The boss said no more messing with the kids. He needs 'em working."

"Ah, I ain't messin' with him much. Just maiming him a little."

"Don't look like this boy will be working tomorrow and it's your fault. So git outta here before you make things any worse."

The guard muttered oaths under his breath, but he moved toward the doorway, walking right past Kaiden's hiding spot. It would take nothing for Kaiden to reach out and break the man's neck. Instead, he stood still and silent, hands clenched, rage roaring through him. Only one thought kept him from acting, made him realize he must bide his time. One man could not take on an entire town to free these children. He needed time to think. Time to plan. Kaiden stayed behind the door flap until the guards left, then crept out. Peering through the doorway, he saw two men keeping watch on the barracks.

With quiet care, he moved to the boy's side, shushing him with a finger to his mouth. Wide-eyed, the boy backed up, or tried to. He had no reason to trust Kaiden. To the boy, he was another adult ready to inflict pain.

"I won't hurt you," Kaiden whispered. "I want to help."

He saw the distrust in the boy's eyes and was gratified when he allowed Kaiden to pick him up and carry him to a nearby mat, vacated by another child.

He laid the boy down with care. "I'm just going to see if anything's broken." Several children gathered around, all grimy and thin, with eyes so forlorn it about tore Kaiden's heart out. It surprised him how quiet they were. He guessed they'd learned the hard way to be silent.

Fury raced through his veins at the atrocities these young ones must have endured. What made people do this? And who did this to children? He could not fathom it.

Trying to calm the rage that seethed inside him, Kaiden ran his hands along the boy's arms. "No broken bones, but you'll hurt for a while," he said. Pulling out his waterskin, he helped the boy take a sip.

The others looked so dehydrated he passed the skin around, admonishing them to take only a sip. Too soon, his water was depleted. He did not have enough water or food to help all these children. There were just too many.

"Who are you?" the boy asked. The others leaned in, trying to listen to the whispered conversation.

Kaiden smiled at them. "I'm here to help. But…it might take me a while." He closed his eyes, aghast at the promise he'd just made, the hope he'd given them when he didn't know how he alone could affect anything. Searching for Tevy remained his priority but he couldn't leave these children in such a deplorable situation. He just couldn't. "I have to go for now. Be patient. Be quiet. I'll be back soon."

They all nodded as the light that had sparked in their eyes dulled, then disappeared. One by one, they turned and, with slumped shoulders, returned to their mats to gather enough strength for another hard day tomorrow.

Kaiden nearly broke down as he watched them. He vowed then and there that he would find a way to free them. They would have a better life, or he'd die trying.

Outside, darkness had fallen, and the guards rested on a bench. Kaiden slipped out without being noticed. He found the men's sleeping quarters and snuck inside. Once settled on an empty mat, he lay there, misery washing over him. He had to protect these children.

And to make the monsters who'd done this to them pay.

~~~

After breakfast, Rianthe set out traps to catch their dinner, then settled beside the fire to repair a damaged trap.

"You only delay the inevitable," Roulf said, coming to stand beside her.

She bent closer to the trap she worked on.

"Ignoring me has never worked for you before, has it?"

"No," she said.

"You must train."

She knew that, but every time she went into that cave, the discordant hum of the magic jarred her nerves. Rianthe sighed. "I'm not sure it would do any good."

"What do you mean?"

Rianthe set the trap down and reached for the book her parents had left her. "I've been through this book twice. There's nothing here except a lot of history and some magic tricks."

"Practice—"

"Makes perfect." Rianthe rolled her eyes. "Yes, I know. I've heard that a time or two. But here's the thing, it's not making perfect for me."

"Did you expect this to be easy?"

"No." Rianthe set the book aside. "I'd work sunup to sundown if I thought it would make a powerful druid out of me. You know that."

Roulf nodded.
~~~

Her worst fear, that she'd never live up to the faith others had in her, sat like congealed porridge in her stomach, souring her and weighing her down. She'd work tirelessly to learn if she thought it would help. Each time she'd tried to tap into the *awen*, nothing came. Even when the need was dire, her power had never been enough to save the day. She picked up the trap and tried to concentrate on the repairs, but her blur of tears made it next to impossible to loop the new leather. Rianthe tossed the trap aside and stood up.

"I can't do it, Roulf. I can't. I'm not who people think I am. I—" She gulped in a breath. "I'm not the prophesied one. How can I be? Nothing works for me. Nothing works from inside me. I—" She turned away from Roulf, hung her head, and let the tears fall. "I don't have any ability, and there's nothing in the book my parents hid so carefully that will help me, either. I need to find Tevy, and find out what happened to Kaiden." She balled up the strap of leather and threw it. True to form, it went about one foot, then dropped to the ground.

Roulf picked up the strap. "I know, child. I know. This is the hardest thing you've ever done, being here when you want to be searching for your brother. You also carry the weight of everyone's belief in you. This isn't easy, but we must have faith of our own. Faith in your parents. Faith in Earth. Faith that our destiny is unfolding as it should."

"How can I do that when nothing ever works?"

"By letting go of the past to focus on the present. The task at hand. That is all we can do."

"Apparently, you're right, because Earth won't let me leave."

She looked at Roulf and saw the gleam in his eyes.

"Maybe practice will help you find a way to leave."

Now that was logic Rianthe could wrap her head around. Maybe, just maybe, practice would show her the way out of there, the way to Tevy. Yes, that was the best option she had for now. "All right," she said to Roulf. "If Earth wants me to practice, I'll practice." She kicked at the trap and strode into the cave, trying hard to calm nerves rattled by the dissonant magic she should be able to access and wield, but so far, could not.

~~~

When they could run no more, Hark stopped his brothers. Marin, Joek, Grog, and he had run for days, not quite toward the rising sun. Each of them lay with tongues lolling out the side of their mouths. Food had been scarce, but at least water was plentiful in these hills.

We must find our brother, Grog mind-spoke. Just the fact that he mentioned something beyond food proved the urgency in this situation. All Grog ever thought of was food. He teetered as he stood, but took no step. Exhaustion won as Grog again sank to the ground.

We will, Hark said. *We must rest first.*

His scent is stronger, Marin said. *We find him soon.*

Hark wagged his head. *We will. After we rest.*

It didn't take long for his brothers to regain their strength. He was proud of how hard they searched. Hark lifted his nose to the air. Yes, their brother was close. They would find him this day.

They each caught the scent, and knew what Hark knew. He saw it in the brightness of their golden eyes. In unison, they howled their knowledge. One family. One pack. With one brother who would soon be missing no longer.

We come, Hark mind-spoke.
~~~

Hark? Tevy's mind-voice was faint.

Yes. We come.

Hurry.

The wolf heard tears in his brother's voice. Tears and great pain.

They set a good pace and found the copse of trees as dusk darkened the landscape. When they found him on the far side, Tevy lay on the ground amongst the trees, grimy from days in the woods. He was curled into a newling's ball, wearing nothing but ragged leggings.

The wolves crept closer.

Hark nudged Tevy's foot with his nose. Tevy groaned.

He lives, Grog said.

Yes, Hark answered, widening his mouth in a feral smile. *He lives.*

He hurts, Joek said.

The wolves stared at Tevy. The boy didn't move, didn't acknowledge them. He stayed still, curled into himself, awash in his own misery.

He is cold, Grog said.

Grog lay down against Tevy's legs. One by one, they lay against Tevy, offering their warmth against the chill of night. After one more look in all directions to make sure no one else was near, Hark lay down at Tevy's head, licking his forehead.

You are safe now, Hark told him. *You will be all right soon.*

The boy hadn't stirred through all of this, but finally, as each wolf settled in to sleep off the long days of searching, Tevy moaned. His arm snaked around Joek, and he gave him a tight squeeze. They all heard a faint *thank you* in their minds, a gift from the brother they'd searched so long to find.

We will wait, Hark said to his wolves, *for our brother to join us.*

We will wait, they all said in response, then lay their heads down, curled up, one big ball, one wolf pack, one brotherhood.

CHAPTER SIXTEEN

Kaiden snuck out of the men's sleeping quarters before first light. A sleepless night had not illuminated a solution to the problem. How could one lone man make a change there? And Tevy's safety weighed heavily on his shoulders, as did the oath he'd given Rianthe. Tevy did not appear to be in Minor Town. A slim chance remained, but Kaiden saw no children outside the longhouse near the mine. He didn't want to consider what might keep Tevy from working. No, Kaiden needed to believe he wasn't there. He prayed his young friend remained safe, wherever he was. That thought had distracted Kaiden through the long dark hours. Should he continue the search? If he did, that meant leaving these children in horrific circumstances, and that went against every fiber of his being.

Once more, duty tore Kaiden apart. His gut churned and his chest burned like someone had sliced him in two with a sword. Helping these children and Tevy at the same time had become an impossible feat. Ignoring either might have dire consequences.

He crouched behind a water barrel and waited for Minor Town to wake up, hoping the town's schedule would help him formulate a plan.

"There you are," Marta said behind him.

"Shh," Kaiden admonished, waving her to squat down. "Do not be seen."

"No one's even awake," she said, her tone clear. She should not be awake, either.

"Then go back to sleep," Kaiden said, shushing her as two men strode toward the longhouse where the children slept. The men walked up to the guards, the same ones Kaiden saw as he'd slipped out the night before. If they had guarded all night, fatigue was a weakness he could exploit.

The men spoke quietly for several minutes, then the night guards left.

"They're going for breakfast. We should find something to eat, too," Marta said. Her stomach growled in assent.

"Not until I see how things operate. Besides, we'll be recognized as strangers."

"Not if we act like we belong here."

Kaiden turned to her. "You know a lot about this town for someone who's never been here. You even slept in that boarding house without being noticed."

"I talked to quite a few people on my way to find you. I listened, and I have a good memory," Marta snapped.

"Find me? You came to New Hope to find me?"

Her eyes widened. "Find anyone who would help

me. Offer me a home," she said, her voice turning from venom to honey as her face softened. She touched his face. "Like you."

Kaiden stared at her. She had a certain beauty about her, especially in those eyes, deep pools of swirling hazel. What had they been talking about? He lost himself in her gaze until a distraction across the street freed him from whatever web she'd been weaving. He shook his head several times, trying to clear the cobwebs covering his thoughts. What was it about this girl that affected him so?

The youngsters file out of the hut. None of them looked any less exhausted than they had the night before. Not just boys, either. He saw a few girls. Their ages looked to be anywhere from True-Naming age down to six or so. All weak, all struggling. He clenched his fists, wondering how many of them would not make it out of the mine today. Who did this to innocent children?

The last child out of the tent limped. Kaiden recognized him as the one he'd helped the night before. The bedraggled youngster worked hard to keep up with the group but fell further and further behind.

Kaiden clenched and unclenched his fists, praying the guards didn't notice the boy. He knew if they did…

"You can't save him, Kaiden," Marta whispered in his ear.

"I can damn well try," he ground out.

Right then, Kaiden's worst fears came true. A guard turned and saw the boy lagging. The sneer on the man's face did not bode well for the child.

As they watched, the boy fell to the ground with a cry. He tried to stand again but the guard knew this child could not work today. Kaiden saw it in his eyes, even from this distance. Kaiden knew, too. If the boy couldn't work, he was useless to whoever had forced him into this slavery.

The guard grabbed the boy by his ragged collar and yanked him to his feet, the sneer still on his face. This was a game to the guard. Fury consumed Kaiden, making him shake with the need to aid the child.

"If you save this child, you'll lose your chance to help them all."

Kaiden knew that, yet how could he stand by and let that guard beat the boy again. Or worse.

"Stay here," he said to Marta.

"This will never work. You'll out us both and won't save anyone."

"I don't care," Kaiden said. He had to do something.

As the guard hauled the child along, Kaiden moved with him, shadowing him. Once behind the longhouse, the guard shoved the boy to the ground.

"You think you can slack off?" The guard leaned down and got in the boy's face. "You think a little limp will keep you out of the mine? Keep you from working?"

He slapped the boy so hard his head lolled to the side. He went limp, unconscious.

"Wake up, you lazy bastard," the guard screamed.

The boy moved his head, opened his eyes enough for Kaiden to see his agony.

"You can't save him," Marta, who'd followed him, hissed. "You'll ruin everything."

Kaiden was past caring, way beyond the point of no return. All he knew was that he couldn't let this child die. The boy looked past the guard and Kaiden knew the moment he saw him. Hope flared in his tormented gaze.

The guard picked the boy up by his shirt and tossed him down again. His head hit the ground with a sickening thunk.

Fists clenched and chest heaving, Kaiden prepared to come out of hiding.

Marta yanked him back. "Don't. You'll get us both killed. Then where will Tevy be?" Her whisper was fierce, but Kaiden barely heard her. Until she said Tevy's name. Rianthe. Tevy. New Hope. They should be his priority. They were what he'd been True-Named to protect. Still, this boy would not be tortured if he had anything to say about it. Kaiden crouched down before the guard saw him, looked around, furious and conflicted, searching for an answer. Even if he dealt with the guard quietly, a sword wound would leave too many questions.

The guard's back was to him as he yelled at the boy. The decision was taken away from Kaiden as red hot fury overrode reason. He would not let this boy suffer any longer.

He grabbed a rock. A big one. He hefted and lofted it in one fell swoop. His aim was true, catching the guard in the back of the head. The brute fell to the ground with a hard thunk, blood already seeping into the soil around him.

Kaiden rushed over, yanked the man onto his back, saw his sightless eyes. It didn't matter. Kaiden hit him. Hard. Again and again, until the man's face was pulp and his own knuckles were bleeding. Still, his fury did not wane.

A sound stopped him, stemmed the insanity that had taken him over. The boy had stirred. Kaiden slumped to the ground next to him, then pulled him gently into his arms, wishing Raisa's healing hands were there to stop this child's pain. Even unconscious, the boy moaned. How badly hurt was he? Where could Kaiden take him?

The boy's eyes flickered open, just once. He looked up at Kaiden, a small smile appearing on his face just before it went slack and his eyes closed. His arms slid away, the droop of death in every lax muscle.

Tears poured down Kaiden's cheeks as he held the boy close. This child had done nothing to deserve this, except to be in the wrong place at the wrong time. So young, so innocent. Kaiden's heart broke for the child.

Kaiden had not saved him. He hadn't stopped a single thing.

The hand on his shoulder reminded him Marta was there. "We're exposed here," she said. "We need to get away from…this."

He shrugged off her hand and continued to hug the child, awash in his own misery. How could he be True-Named protector when he wasn't able to protect a small, defenseless child?

"I'll pile some rocks nearby, make it look like they slid from that ledge above us, so this looks like an accident," Marta said.

Kaiden didn't listen. There was nothing but the poor, innocent child he'd just watched be murdered by the beastly guard. Kaiden should have died in his stead. Not this child, an innocent with no sins to atone for.

Nothing else mattered as Kaiden rocked back and forth. Nothing but the waste of this life. This could not be allowed. Not one more child would die for this mine. "No one else dies." He mumbled the words over and over, smoothing the boy's hair as he did so.

"Come on," Marta growled. "I hear someone coming." She yanked on Kaiden. "We've got to get out of here."

She kept tugging until finally, he stood, still carrying

the boy. But he didn't move. He couldn't. Grief and guilt held him frozen in place.

"If you don't come with me, the men here will toss that boy's body unceremoniously in a ditch to rot." Marta's whisper was furious as she yanked Kaiden away.

She was right. Kaiden looked down at the innocent face. The child at least deserved an honorable passing through the *kenaz*, the death rite. He nodded, pulling his arm from Marta's grasp. "All right. All right," he said. "Let's get out of here."

They climbed out of the valley and walked. Kaiden never stopped, never slowed, never slumped from the small weight he carried. He kept walking. A mile. Two. More. He intended to walk until they were far enough away that no one would see the fire.

"We've gone far enough," Marta said.

Kaiden kept walking.

"Why does this child mean so much to you?"

He stopped then. Staring ahead, seeing nothing except the vision that had haunted him his entire life. "I was sold as an infant. For a bit of food."

The simple act of uttering those words drove the dagger, already lodged in his back, even deeper. Like the boy, Kaiden hadn't deserved being sold like a commodity. Had the boy ever known the love of a family in his short life? Kaiden knew that love, but finding out he'd been handed over like baggage had destroyed his sense of self-worth. At least Kaiden's adopted family loved him with a fierceness that had offset the reason for his arrival in New Hope. Still, it rankled. And this child's life had been devoid of that care.

It took several hours to build the pyre. Kaiden took his time. He would honor this child. It was the only thing left to do.

The boy did not deserve this.

Kaiden nodded.

You let him die.

The words pounded into his brain like spikes. Kaiden whipped around, searching for the person who'd said them, only to find no one there but Marta. "What did you say?"

"Nothing. I didn't say anything," she said, her voice calm and quiet.

The child is dead because of you.

He watched her as the words screamed through his head, but her lips never moved. Kaiden searched the area, sensed nothing in the vicinity, no other person, no wolf that might mind-speak.

Where were these accusations coming from?

Your inaction killed him just as if you'd beaten him with your own hand.

"No, no, no." Kaiden grabbed his head, willing the words to go away.

You killed him.

Over and over the words came at him, until he mouthed them himself and screamed them. When he stopped, he knew them to be the truth. He had killed the boy with his inability to make a decision. The boy's death was his fault. His responsibility.

Kaiden laid the child on the pyre with a heavy heart. He lit the pyre and watched it burn until nothing but embers and ash remained. He cried until there were no tears left to cry. Then he made the only choice left to him. While he would never forgive himself for standing by and watching the child die, he vowed there and then that the people responsible for bringing the boy to Minor

Town, who'd left him to this torture, would pay.

Resolute for the first time in months, Kaiden unclenched his fists. He had no choice now but to see this through. Then he would continue his search for Tevy. First, he must make certain no other child died there.

He prayed to anyone who would listen. *Please keep Tevy safe. I will come for him. I will find him. But I have to do this first.*

I have to.

With one last glance at the embers, he strapped on his sword and strode back the way he'd come only a few short hours ago. He barely noticed Marta following and never saw the small smile on her face.

He was going back.

To Minor Town.

Where people would pay dearly for what they had done.

~~~

"Try again," Roulf said.

"I *am* trying."

Couldn't the little man who stood so close to the ground see how hard she had been working for the last several hours? Rianthe sat cross-legged in the clearing outside the cave. She'd been trying so hard and for so long, her bottom was about frozen from sitting on the cold ground. It hurt, too. She swore a tree root nudged the surface right under her left butt cheek.

She jumped up, brushing the dirt off her pants with her gloved hands. "I need a break." She glared at the rock that sat on the ground in front of her. "I've tried everything to move that thing. I've tried seeing past it, into its core. I've imagined it floating in the air, and I've dug deep into my soul looking for some iota of magic.
~~~

I've cajoled, I've asked. I've even tried pain." She rubbed her sore butt. "All the same ploys that I used to push back against Deakon's power. The rock hasn't budged. Not even a wobble. I can't lift it unless I pick it up."

Roulf paced back and forth, running hands over his bald head. "I don't understand. Something is blocking the *awen*."

"You've read the book. There's nothing indicating they hid the power I'm supposed to have by magical means."

"You're too easily distracted," Roulf said.

Rianthe threw up her hands. "Of course, I'm distracted. How can I not be? I'm worried about Tevy. Things are not well with Kaiden. How am I supposed to concentrate?" Tevy was never far from her mind. And Kaiden… This morning she'd woken up with a horrible feeling about him in the pit of her stomach. Something was wrong.

Roulf stared at her, at the ground, then at the cave. When he looked back at Rianthe, she knew she would not like what he said.

"I know you're worried. If you can try to trust in Kaiden, it will help you."

"I do trust him, but something seems…off."

"What?"

"I don't know!" Dram. Rianthe wanted to hit something. Run somewhere. Anything to get rid of her pent-up frustration.

"Maybe you should look at it another way. The sooner you have some sort of breakthrough, the sooner you can go help Kaiden find Tevy."

Rianthe bit her lip, almost hard enough to draw blood. She needed to be out there searching. She hadn't even been able to connect with Tevy's wolves for days.

I cannot speak to them either, Taschia mind-spoke. *I worry.*

That meant they were too far away. Had they found Tevy? Were they still searching? Rianthe scratched the wolf's head. "Me, too, Tasch. Me, too." With a heavy sigh, she turned to Roulf. "What else can we try?"

"I think we need to work inside the cave."

Rianthe had not gotten used to the discordant hum that radiated through her body ever since they'd found this cave. The closer she got to the stream of white light inside, the worse it got. The last time, her teeth had chattered like they would shake right out of her mouth, so she'd opted to stay outside. The prospect of going back in didn't thrill her, but she had no choice.

So be it. If this is what was needed to be free to find Tevy, she'd do it. Or, at least, try. She followed Roulf into the cave. The closer she got, the harder her body pulsated. A column of white light shot straight up, brighter than the one she'd seen in Taegar's cave. It lit the cavern, but not enough. From what Rianthe had seen, Taegar's magic funneled through the light in her cave, so if she could tap into Earth's power through this radiance like Taegar, logic dictated that she'd be just as powerful. Maybe even more so. The funny thing about logic, though, was that it rarely helped when you needed it to. And right now, there was a dissonance in this light, an unhappiness that jarred Rianthe's whole body. Touching it was out of the question, at least for now.

Roulf followed her inside, the dratted rock in his hand. He set it down a few feet away from her. "Try to lift the rock now. You have the power within you, Rianthe Royan. Believe in it. Dig for it. Use it."

Rianthe sat, shivering as a rush of cold infused her, then waned. Her prescience warned of danger. She looked around but saw nothing. Shaking her head, Rianthe tried to set aside the reverberations and focus on the rock. Gray, with light and dark striations, its surface mottled with indentations. She stared at it, willed it to be lighter than air, to lift.

Lift. Lift. Lift. She said the words over and over, seeing the rock, seeing inside the rock.

When it wobbled, Rianthe was so shocked she lost her concentration and fell backward.

Roulf whooped and, when Rianthe sat back up, he was dancing a little jig. "It was only a little wobble," she said, laughing.

"That was a very big wobble, child. Do not demean it. You touched the *awen on purpose*."

"Maybe. Maybe that rock got tired of playing around." Inside her, deep down, Rianthe knew he was right. She'd tapped into a power!

"You moved it. I'd like to see what you can do if you touch the light stream."

Rianthe shook her head. The rock had reverted to its still, silent position. Could she do more with direct contact? "I'm not sure that's a good idea. At least, not yet. We don't know what will happen when I do. I'm not ready. And what if…what if the same thing happens as when I touch Earth? What if I have another vision?"

She saw the concern on Roulf's face, tinged with a little disappointment. "It's a worry, but we must try it eventually."

"We?"

He shrugged. "You're not here alone."

"But I'm doing all the work." Rianthe chuckled to

ease the sting of her words. "I'm willing to try, eventually. But let's see if I can control it a little first. I think maybe a few more wobbles are in order before we up our game."

Roulf's grin lit up the cave. "Deal." He pointed at the rock. "Have at it, Druid Rianthe."

It startled her to have the druid title attached to her name. Rianthe turned the signet ring on her forefinger, the one Bhren had designated as hers to wear. The sign of the Guardian circle of druids. The whole town believed from then on that she would save them.

Druid Rianthe. For the first time, a spark of conviction settled in her heart. Maybe she really could become that person. With a satisfied sigh and renewed enthusiasm, Rianthe stared at the rock, moving back into a meditative state to focus on lifting it. It wobbled but did not rise.

Rianthe tried not to let it faze her. This would take practice. A lot of it. She had much work to do to earn the title everyone thought she deserved.

Hours later, Rianthe stood and stretched muscles that had been frozen in one position for too long. She looked outside, her teeth chattering. "I need a break, Roulf. I'm tired. And… don't you sense the vibrations in here? How… off it feels?"

"Only a small bit. Not like you do." He glanced outside. "It's getting dark anyway. Rest for tonight and we'll begin fresh tomorrow." He patted Rianthe's shoulders. "You did well today, child."

She didn't exactly agree, but she'd tried. Hard. And had raised the rock a couple inches off the ground on a few attempts. Right now, she didn't want to remain one more second in this cave so she quick-stepped outside and breathed deeply of the early evening air. "I'll go check the traps to see if we've something for dinner."

"I found some root vegetables earlier. I'll start a stew."

And I will hunt, Taschia mind-spoke to Rianthe.

She laughed. Her wolf always preferred her own hunting to human food. She never understood why people chose to cook their food before eating it.

It is better my way.

Rianthe chuckled again as she headed off in her own direction, happy that she could still laugh. How long had it been?

The rabbit she found in one trap would make a nice stew. She reset the traps, thankful they caught enough game to fill their stomachs. She wondered how New Hope fared. They'd hardly settled from the earthquake when she and Roulf had left, and it seemed like food became scarcer by the day. Not only game. Vegetables and greens didn't grow as well as they had before. Part of that, she knew, was the time of year, plus the fact that Uja's hands were not there to nurture growth. Fraka did what she could, but Uja's abilities had been so much stronger. Rianthe hung her head for a moment, covering her heart with her hand as she thought of her brother. He'd never gotten to meet his son and that cut deep.

Ujami, with his sweet smile and soulful eyes, helped diminish Rianthe's pain. And hope in Ujami's ability to take his father's place eased her worry. Already, as a newling, when he touched a plant it grew faster. He seemed to have powers greater than his father had at that age. Except his ability to provide much help lay years down the road. For now, they'd have to find another way to sustain themselves, as a village, and as a society.

Rianthe frowned. If she didn't find a way to heal their foundering world, the consequences would be dire. Changes for the worse seemed poised to happen. The world appeared to be near some sort of tipping point. Soon, Earth would not sustain any life, including its own.

No. She would find a way. She must. Maybe she shouldn't have stopped practicing. Promising herself that she'd start earlier and work longer tomorrow, Rianthe carried the game back to their campfire, ready to help Roulf cook the stew.

For tonight, she'd try to relax, but she doubted she could tamp down her worry. Whatever omen had soured her mood when she woke up that morning hadn't been good. Rianthe wriggled her fingers inside her gloves. Maybe she needed to search out Tevy again. She'd done that in her vision before, but nothing had come of it. Maybe she'd have better luck with Kaiden. She'd thought of him this morning. Dram, but she hoped he was all right and that he'd found Tevy.

Because if he hadn't, and he was in trouble himself, the additional tear to Rianthe's soul would be unbearable.

~~~

The girl was taking too long. She should have brought the boy by now. Taegar paced, clenching and unclenching her bony fists. She needed a bigger outlet, but couldn't trust her own powers right now. The light emanating from the altar had weakened more. Taegar did not dare waste power, or she would succumb to the Forever breath before attaining her destiny.

She'd given the girl precious amounts of her own magic. If it didn't work… If she hadn't found the rest of the talisman, Taegar would use every bit of her remaining energy making certain the girl paid for that mistake.
~~~

She needed to make plans. To do that, she must know what had happened. Taegar unfolded her hand, staring at the runes she held. They were the only thing that infused her with the *awen* these days. She must have the rest of the set.

Taegar reached into the yellow light with her hand, reaching for the *ehwaz*. She must know what was happening.

It surprised her when she did not find the girl, Marta. Instead, the one she'd met in prior visions sat before her, only she did not see Taegar. She sat on the ground, facing—

Another cave, much like her own. Taegar gripped the runes as she searched the vision. A light streamed from Earth. Earth's *awen*, white and pure and much stronger than the one there. Where was this?

A long time ago, Taegar believed Damian Royan had hidden a wellspring of power somehow. Could this be it?

Someone out of her sight spoke. "You have the power within you, Rianthe Royan." Fury, immediate and strong, filled Taegar. She shook with the need to reach through the *ehwaz* to the girl. This must be the child of Damian and Valena Royan. That explained so much about her powers. She was a threat, the only person who could possibly thwart Taegar's plans. She must die. Taegar tried again to reach the girl. She tried, but her strength waned.

"Argghhh!" she screamed, pulling her hand out of the light, the vision disappearing. Taegar needed to conserve all her energy, for she was about to travel. Physical movement across this land that fought her took an excess of her magic. This, however, was too important to pass up. She'd gotten a strong idea of where Damian

Royan's cave was. She would go there. The *awen* in that cave would rejuvenate her, and she could get rid of the Royan girl, who stood between her and her place as the rightful heir of Earth's powers.

She would regain everything, then kill Rianthe Royan and be ready for the final battle, where she would win. All would be hers. All would bow to her.

All would die as she decreed.

CHAPTER SEVENTEEN

Kaiden sat on the hillside above Minor Town, unable to shake the dark, morose mood he'd settled into. He needed to do something, anything. Torn between rescuing Tevy or these children, he seemed unable to take action of any kind. He needed to do *something*. Anything that would get the heavy rock off his chest.

Instead, he sat imagining that child still in his arms. Dead. And how he could have stopped it. That was his job. He was a protector. Lately, he hadn't been protecting anything very well.

"Do you plan to sit there all day?" Marta asked.

"If I choose."

She blew out impatient air. "This isn't getting anything done. If your friend's brother isn't here, maybe…" She ran a finger along his upper arm. "We can find him elsewhere."

"I can't leave these children."

"Why are they so important to you?" she asked.

Something compelled him to remind her. "I told you already. Some guy sold me, just like these children." Except, had they all been sold? Could some have been kidnapped instead? Torn away from their families to be worked to the bone in this mine?

"That was different. You were a babe."

"Different circumstances. Same lack of choice."

Marta shook her head. "I don't get it." Her voice sounded like a note sung off-key. She took a deep breath, then another. "I think," she continued, now quiet and calming, "I understand why this is so important to you. But you're one person, Kaiden. What can you possibly do?"

Rianthe would have jumped right up, ready to take on the world to save them. He grew tired of Marta's selfish whining. But he might need her. She was right. How could only one person rescue those children?

"I'll figure something out."

"You've been sitting here for hours. Got any ideas yet? I'm tired of waiting."

He waved in the direction they'd come from. "Then leave."

That fleck of gold touched her eyes again as they narrowed. Was it real or was he seeing things?

"You know I can't leave you," Marta said with a laugh. More of a purr, really. Whenever her voice changed like that, a fog reached for him, tried to ensnare him, pacify him.

"I wouldn't know where to go, who to rely on," she continued. "You keep me safe."

Kaiden shook his head. "Stop that."

"Stop what?"

"Whatever you're doing that makes me lose my ability to think."

Kaiden removed her hand from his arm, surprised to see her face turned ugly for an instant before returning to the Marta he was used to seeing. Had he imagined it?

"Honestly, Kaiden," she tried one more time. "I know a place we can go. Where we'll be safe. You won't have any concerns. Where you won't have to worry about protecting anyone ever again."

Despite his better judgment, she'd piqued his interest. "You know a place?"

"Yes. Come with me," she said. She didn't touch him this time, but her voice could beguile a sailor tied to the mast of his ship. It sounded nice. In theory. Kaiden longed for the day when he wouldn't worry. At least, not as much. He longed to open up about his feelings. For a place, or time, when the weight of the world didn't sit upon his shoulders. He'd grown so tired of always being the protector. Why should everyone be his problem? He looked down at the town. Why were these children his problem?

No. Running away from his destiny wasn't the answer. He'd been born to protect. And he would. Starting with these children. Then Tevy. Then Rianthe. The worry that she'd gotten herself into trouble lay like a stone in his gut. The knowledge was always there, in his mind and heart. If he couldn't protect her, them, the rest would be the least of his concerns.

Kaiden watched a man leave the two-story building he'd decided housed the people who ran this slave camp. That was the man he planned to capture. This leader must pay for the suffering he'd inflicted.

Four men immediately surrounded the man.

Bodyguards. Kaiden could take all four on at once, but that would take precious time and the leader might get away. He needed a distraction to draw a couple of them off. But what?

Kaiden looked at Marta. "You stayed in that so-called boarding house last night, right?"

"Yes," she answered carefully.

He nodded toward the group crossing to the mine. "Did you see any of them there?"

Marta peered at the men. "Maybe one or two. And not the one in the center."

Distracting them with a girl may not work, then. At the mine, all the guards stayed outside except for one. Much better odds. If he got into the mine first and waited for the boss to enter, he had a better chance of taking out the guard and keeping the leader quarantined.

It was as good a plan as any.

At dusk, he and Marta slipped back into the town. While she went to eat, he snuck near to the mine and watched the children file out. All bedraggled, all tired, and all in pain. Their appalling circumstances hurt Kaiden almost as much as it must hurt them. He thought of the little boy. The man who had done this must pay. Would pay. Soon.

After the children left, two guards stayed behind at the mine's entrance. Kaiden could take them out if he needed to, but if last night's guards were the norm, sleep would distract them at some point, giving Kaiden the chance to slip inside and wait for his chance tomorrow.

"All night. We gotta stay here until dawn," one guard moaned. "It ain't right."

"We all got to do our part. Everyone does dark duty." The second guard's voice was quieter, timid.

Probably just as lethal in a fight though. He wouldn't have been hired otherwise.

"Yeah, but I didn't sleep so well last night. I don't see how I'm gonna make it through. And no one would cover for me."

"That's because you never help them when they need a break. You get what you give."

"Well, Tank said we'd live the life of luxury. This ain't that life."

"There's food in your belly, drink to warm you, and a bed to sleep in. That's more than most have. I, for one, don't mind a little work to keep all that. Our boss isn't an easy man to work for, but I'll still take this over starvation."

The disgruntled guard continued to mumble as they moved off to the side and pulled out a cask of drink. Kaiden gave them an hour. He waited until their words were slurred, then slipped by them without notice.

Once he got far enough inside, he unwrapped a glow and explored the mine to make sure no one lurked there. He'd been in caves before, but a man-carved mine was a different creature. This tunnel was narrow, the walls straighter. Wood bracing every few feet told the story of a mountain that fought man's invasion. Openings showed where veins had been chipped out. Kaiden reached for a piece of shale forgotten on the ground, hard and not quite as black as coal. He found it difficult to believe this could become something that nourished the soil.

He searched until the tunnel narrowed, then returned to the entrance, covered the glow, and found a niche to wait out the night. Kaiden chewed on hardtack, settling in for the long, cold hours ahead. The darkness remained unbroken save for the eyes of the child he'd failed to save, who stared at him, filled with one last ray of hope before his life had been brutally snuffed. Kaiden's responsibility. Kaiden squeezed his eyes shut against the pain, but the boy's face would not go away.

"I'm sorry," he whispered to the darkness. He curled up into a ball of misery, unable to shake the worry that he might fail on the morrow. That he might not avenge the boy's murder. That everything—these children, Tevy, Rianthe, the world—might come crashing down because he could not protect one single thing. He pulled his cloak tight, but it didn't keep the darkness from chilling him right down to his soul.

Shortly after sunrise, the boys and girls who slaved in the mine filed in. Kaiden hugged the wall in his little alcove, trying to remain unseen, but one boy looked right at him, his eyes widening. Kaiden put a finger to his lips and the boy hurried to look down and away. He would keep Kaiden's secret.

Soon, the regular staccato sounds of mine work filled his ears. He wanted to spare them this work, but he dare not leave his hiding spot or he might miss the one chance he had to capture this Tank fellow. *Soon. Very soon, your life will improve.*

Some shuffling outside drew his attention. The guards were shifting, probably straightening up. That meant only one thing. The boss was coming.

Kaiden moved further into the cave. Soon, two men entered. The man he'd seen yesterday—Tank, they'd called him—and one guard. Kaiden waited until they passed him, then attacked, shoving the leader into the alcove behind him. Tank's head hit the stone wall and he crumpled to the ground. Kaiden didn't have time to check if he'd knocked the man out because the guard turned, ready for battle. In close quarters, Kaiden only had his short knife to rely on. And his strength and wits.

The guard lunged for him. Kaiden barely side-stepped, driving his knife into the man's shoulder, forcing him to drop the club he carried. The man didn't scream or even groan. Instead, he came at Kaiden full bore.

He could fight, but Kaiden fought better. The man had no weapon but his fists, so Kaiden crouched low, rising up as the man got to him, coming up underneath with fist and knife. He gutted the man and hit him under the chin in one sweep.

The guard's head flew back as blood spewed from the belly wound, then he slumped to the floor unconscious. He would not wake up.

Breathing fast and hard, with adrenaline surging through his body, Kaiden turned to Tank, who was no longer slumped on the floor. He was also prepared, with a knife in each hand and cunning in his eyes. He hadn't risen to his role in all this without thought or ability. The man looked smart and would fight that way, too.

Kaiden advanced, blood from his last victim still dripping from his knife. He and the leader circled each other, both searching for weaknesses. The man feinted with his left arm. Kaiden didn't budge, knowing it for a ruse. But it told him the man was right-handed. That was where the most danger lay.

Kaiden crouched lower.

So did the leader.

Circling, searching for a way in.

When Kaiden dipped his arm, the man lunged with glee in his eyes.

Except Kaiden hadn't made a mistake. He'd drawn Tank out. Ready for the lunge, he slammed down on the man's wrist and jabbed with his other arm, catching Tank in the side with his fist.

Air whooshed out of Tank's lungs. He threw himself backward and came at Kaiden again. Arm to arm, face to face, they grappled. Around and around they struggled, sweat dripping from them both.

Slowly, Kaiden got the upper hand. Slowly, Tank's arms inched back as Kaiden's hands got closer and closer to his neck. When the man screamed, it startled Kaiden. He almost lost his grip, barely managing to keep the pressure on.

A commotion broke out behind him, but he couldn't look. His total focus was on the man he battled, somehow as powerful as he himself was.

Then, Tank's strength broke and he fell back. Kaiden landed on top of him, and again the air whooshed out of his lungs. Kaiden's hands encircled the man's neck. He squeezed.

This is for you, child. He kept squeezing, remembering all the pain the man had caused. Blood pounded in his head. Out of the corner of his eye, he saw others. Kaiden turned and found the children there, maybe all of them, one big crush holding off the remaining guards with crude spears and bulk mass. But the guards were advancing.

They needed help.

Tank had lost consciousness. With great reluctance, Kaiden released his hold. The man still breathed, which Kaiden planned to take care of soon enough.

He joined the boys to make quick work of the remaining guards. Kaiden shook with the need to vent his rage and barely reigned it in. He didn't understand what was happening to him. He'd always been able to harness his anger before. But now, he hungered to kill someone. To make them pay for what they'd done.

He must make them pay. Nothing was more important.

~~~

The rock, the same orange-sized one Rianthe had stared at for days, hovered in the air about three feet off the ground. Sweat dripped down her back with the effort it took to hold it there. It tired her out, this magic thing. Plus, the heat from the nearby Earth-light could warm even the coolest grotto. Focusing, Rianthe pulled off her gloves. Sweat and gloves did not mix well. The rock wobbled but held its place in the air. Roulf had been teaching her to focus despite distractions. Pleased that she'd done two things at once, Rianthe smiled.

"We need to test whether you can direct it," Roulf said. "Do you see that tree outside?"

She grunted. So much for her fleeting sense of accomplishment. Onward to the next level of magical competence. "If I look, I'll lose my concentration."

"You know the tree is there. You remember it."

"Yes." She could picture it.

"I want you to throw the rock at that tree."

They'd been at this for hours. Roulf was not letting up on the training. Rianthe knew her ability had grown steadily in the short time they'd been there because of his direction. She'd been able to summon bits of power on demand. Sometimes, it all overwhelmed her. She longed for a day off to just relax and stare at the stars. To lie beside their lake back in New Hope. To not have the problems of the world on her shoulders.

No one else got that kind of day though. There was no feast one day and famine the next. Everyone worked
~~~

all the time. In New Hope, and around the world, from what little they'd heard. With food shortages approaching critical, a day of relaxation was a dream, and something that wouldn't be her reality any more than anyone else's. Plus, the more she learned to do, the quicker she could leave. She returned her focus to the rock.

"Concentrate. Send it to the tree."

Rianthe tried. She willed it to hit the tree. When it moved, she shouted her glee, until the rock moved about one foot, then dropped to the floor with a thunk.

Roulf was in front of her immediately. "You must not let your thoughts distract you. You cannot break your concentration."

Her muscles throbbed from being too long in one position, so Rianthe stood and took a well-needed stretch. It grated on her that he was right. "This isn't easy, you know."

The rock lifted and shifted slowly and smoothly until Roulf held it. "It is if you focus."

"Show off," Rianthe muttered.

"Again," he said, setting the rock on the cave floor about five feet from her. "Focus. First on the rock, then on where you want it to be."

Rianthe was very close to being done with rocks. Besides, how did this help her defeat Taegar? Maybe the time had come for them to move on to something else. Although, if she didn't get a hold on this, how would she ever work with something bigger?

Baby steps, she reminded herself as she sat cross-legged on the floor again, glaring at the rock.

Move to the tree.

It didn't budge.

For a full minute, she focused on the task, her

frustration growing.

Nothing happened.

"Emotions will hold you back, child," Roulf said. "If you cannot control them, they will block you."

She looked up at him. This was the crux of the matter for her and the thing that worried her the most. Was her own fear holding her back? "Is that why I don't seem to have much ability? Because my mind and heart are blocking the *awen*?"

He cocked his head. "Maybe. I've told you before. I sense great power in you. Only time will tell if you can unlock it."

And save the world. The unspoken words hung in the air. Rianthe had come a long way, she knew that. Still, the world was in a lot of trouble if it only had her to save it. At least if it needed saving anytime soon. This was going to take a while.

"Concentrate." Roulf nudged her.

Rianthe looked at the rock. Looked into the rock. Solid stone, with smooth, rounded edges, yet turmoil lay inside. Different shades of gray tumbled and twisted in a chaotic dance.

The rock rose in the air, hovering where it had been before.

Rianthe held the rock with her eyes, waited until it stabilized, then visualized the tree. And focused, more and more. *Hit the tree. Go to the tree. Be the tree. Join with it.*

Nothing happened.

Dram. Couldn't just one thing come easily to her? Rianthe hit the ground beside her. Without her gloves to protect her.

Two things happened simultaneously. The rock

disappeared. It didn't fly away, it vanished. And the vision hit her with a vehemence that stole her breath away.

A man. In a dark place. Hitting something. No, someone. Beating someone to a pulp with a glazed look in his eyes. A look so dark and feral Rianthe didn't recognize him at first. Kaiden!

She gasped and jumped up, losing her connection with Earth. Breathing hard, she rushed out of the cave and stared south. That was where he'd gone in search of Tevy. She knew it. Felt it in her soul.

"What happened?" Roulf asked, coming up beside her.

"I saw something. Kaiden. He… didn't look like himself." She continued to gaze into the southern skies. "He looked…angry, full of pain. Oh, dram," Rianthe said, clutching her stomach and sinking to the ground. "What if Tevy—"

"Did you see him?"

"No," she cried. "But Kaiden looked so angry."

"Do not assume happenings you did not see."

"What would make Kaiden that upset?"

Roulf patted her back. "I do not know, child. These visions, they are sometimes real, sometimes an echo of what can happen. There's no way to tell which is which."

"I need to go to him, Roulf. I need to help. To find Tevy."

"You need to work on your powers. That is your journey."

"I can't. Not right now." Rianthe strode back into the cave, Roulf following close behind. She whirled and dropped to a knee, grasping Roulf's arms. "I've worked hard at this. I have."

"You have," he agreed.

"And my power is coming along, but so slowly that at this rate, it will be months before I can take on anything bigger than that rock."

"You need to have more faith in yourself, child."

"I do have faith. You've helped me with that, and I'm grateful. But… Right now, I need to be out there." She waved. "Helping. Doing something. I can't do this anymore." She yanked on her gloves, her eyes darting around the cave.

"If you're set on this, so be it," Roulf said. "Your pack is out by the campfire.

"I wasn't looking for my pack."

"What?" He'd gone quiet, deep in thought, probably searching for a way to convince her to stay. Not going to happen.

"Roulf, where's the rock?"

That yanked him out of his contemplation. Both Roulf and Rianthe looked around. The rock was nowhere in the cave.

"I didn't see it move," he said.

"I didn't see anything. It was there, and then it wasn't."

"Where did it go?"

In unison, they both turned and stared out the entrance toward the tree about one hundred yards away.

They walked to the tree. Rianthe expected to find the rock sitting at its base so she searched the ground. Roulf's surprised gasp pulled her gaze upward.

There, in the middle of the trunk, lay the rounded edge of the rock. Except not like it hit the tree. It was embedded in the tree, as if the tree had grown up around the rock.

Rianthe figured her eyes were as round and wide as Roulf's were. "Did I do that?"

Roulf stepped back and clapped his hands together, laughing. "I knew you had it in you."

She gulped in wonder, touching the bit that still showed. "Wow."

"Yes, child. Wow."

"And I'm not tired. Well, not as much."

"That is the best news yet."

Rianthe looked down at her hands, now safe inside her gloves. "I touched Earth."

Roulf nodded. "From whence comes your magic."

"So my magic is stronger when I touch the soil?"

"Makes sense," Roulf said. "Earth is the source of magic. If you are destined to heal Earth, there must be a symmetry between you."

"Which means anytime I want to use power, I have to chance a vision."

Roulf nodded. "It seems so."

Rianthe rested her hand on the rock in the tree, searching for any silver lining to this revelation. "I guess we know what I need to do."

"Yes. This is a breakthrough. We must continue working on your abilities."

"I can't. I have to go to Kaiden. I must find Tevy."

"You have to stay." Roulf turned her to face him. "Can't you see how important this is?"

She backed away. "I do see. I still have to go. Roulf—" She moved back to him and grasped his shoulders. "I can't concentrate like I need to. Not with Tevy out there lost…or worse. And Kaiden…" The look she'd seen in his eyes scared Rianthe more than just about anything. "I have to find them."

Roulf hung his head for a long moment, then nodded. "I understand. I can't help but believe that leaving now is a mistake, though. That we will lose something barely gained in deserting this place."

"Then you stay. See if you can find anything else. Plan my training. I promise, once I find them, I'll work sunup to sundown every day. I'll get stronger. I know I will."

Pacing in front of the tree, Roulf stared at the rock for a long time, then turned back to Rianthe. "All right. I accept your promise." He waggled a finger at her. "Do not be gone too long."

"The day's about disappeared. I'll leave with Taschia first thing in the morning. If Earth will let me." She chewed her lip, sending silent prayers. *Please.*

"It's not the best idea," Roulf said. "But it's the best we can do for now. So be it."

Agreed, Taschia mind-spoke.

With their plan set, they turned to the tasks around camp, checking snares, searching for greens and berries. Taschia left to hunt her own dinner.

Rianthe couldn't stop worrying about Tevy and Kaiden. Were they together? Was Tevy all right? And Kaiden? Would Earth see the urgency and let her help? She needed answers.

That night, in darkness broken only by firelight and stars, Rianthe knew there would be no rest without answers. So, with Roulf asleep across the fire from her, she slipped quietly from her bedroll. Taschia raised her head, but Rianthe signaled her to stay put. *I have to do this for myself,* she mind-spoke.

I should be by your side. In case.

I will call for you if I need help.

Taschia sniffed the air. *Agreed. Do not be too long.*

Rianthe stole off into the woods and sat on the ground, pulling off her gloves slowly. She needed to determine where Kaiden was and if Tevy was with him. She'd directed the visions before and planned to try that again. If she failed... If she met Taegar in this otherworld...

She wasn't ready for that. She needed time to gain strength and belief in her magic before she took Taegar on again. She must focus on Kaiden and Tevy, and she must not fail.

Focusing on their faces in happier times, Rianthe settled her hands on the ground, reaching for the *ehwaz.*

Instead of Tevy or Kaiden, though, she saw herself.

Standing in a dark place, her hands plunged deep in the soil, stuck in an epic battle with Taegar. Her body writhed in pain as bolt after bolt of raw power hit her. Again and again. So much pain.

Rianthe tossed the pain back to Taegar, but it wasn't enough. She could feel herself weakening. Finally, in a last gasp, she dug deep into the soil, deep into her soul, calling up all the magic she had, calling for Earth's power to aid her. She gave herself to the magic, let it use every last bit of her energy in one final volley fired at Taegar. Rianthe did not see if it helped. She slumped to the ground, her hands slipping from Earth's sustenance.

She saw herself, there on the ground. Not moving. Not breathing.

As suddenly as this vision began, it disappeared, morphing into Kaiden. His eyes were red with a fury she'd never seen in him before. He stood in the middle of a group of buildings, some small, some larger. He faced a man's back, a man tied to two poles.

Kaiden held a whip. He raised it without hesitation, bringing it down on the man again and again. Blood flowed from rips in the man's raw skin. Still, Kaiden did not stop.

This was a Kaiden she'd never known. An unleashed Kaiden. Something had happened. Something that made him lose control. She needed to get to him. Soon.

Was Tevy with him? Rianthe's focus changed, to an even darker place. A black void. She saw nothing, but heard faint howling. Wolves. Tevy's wolves? It was too dark to tell. She got no visual and could only listen until the plaintive howls lessened, then disappeared.

Rianthe felt a nudge. Taschia. She pulled her hands from the dirt, returned to the reality of her night, more confused and scared than ever.

You scented my brothers?

Rianthe touched her own cheek, swiped at the tears there while she shook her head. *I heard them. I think.*

Taschia licked her. *Then they are alive. That is good.*

Rianthe wasn't so sure. Too many scenes had flashed through her, all bringing more uncertainty. Were they happening now or were they portents?

And the battle with Taegar. Rianthe had always known they would meet again. This had been beyond anything she'd imagined. And there, at the end, she'd looked dead.

Do not let the magic use you up. Roulf's words came to her mind unbidden. In the vision, she'd lain on the ground unmoving, no rise and fall of her chest to signal breath.

The final sacrifice, giving everything of herself so others would survive.

Rianthe held out shaking hands, wrapped them

around Taschia, and held on tight. Then she closed her mind to keep her sister-wolf from knowing what she now knew as truth.

That she would die.

That saving Earth and humankind meant giving everything she had.

Rianthe resolved to bury that knowledge deep. Now was not the time. For now, Kaiden and Tevy were all that mattered. She'd gotten no sense of Tevy's whereabouts in her vision. Refusing to consider reasons why she hadn't been able to see him, Rianthe focused on Kaiden. He was south of there. And he needed help.

She must go after Kaiden. Hopefully, in helping him, she would find out more about Tevy. Maybe even find Tevy with Kaiden.

All she had now was hope.

We head south at first light, she told Taschia.

I am with you, the wolf replied.

The next morning, Roulf watched her with sadness on his face as she tucked the book into her pack. She hugged him tight. "I'll be back. I promise."

With a deep sigh, he reached up to cup her cheeks. "Come back safe, child." He tapped Taschia on the nose. "All of you."

"That's the plan."

She walked away. Two steps into her journey, the sludge that had kept her from leaving before returned. Each step grew more difficult, and Rianthe more forlorn. "Please," she cried. "Let me go. I have to find them."

She turned back to Roulf. "I cannot believe Earth would keep me here against my will."

"Maybe it's not Earth," Roulf said, joining her. "Give me the book."

Instinct made Rianthe clutch her pack tighter. That book was a gift from her parents. "Nothing in here deals with this situation."

"I know," he said, admonishing her with his outstretched hand to give him the book.

Rianthe pulled the book out and reluctantly offered it to him.

"Step away."

She backed up several steps with no hesitation, no slowing of her steps, no quicksand to hold her captive. She took more steps, again with no issue. "It's not Earth?"

"I wondered, when this happened the first time, if your parents had coupled the book with Origin Cave. The book will not open for anyone but you, and it cannot leave this place."

"Then I am free to follow the path ahead of me," Rianthe said. Her whole body shook with gratitude. She could go. Earth wouldn't hold her back. Indecision disappeared along with the weight of her choice. She'd chosen the right battle.

Now, she only had to pray it didn't mean losing the war. Though Rianthe knew she was doing what she needed to do, it felt like she was running away. Leaving something important behind. She stared at the book in Roulf's hands. *Thank you,* she told Earth. *I'll give you everything I've got once I find Kaiden and Tevy, put everything aside to focus on you. I just...I need them out of harm's way while I do that.*

"Go, child," Roulf said. "I will keep this safe."

After rushing back for one more quick hug, she and Taschia turned to the south.

To Kaiden.

To Tevy.
To her destiny.

~~~

Tevy did not understand what was happening to him. The pain hurt beyond imagining. Horrible, bone-crunching pain. Moving was all but impossible. He lay still, grateful to be encased by the warmth of his brothers.

Suddenly, the pain disappeared. Tevy lay there, curled up and panting, trying to figure out what had happened. A sound so slight he shouldn't have heard it drew his attention. Tevy's head whipped around and he saw the rabbit, sitting up, chewing on a leaf, unafraid. Saliva filled Tevy's mouth and drool dripped down his chin as his appetite returned. He looked away, surprised to see so well in the darkness. His sense of smell seemed stronger, too.

What happened to me?

You are our brother.

Hark! Tevy's joy was insurmountable at being able to converse with his wolves again. He wasn't alone. He'd known that, but it seemed like ages since he'd spoken to someone.

You have not been alone for a long time. We were always with you.

Grog nudged him. *You feel better?*

I do. In fact, Tevy felt great. No pain, nothing. And that worried him. Had he…

Was he…

Dead?
~~~

CHAPTER EIGHTEEN

Once Kaiden took down the leader of Minor Town, the most hardened of his guards fled. At least the ones they hadn't already captured. The others agreed quickly to their new leadership. Kaiden. He called the shots now, albeit through a red haze of anger. Marta watched him order food and care for the children, barely suppressing his baser need for retribution. The oldest of the kids helped him identify who'd treated them the best. Kaidan had two of the cruelest guards tied up and guarded until they could be made to pay for their treatment of the children. Pay they would, but for completely different reasons than Kaiden's self-righteous ones.

Marta had searched everywhere except on Kaiden's body for the runes Taegar wanted her to find, to no avail. Kaiden wouldn't let her get close enough, so she'd have to take him to the Dark druid and let her solve this riddle. She needed Kaiden pliable and willing, but he'd shown an irritating immunity to her powerful, magic-enhanced charms. Now, though, he was close. He would succumb, she could tell. She just needed to push him to get angrier, to feel worse. He'd be too weak to resist her. Then, he'd be putty in her hands.

After directing the erection of several poles in the middle of the town center, Kaiden skulked off to a dark corner and crouched down. Marta followed, though he didn't acknowledge her presence.

Kaiden was quite handsome. In fact, he looked eerily like Drohan, the boy who'd stolen everything from her, turning her from a smitten young girl to a cynical and angry woman. The day Drohan had arrived in her village, Marta had fallen in love for the first and last time. With his dark looks and tall, strong body, he'd swayed her tender heart. Arms that bullied her friends held her with a tenderness she'd never known from her parents. Her mother had died when she'd been a child. Her father had put her to work as a child and piled more chores on her with each passing year.

Drohan was the respite from the drudgery of her days.

"Come away with me," he begged with that dimple of his. "Just for the day. Everyone deserves a day off."

Marta bit her lip. "I don't know."

"It's one day," Drohan said. "What can your father do? Fire you?"

"Worse." Marta was all too aware of her father's wrath.

"If he comes near you, I'll take care of him. I'll protect you."

She chewed her lip, then decided. She went with Drohan, safe in his arms, learning the love she'd given to no one else. The perfect day.

Perfection she'd paid dearly for every day hence. Her father's ire had been beyond anything she'd known before. And Drohan? He'd stood back, laughing, and watched her father beat her. Every day since, she'd seen that scorn and laughter upon his face. She'd felt the shame of everyone's eyes on her, knowing what she'd done, how she'd been duped. Branded as a harlot, she'd been forced to work harder, with longer hours, until her hands bled. All to learn her place, a place she did not belong. A place she knew she would never return to again.

Except once. She'd go back, this time with her powers, to show them that humiliating her had been the worst mistake of their lives.

Marta saw Kaiden angst in his stooped posture and mumblings. He was awash in fury over the injustices he'd seen in this village and she planned to use that. She let quiet words snake inside him and wrap themselves around his heart, his mind, his soul.

"They enslaved children, Kaiden. They must be made to pay."

He stared at the ground, not answering.

"They killed them, all in the name of greed."

This time, he nodded.

"They must die," she said. "The same horrible death they inflicted on these innocents."

"They will die," Kaiden whispered. He said the words over and over again, developing a cadence, a banner of action he hoped would soothe his raging pain.

Except Marta knew his actions would not soothe anything, but instead fan the fire she'd built in him.

"Horrible deaths," she said.

"Horrible deaths," he repeated. "I will show her I am worthy."

"Her? That girl?" Marta swallowed her hatred of Rianthe and tried to keep the venom from her voice.

"Yes. I am the protector."

"You protect the children."

"Yes."

"You protect her." Marta sneered behind Kaiden's back. She worked hard to keep her voice even, but it galled her that, even with her extensive attempts to bring Kaiden under her will, he still thought of that girl.

"Yes."

"You are the protector. These men must die. Slowly. They must feel the children's pain. They must feel your wrath."

Kaiden stood and punched the wall next to him, his hand pounding straight through the thick wood. "They will." He crouched back down, mumbling to himself and staring at nothing.

~~~

With quiet precision, Kaiden closed the door behind him. He wanted more than anything to pick up where he'd left off in the mine, beating this man to a pulp, but he must be certain these crimes against the children never happened again. For that, he needed information.

The man, the leader of Minor Town, sat on the floor with his back propped against the wall. He peered at Kaiden through a swollen, bloody eye. He still managed to sneer, showing a couple missing teeth. Kaiden pulled a bench over and sat in front of him.

"Come for round two?"

"Not yet," Kaiden said, although the need to make the man pay thrummed through his every nerve and
~~~

thought. "I've come for some answers."

"And why should I give you any answers?"

Kaiden shrugged. "Maybe, just maybe, the end will come quicker for you if you cooperate."

"Ha! That's not much incentive."

Kaiden clenched and unclenched his hands. "It's the best I can do." He leaned forward, stared into the leader's good eye. "I hear they call you Tank."

It was the man's turn to shrug, unable to do more with his hands and feet bound. "So what. I've got a name."

"How long have you been doing this? Enslaving children."

"A while."

"Where do the children come from?"

"All over. The word's out," Tank said. "Food and a bed to flop in. Fertilizer for plants. A trade."

Kaiden's hands pumped faster. Fist. No fist. Fist. No fist. "Children are sold for nothing more than a meal?" Exactly like his father had done, or whoever that was who'd sold him.

"Just like you, Kaiden," Marta said, as if reading his mind.

He turned his head as she stepped out from the shadowed edges of the room. "Weren't you sold to some village?" she said. "For food? Haven't you been waiting all these years to understand why? To get revenge?"

"Be quiet," Kaiden said, but her words echoed his own thoughts. Being tossed away as a babe had haunted him his entire life. He wanted vengeance but would never get it because no one knew who the man had been or where he'd gone.

"Now I understand why you're so angry," Tank said,

smirking. "You were in the same situation as my…workers. Enslaved for a bite of food?"

"Worse," Marta said. "He was a newling. A still-wrapped babe."

Kaiden stood and grabbed Marta's arm, intent on seeing her out of the building. He wouldn't get any answers with her stirring the pot. Plus, she had no right to his secrets. She knew more than she should already.

"Twenty-some years ago, by the look of you. Up near that Rushmore Mountain, perchance?"

Kaiden whipped around, yanking Marta along with him as he closed in on Tank. He let go of Marta and grabbed Tank's shirt, yanking him away from the wall. "How could you know that?"

Tank cocked his head for a better look at Kaiden through his one good eye. "Yep. I think I see the resemblance now," he said. Then he laughed right in Kaiden's face.

Incensed, Kaiden threw him against the wall but the man didn't stay there. He slid to the ground, laughing until he coughed up blood. "Oh, this is priceless," he gasped out in between guffaws.

"What the hell are you talking about?" Kaiden demanded an answer even though, deep inside, he knew he didn't want to hear it.

"You… You are the…one who started this. It was all…because of you," the man said, coughing up more blood as he continued to chortle.

"Me? I've done nothing this detestable. How could I have begun it all?"

"Well," Tank said, "that's got a story to it. And I'm a bit dried up from all this blood loss."

"Tell me." Kaiden grabbed his shirt again, getting up

close and personal. "Tell me now." He tossed Tank back to the ground.

"Seems like the power's flipped back to my side, hasn't it? Tank wiped his mouth with his tied hands. "I want whiskey to quench my thirst. Won't be saying nothing until that happens."

Kaiden's nostrils flared. He hated giving in, but he needed to solve this confusion, to understand what this was all about. Did this man have knowledge about Kaiden? He couldn't stand not knowing. Kaiden glanced at Marta, who leaned against the wall. "Get him his drink."

Her eyes narrowed. She didn't like taking orders. Frowning, she turned and stomped out of the room.

Tough.

Until she returned, Kaiden settled back on the bench to glare at Tank. This man would not get the upper hand. Kaiden held all the cards and this man must not win. He would tell Kaiden what he wanted to know or he'd get another beating. "You'd better not be playing me."

"Or what? You'll make my punishment even worse than whatever you already have planned?"

Marta returned with a skin and dribbled some into Tank's mouth.

He smacked his lips in pleasure. "Nothing better than a good whiskey," he crowed.

"You've had your precious grog. Now, what do you know about the Rushmore Mountain…and me."

"You don't see it, do you?" Tank said, wiping his lips again. "The family resemblance."

Family? Blood pounded in Kaiden's ears, but he kept his silence and waited, albeit impatiently.

"I'm your uncle, boy." He said the words with glee,

snorting his laughter as if he'd gotten the last word in an argument.

Frozen in shock, Kaiden didn't know how to process what he'd just heard. It couldn't be true. Could it? Dram. He didn't know who to believe these days. If this was true, Kaiden might be about to get the answers he'd waited his entire life for. Even if they were from this degenerate, the answers might be a salve to his soul. But this? It was too much. To implausible to be true.

"You're not my uncle," he spat out.

"You can say that as many times as you want, but truth's truth."

"Prove it."

Tank gestured for another drink. Marta obliged him, wisely keeping quiet.

"You look a lot like your father, you do. He was a strapping lad, my brother. We were born about forty years after the Great Magic War. Things wasn't as good then as they are now."

"Things aren't good now," Marta said.

Kaiden glared at her, but she stood her ground defiantly.

"Whatever they are now, they were worse then. We didn't have seeds to grow anything, and most of what the old world created had been used up. We was starving."

"Like I said. Same as now." Marta gave him another sip of whiskey and leaned against the wall.

Tank shook his head. "Was worse. Way worse. My brother and me, we grew up hard. Fought for everything we got. Learned to fight well." He nodded at Kaiden. "As good as you.

"Then, he went and found some woman. Fell for her hard, he did. Stupid man."

"My mother?" Kaiden had steeled himself against asking anything. He refused to show any interest or that he might believe anything the man was saying. But the pull of this was too strong. "What was she like?"

"She wasn't pretty, not really."

Kaiden clenched his fists, hating that he wanted to defend a woman he knew nothing about, including the reason she'd abandoned him.

"Her hair was brown, like yours. And long. He always said he loved playing with her hair."

Just like Kaiden did with Rianthe's hair.

"Stupid fool. Got the girl pregnant."

With him.

"He was actually happy about it. Happy. Weak, more like. He gave her almost all the food we found, keeping little for himself. Or for me."

He sneered again, gesturing for another sip. "I didn't like that he did that," he continued after a gulp that caused a coughing spell. "Nope. I didn't like that much at all. Didn't even matter, either. Because she only lasted about a month after giving birth. There wasn't enough food to keep her healthy enough to feed you. My brother, still the fool, gave her all his food. She still died. Then he followed her, leaving me with a newling and nothing to eat."

Kaiden couldn't talk, couldn't even move. His parents died trying to save him. All this time, he'd thought they'd given him up. But they had loved him. They had died trying to give him a chance at life. And he'd never known them.

When Kaiden found his legs, he paced, clenching and unclenching his hands. "What were their names?" he asked, hating the plea in his voice.

"What's it matter?"

"I will not ask you again. What were their names?"

Tank hesitated a minute, stringing out his answer, goading Kaiden. It worked. He would have beat the man to death, except he wanted answers. Needed answers like he needed air to breathe.

"The girl's name was Cait. Aiden was my brother." Tank beckoned to Marta for more whiskey.

Aiden? Kaiden, who'd been called Aiden before his True-Naming, had been told Fraka and Jonah picked out his name. What cosmic force helped them name him the same as the man who'd sired him? Kaiden couldn't wrap his head around it.

"So you found a village and gave me up for a meal?"

"I did. Well, sort of. I found that place, New Hope, I think it's called. I was about dead on my feet. You weren't much better off. Some black man with long white hair took you out of my arms and told the villagers to get me food. He talked to me while I ate. Asked about you."

"Me? And you told him?"

"Everything."

The breath whooshed from Kaiden's lungs. Bhren had known who the man was? Known who Kaiden's parents had been? Kaiden sank onto the bench, unable to think about anything, hear anything, the blood pounded so hard in his ears. Bhren, the master who'd taught him everything, protected him, loved him. He'd known everything and had never told Kaiden any of it. He'd let Kaiden wonder and worry for his entire life. He'd betrayed Kaiden. Just like he'd convinced Kaiden to betray Rianthe.

Tank asked for another swig of whiskey. "I told him you weren't nothing. Would never amount to anything.

He'd be better off just letting you die."

That hurt more than Kaiden wanted to let on, though a part of him agreed. He'd made so many mistakes. Maybe he should have died back then. Maybe Tank hadn't done him any favors, leaving him in New Hope. "Why would you say I'd be better off dead?"

"Because there's no good in our family. Our blood's bad. Always has been. You see…" He paused to leer at Kaiden. "We're the reason the world's in the state it is."

Kaiden leaped up. "How the hell can we be the cause of that?"

"Because my grandfather, your great-grandfather, is the man who started it all. Leastways, that's the way I heard it. He convinced some druid that all that magic they found back then shouldn't be for everyone. That it would be better serving a more…personal agenda."

Kaiden had heard the stories. Rumors, really, about how and why Taegar had turned. Taegar had been a Guardian druid, then split off to form the Dark druid circle. These were facts handed down through the Studies, but only rumors remained as to her motivation, whispers that she'd lost her heart to some man who'd used her for access to her power.

Could that be his heritage? That he came from the line who had destroyed all that humankind held dear? Everything from Kaiden's past coalesced. Bits and pieces of things he'd done wrong all gelled with what Tank was saying. He hung his head, unable to come to terms with this information. It was too much. His heart swelled with the pain of truth, ready to explode.

"So you see"—Tank sneered—"you're a bad apple from a diseased tree. Never gonna amount to much. Always up to no good. That's what our family's all about.

That's why I am the way I am. It's in our blood."

"Noooooo," Kaiden screamed. He would not be that person. He could not be. He hit Tank in the cheek with his fisted hand. "I am not who you say I am. I will never be that person."

Tank struggled up from the ground. He spit out blood and a couple more teeth. "Seems like you already are, nephew."

Kaiden couldn't stand it. No way Tank was right. Kaiden was the protector. He was meant for something better. Something greater. What Tank said wasn't true. "I don't believe you. You and your ancestry are not mine. You're playing me."

"Say what you like, boy, but you know. I know you do. I'm your uncle. Nothing you can do about that. And you come from a long line of bad blood. You ain't going to be nothing. Better get used to that now. In fact, you should come along with me. We got a good thing going here. You'd see that if you'd set aside that moral code of yours and take a closer look."

"Never!" Kaiden refused to listen to any more of Tank's ramblings. He needed out of there. Needed air. To breathe. To try to make sense of it all.

He turned to Tank. "You die within the hour," he spat out, then strode to the door, never seeing the satisfied look on Marta's face.

~~~

Marta pushed off the wall she'd been leaning against, a small smile on her face as she followed Kaiden out. Everything had gone exactly as she'd planned. Soon she would have him right where she needed him to be. He would understand his place. And very soon she could take him to Taegar and would be gifted with the
~~~

unlimited power she deserved. The power to make those who had hurt her pay.

Marta watched and waited. It wouldn't be long before she had what she wanted. Scant seconds after she settled on a barrel to watch the coming spectacle, Kaiden turned to her, fists clenched.

"It's time. Have the men strung up between the posts."

CHAPTER NINETEEN

Rianthe and Taschia pushed themselves hard, but still, it took three days to reach the outskirts of civilization. A town lay ahead, set in a narrow valley accessed by a single, thin lane at only one end. A barricade lay over the road, but no guards stood to prohibit entry. In fact, as they walked past the barricade it was eerily quiet. Too quiet.

Something had happened there, and it looked familiar. Like when she, Kaiden, and Taschia had walked through downtown Minnie Apples, waiting for danger to leap out from behind the rubble. Her gut and her sense of danger told her this was the place she'd seen in her vision. She was close. To Kaiden, and hopefully to Tevy.

Taschia whined.

I sense it too, Rianthe mind-spoke. There was a sour taste to this place, as if it were tainted.

Noise stilled them. Crows cawing, or a lot of people

shouting. Up ahead. Whoever was making all the ruckus didn't seem worried about the noise, but Rianthe had learned the hard way to let caution lead. She and Taschia inched their way around the barricade, using buildings as camouflage to get closer to the growing crowd. The sounds grew wilder, more frenzied, the closer they got to the center.

Rounding a corner, Rianthe got her first real look at what was happening. A throng of mostly children surrounded three men, who were tied between posts and bare-chested. Youngling and adult alike were yelling and screaming at the men. They pelted them with rocks. The men were bloodied, but alive. The horror of what she watched rolled over Rianthe in waves of revulsion. Children were stoning these men. What had made them stoop to such violence? She glanced at Taschia. The wolf's ears were flat.

I do not like this.

Rianthe reeled from the evil and hatred emanating in waves from this spectacle, appalled that they came from children.

Snap! Rianthe's head whipped toward the sound. She clapped a hand over her mouth to silence her scream. A lash struck the man in the center. He arched, yowling as the leather bit his skin, tearing a crimson welt. Nausea churned in Rianthe's stomach and acid bile rose to her throat as she watched blood ooze from the newly inflicted wound. How could anyone do such a thing to another human being? She turned her head toward the instigator of the brutal torture and everything inside Rianthe froze. The man wielding the weapon, the man inflicting this pain, was Kaiden.

Rianthe had seen this in her vision. Her worst fear.

Kaiden, his face a mask of fury, doing things he'd never done before. Heinous things. Sins against humanity. What had tipped him over this precipice?

Looking around, she saw the children. Really looked at them. Dirty, thin, and bedraggled, their eyes held a wealth of emotion. Some threw stones in anger, some seemed to want answers. They shouted questions, screaming at the men.

"Why did you do this to us?"

"Why do you hate us so?"

The ones who truly broke her heart stood or sat at the periphery, silent and watching, tears streaking the grime on their faces.

Pain raked through Rianthe with each snap of the whip. She skirted the crowd for a better look at Kaiden. What she saw worried her even more than his actions. He didn't seem aware of anything around him, focused solely on the man strung up in front of him. Kaiden's eyes were like someone possessed. Wild, crazy, driven to the edge.

Kaiden pulled back, ready to lay another stripe on the man's back. What had happened there? What had led Kaiden to the edge of insanity?

This is not our friend, Taschia mind-spoke, distaste apparent in her internal voice.

No. It's not.

The whip came down on the man's back again and Rianthe flinched as if hit herself.

She had to stop this. Maybe, if he saw her, saw that she was safe, he'd pull out of the fugue that trapped him. She needed to divert Kaiden's attention, to get him to see she was there. But how? Rushing in would only add to the frenzy. Rianthe searched for something, anything that would help her. Nothing stood out. Since everyone seemed gathered there in the center, participating in this horror, she knew no one would help her. In fact, they might turn their stones her way.

Wait. There. Between those two buildings. Was that a shadow?

Rianthe couldn't see who or what it was. *Taschia? Can you see?*

It is the woman.

What woman?

The new one.

New one? New where? When?

She came to our home.

Marta?

That is the name she used.

Rianthe's brain shut down as a primal rage consumed her. Marta, whose eyes had turned yellow. Who'd tried to dig her claws into Kaiden. Who'd apparently caught up to him and done just that after he'd gone off in search of Tevy.

Tevy! Rianthe searched desperately over the crowd of children, her pulse pounding. She didn't see him. Tevy was not there, meaning Marta had put his life further in danger by diverting Kaiden to this place. The bold rage that filled the children of this town sunk into her, her body and soul overflowing with the same buzzing red hatred.

It had to be Marta. That woman must be at the center of all this. Rianthe moved out of hiding, her only thought to disrupt whatever spell or magic Marta had used to enthrall Kaiden.

Taschia tugged at her sleeve, stopping her at the edge of the buildings. *Anger is not the way to fight. Kai-den says this.*

"We have to stop her."

We are only two and must plan first, then act.

Before they could do either, Marta stepped into the middle of the short alley where they stood.

"I thought I'd seen the shadow of some dung monster," Marta crowed.

"What have you done to Kaiden?"

The girl actually laughed. "Absolutely nothing, except to show him who he truly is."

"That"—Rianthe pointed to the center of town, where Kaiden stood in a trance, staring at the whip he held as he prepared for the next strike—"is not Kaiden."

"Maybe not as you remember him. This is the man he's destined to become. And you..." Marta moved closer. "You can't stop this."

"I *will* stop this. And you."

"Go ahead. Try." Marta laughed again. "I dare you." She raised her arms and fire spat towards Rianthe.

Golden fire. Just like Taegar's.

Rianthe's sword was out in an instant and proved a worthy shield to Marta's magic. Fireball after fireball shot from Marta's hand and each time, Rianthe's sword protected her. Until the ground dropped from underneath her. Lifted, as if by air, Rianthe was thrown across the center of town, over the whippings, the children.

"Kaiden!" Rianthe screamed as she landed with a thud against a building, all wind knocked out of her. She lay there gasping, certain she'd broken every bone in her body, the pain was so great.

The children parted, giving Marta a path to advance on Rianthe. She strode past them, intent on Rianthe, golden eyes blazing.

Rianthe struggled to rise. She barely made it to her feet before the next volley hit her. Taschia circled them both, searching for a way to wound Marta.

"Ugh." Rianthe grunted as she hit the ground again. Where did this woman's power come from? If she didn't find a way to fight back, this would be a very short battle. She must defeat Marta or she would not be able to help Kaiden. Or find Tevy. Or become what she was on her way to becoming.

With those thoughts spurring her on, Rianthe struggled to her feet. She focused and dug deep for the *awen*, like she'd learned to at Origin Cave. She needed protection, or she'd never be able to attack.

The tingle grew within her slowly, building for precious seconds until it burst forth, a blue-white translucent barrier against Marta's powers.

It came too late. Marta's energy got through before the shield strengthened. Everything Rianthe had, she'd poured into creating the barrier. Nothing remained to defend her against the energy that hit her.

The ball of light raised her up, then tossed her against the brick wall like a rag doll. Rianthe couldn't help but scream in pain. No part of her was unscathed. Everything hurt, the pain so great she almost succumbed to the relief of unconsciousness.

She must fight. Losing wasn't an option. All would be destroyed if she did. Kaiden. Tevy. Humanity. She was not supposed to die in this grim town. Rianthe pushed the darkness aside and struggled to stand. Somehow, she had to defeat Marta.

There was no other choice.

~~~

Kaiden's whip laid another stripe on Tank's back,
~~~

red filling the wound almost immediately. Full of blood fever, he was intent only on what lay in front of him. Men who'd done wrong. Men who must pay.

He had to protect the children.

From his peripheral vision, he saw something, or someone, fly overhead, breaking his concentration. He glanced toward the movement, saw someone hit the side of a building and slump to the ground. Some new threat? It didn't matter. He would fight it. He would make sure no one would hurt these children ever again. He broke from his position in front of the tied up men and advanced on whoever it was just as the children parted and Marta passed him, fast and smooth, almost as if floating. Kaiden looked beyond her, to the person struggling to stand up. Dark, familiar hair covered the face until she swept it aside and he could see.

Rianthe!

Rianthe? There? She'd gone north with Roulf and—

Taschia sped by with a quick glance spared for Kaiden. *You must help.*

The words, foreign and yet familiar, stopped Kaiden in his tracks. He *was* helping. The children.

Help Rianthe. We fight the bad woman.

Balls of fire spewed from Marta's outreached hands, aimed right at Rianthe, who only just got her sword up to deflect the magical blows. Flame after flame shot from Marta, directed solely at Rianthe.

No! Kaiden shook his head, trying to clear the fog that held him prisoner. He needed to help Rianthe. But... He turned back to the men hanging from the posts, none standing on their own any longer. This was why he'd gone there, wasn't it? He must make them pay for what they'd done. For the little boy who'd died in vain, and so many others before him.

"Kaiden," Rianthe screamed. "Help!"

Rianthe's voice ripped any remaining cloud of indecision away. The horror of what Kaiden had done flooded him with remorse and grief, freezing him in place. He was neither his uncle nor his ancestor. He was not this darkness. Not the one who meted out punishment. He was Kaiden, protector of Earth and all humankind. Friend of Rianthe and so many more.

When Rianthe went to a knee, he yanked himself out of his chasm of darkness. Indecision fled in the face of need. The woman he loved lay in danger's way. Kaiden drew his sword, ran past the children, yelling at them to go hide, to get somewhere safe, and rushed to Rianthe, toward the real battle he should be fighting.

CHAPTER TWENTY

Each blast from Marta stole more of Rianthe's dwindling energy. She managed to hold her sword as a shield in front of her, nothing more. Magic eluded her, even though Rianthe begged Earth to help her. No help came. Wait. The rock, back at Origin Cave. She'd embedded it in the tree when she'd touched soil. Rianthe tore off her gloves and reached down, grasping a handful of dirt.

The change was drastic and immediate. Magic flared within Rianthe. Potent energy flowed into and through her. Her sword's ability to deflect Marta's powers strengthened and Rianthe unfolded her body, straightening to her full height as she glared at Marta. Her nemesis continued to throw fireball after fireball, no less powerful now than when she'd started. With the *awen* barrier protecting her, Rianthe envisioned a fireball in her dirt-filled hand. Though she was a little shocked to see the white light form, she wasted no time in hurling it at Marta.

The girl dodged the white heat. Rianthe almost laughed at the stunned look on her face, but there was no time as Marta renewed her fight. Rianthe fired back. Again and again.

Rianthe tried to up her game, to dig deeper into the well of power she'd summoned. She had to break this impasse and kill Marta's magic. No extra powers came to her, and she felt herself weakening. Then, suddenly, the barrage halted. Rianthe, who'd been concentrating on the dirt in her hand, looked up to find the space in front of her empty.

Marta had disappeared. She must have ducked around the corner of the building, but she couldn't be far.

While Taschia went around the other way for a classic two-sided attack, Rianthe strode around the corner, ducking back when a fireball just missed her head.

She straightened, ready to fire her own energy at Marta. Then she froze.

Marta held Taschia by the throat.

"Noooo!" Rianthe screamed. Not Taschia. She could not, would not lose her sister-wolf. Her friend. Fury and fear churned inside her like a cyclone as she rushed forward. She must free Taschia.

An arm around her waist stopped her and yanked her back. Rianthe screamed, whirling, sword up, to clash with another sword. She gasped when she saw who her new opponent was.

"Kaiden!" His eyes were clear, the crazed look gone. Whatever had possessed him had disappeared. Rianthe took precious time to search them, to see the clarity there.

She hung her head as tears of gratitude stung her eyes. Kaiden was back.

"She'll kill Taschia if you rush in. Think, Ri. Think."

"I can't beat her. At best, I can only hold her off."

"You can. You just need help. Me."

"I've been trying. My magic is waning."

"Believe in yourself, Ri. And connect. With Earth. With me. We'll do this together." Kaiden held out his dirt-filled hand.

You…can…save…me. Soon. Taschia's words were slurred and slow. There was no more time.

Rianthe reached for him, grasped his hand, and a surge of power, more than ever before, roared through their connection. Magic filled her. Earth's *awen*, but more. Earth and Kaiden, intertwined. Words echoed in her mind. Kaiden's voice.

I am with you.

Rounding the corner once again, Rianthe saw everything at once. Marta, standing triumphant with Taschia still in her grip, a ready fireball in her other hand. The wolf, weakening but biding her time, waiting for the second Marta's grip loosened.

Rianthe reached out with her mind. Pushed against Marta's magic and hit some sort of force that took her precious long seconds to break through. She finally did, concentrating on the fireball until it got smaller and smaller, then disappeared. She turned her magic toward the hand holding Taschia, mentally prying Marta's fingers loose from around Taschia's neck until the wolf dropped to the ground. Taschia did not wait to get her breath back, but attacked, ripping into Marta's ankle.

Marta's surprise wasn't finished, though. Rianthe picked her up with air, exactly as Marta had done to her, and threw her against a wall. Marta's head hit with a *thunk,* then she slumped to the ground unconscious.

Just like that, it was over.

Dropping Kaiden's hand, Rianthe rushed to Taschia, who hacked and coughed to get her breath back. "Are you all right?"

I am alive. Swallow hurts. I will heal.

"I'm so sorry," Rianthe said. "I was trying. I couldn't stop her from hurting you."

Taschia pressed her nose against Rianthe's throat. *You saved me. You have strong magic. Powerful.*

Rianthe hugged her tight, not sure she ever wanted to let go. She'd been so afraid of losing her friend. She couldn't lessen the frantic beating of her heart, the fear that still pounded through her.

We are well. You saved us. Taschia reminded her.

They'd defeated a powerful adversary. Worse than Deakon, worse than any of the brigands Taegar had sent after Rianthe. She found it hard to believe.

They'd won. That this was only one more battle in the war to free Earth wasn't something Rianthe chose to dwell on. For now, winning this skirmish was enough. She turned to Kaiden, who looked both awe-struck and remorseful. He stood back. Rianthe saw the uncertainty in his eyes. And the pain. Because of their connection, everything he'd felt had flowed through to her. Rianthe saw it all, suffered it all. The little boy he couldn't help, the darkness encroaching, consuming him. Marta always there in the background, whispering, pulling him deeper into the chasm.

Such pain. Only a person with his strength could pull out of that darkness. Only Kaiden.

A world of hurt backed up the turmoil in Kaiden's

eyes. Rianthe didn't know how to help him, and there wasn't time to deal with it now. "I know what you've been through."

"Ri—"

"Shhh. Not now. We can talk later. Right now, there are more pressing things to deal with." She held out her hand. He reached out, then hesitated. "Ungloved? I'm not sure I can take someone in my head again right now. Too many…shadows to deal with."

Rianthe agreed, so she dropped her hand and pointed to the ground beside her until Kaiden sat down.

Slowly, as the trio sat recovering, what had just happened sank in. Scenes of the battle roared through Rianthe's mind. She'd stopped Marta, whose magic had seemed much more powerful than her own.

Stopped her with magic, a gift no amount of training had dredged up. Not by herself, though. She'd needed Earth's help. And Kaiden's.

He looked…wary. And sad, though the red fury she'd seen in his soul only minutes ago had disappeared. Rianthe laid a hand on his tunic. "You saved us, Kaiden."

"*You* saved us," he said, shaking his head. "I only gave you some of my strength."

"You gave me magic. Magic!" She almost laughed at the absurdity of it all. After trying so hard to break loose the power within her, all it had taken was for them to clasp hands. She could still feel the dwindling rush of the *awen* inside. It had been a heady thing. Her aftermath exhaustion didn't seem nearly as bad this time, either.

"We defeated Marta together, didn't we?" Kaiden said with wonder in his voice.

They turned to where the girl had slumped to the ground. Rianthe gasped and leaped up. She was gone. All three of them ran to the wall, where only a bit of blood on the ground remained. Marta had disappeared.

"That hit should have knocked her out for a long time," Rianthe said.

Kaiden nodded. "She's dangerous. We need to find her."

"Agreed. Kaiden, there were times when it seemed like her eyes were almost golden."

"I caught glimpses of someone more sinister, as though she wore a mask."

"I think she was sent by Taegar, endowed with magic like Deakon was."

Kaiden nodded. "That seems to be Taegar's tactic. And each time one of her acolytes finds us, she gains something. Like the runes she got from Deakon."

Rianthe's hand covered the mostly empty bag beneath her tunic. "Which means we need to find Marta before she can get back to Taegar." Rianthe tried to pick a direction for their search. When she saw what was behind them, she placed a hand on Kaiden's shirted arm. "I think we have bigger problems."

Kaiden followed her gaze. All the children he'd been trying to save stood at the end of the alleyway, big-eyed and hopeful.

"Where did all these kids come from?"

"I don't know," Kaiden said. "Everywhere. The leader…Tank,"—Kaiden grimaced—"advertised for workers all over. Some of these kids were conscripted, some were kidnapped." His voice shook with emotion.

"Is that who— Are the leaders the ones tied to those posts?" she asked quietly, slipping on her gloves.

Kaiden nodded, his eyes darkening. "I'm not proud of what I've done, Ri. I don't know what got into me, or how I'll ever atone for this." He hung his head.

She touched his cheek. "That wasn't you."

Kaiden shook his head. "It was."

"Well, it wasn't the Kaiden I know. And you crawled your way out of the darkness." She tapped his chest with her finger. "You."

He didn't answer right away. Instead, he kept his head down, as if he were silently begging for forgiveness. When he straightened, he let out a big whoosh of air. "I feel like I've been to the top of the highest mountain and the depths of the deepest ocean. You're right, though. I did it. I found my way back to daylight."

"You're a protector. You saved yourself."

A brief smile touched his lips and Rianthe's heart skipped a beat. She'd missed this man so much. Her strong, duty-bound, green-eyed man that only she knew held a multitude of emotions deep inside. When his smile faded, she almost reached up, wanting it back.

"I've got to make this right. Somehow."

"You'll find a way. And I'm here when you want to talk about it."

"We do need to talk. I've learned things. But not right now."

She'd caught glimpses of those "things" when they'd connected through the magic. She nodded. "At the moment, we need to help the children," she said, holding out her gloved hand. "Together. Then, we're going to find Tevy."

"Agreed," Kaiden said, this time taking her hand without hesitation. "We'll find him together."

~~~

They walked down the alley toward the children. As they got closer to the town's center, the crowd split to
~~~

give them room to pass. A cheer started, growing to a crescendo of happiness that lightened Kaiden's mood.

Until he saw the poles. Three men hung there. Two still moved, but the one in the center, Tank, hung lifeless. Everything Kaiden had done in the name of "protection" rushed back to him, congealing in his stomach and making him weak with regret. How had he ventured into such a dark place? How could he have done what he'd done?

"The forces at work here were beyond what you and I know," Rianthe said. She turned his face to hers. "I saw a man, holding this whip." She pointed to the loose coil that still lay where Kaiden had dropped it to run save her. "He was not you, Kaiden. Someone else did this. Someone I've never seen. Or known."

Taschia nosed Kaiden's hand. *That was not Kai-den. That was the other one.*

"Marta?" Rianthe said.

Taschia nodded. *That one's magic is strong. Strong like the golden one.*

Kaiden wanted to agree, but deep down inside, he knew the truth. That person, the one who'd held the whip, was a part of him. An ugly part, and grounded, he now knew, in hereditary darkness. It would take a long time to bury this memory and feel some happiness again. No, not bury. He needed to remember, so he never returned to that place again.

Ever.

"Help me take down these men," Kaiden said to the people around him. "It's time to treat our injured, bury our anger, and turn our lives back toward good."

Most of the guards in town had disappeared after Kaiden and the children won their battle. Those who remained had performed menial chores other than guarding and heavy-arming. Workers and cooks, men and women. They'd stayed, and now, they asked to help.

After Kaiden and the older boys released the men hanging from the poles, the women tended to them, as well as to the children's injuries, both from mine work and from fighting. Kaiden was more than grateful that no one else had died that day.

Rianthe helped Kaiden carry Tank's body out of town and build a pyre. Even the worst of humanity deserved the *kenaz* so they might return to the Earth from whence they came. Kaiden stood watching the fire burn, filled with sorrow for his part in this death. He still found it hard to believe he was related to this man, and that his ancestors were responsible for the Great Magic War that had destroyed civilization and changed everything. If it were true, he'd killed his own uncle. His only blood family. It cut deep.

A wave of homesickness caught him out of the blue. His mother, Raisa, cutting his hair, soothing his hurts, singing him to sleep at night. And Jonah's strength, teaching Kaiden survival skills, sparring with him until Kaiden became stronger. He was not alone. In fact, he'd been surrounded by family his entire life. The right kind of family. The loving kind.

He looked at the fire and he recognized that he was not his uncle. He was not his ancestors. He was Kaiden, True-Named protector. Remorseful that he'd chosen this way to avenge the child's death, Kaiden vowed that he would never again allow that kind of darkness to consume him.

Back in Minor Town, a large cache of food stores no one knew about had been found. Large tables were soon set up outside the building that used to be the leader's quarters. No one cared about the chill in the air. A feast lay before them, although the adults cautioned the children to eat slowly. Their stomachs were not used to a lot of food.

For a day that had started out so dark, the lightness and laughter surrounding Kaiden seemed surreal. This kind of joy seemed foreign to him. Plus, he wasn't sure he deserved to be happy. Not quite yet.

Rianthe leaned over. "It's all right to smile, Kaiden."

"I'm not sure I remember how."

"Then use this night to help you remember. Tomorrow, we search for Tevy. Tonight, we rest." She squeezed his hand.

He nodded. She was right. Tonight, for this little while, he should let go of it all and just be. Now. In the moment. With her.

That is a good place to be, Taschia mind-spoke, tearing into a leg of some meat that obviously tasted very good to her.

"Yes," Kaiden said. "It is."

CHAPTER TWENTY-ONE

Over the course of the evening, Rianthe and Kaiden realized that every one of Tank's remaining men had slipped out of town during the struggle to gain control of Minor Town. Those who remained had been treated as nothing more than servants, even those there to provide pleasure. None were paid, and no one got out from under Tank's thumb. All had good reason to celebrate, but before they did that, they worked together as a group to take care of the younglings.

Rianthe walked with Kaiden around the town, taking stock of what remained and wondering how they could help Minor Town survive.

"We need to find Tevy," she told Kaiden. He'd told her at dinner about Marta's misdirection, bringing him here in a futile effort to find her brother. Rianthe didn't blame him, but finding Tevy was still her highest priority.

"We do," he said. "But I can't leave all these children here to fend for themselves."

"I understand that, but..." Rianthe chewed her lip, uncharacteristically timid. "Kaiden, things don't seem to go too well when we separate."

Kaiden's eyes clouded over. Would he ever get past the darkness that had descended on him these past few days and weeks? It haunted him, lingering there in his gaze, and at the edge of his voice. Would it return? And, if it did, could they get past it? This worry would stay with Rianthe for a long, long time. With him, too.

"Agreed," Kaiden said. "I'm not willing to let you go off on your own again. It was hard enough last time."

"So what do we do?"

Rianthe looked around. Dinner was being cleaned up, tables pulled back inside. The poles at the center of town were being torn down. Man, woman, child. Everyone pitched in. One woman took dirty dishes from a boy who couldn't be more than six or seven years old. He was so thin, with the look of a frightened rabbit in his eyes. The woman stopped, set the dishes on the ground, and pulled him into her arms. After only a slight hesitation, he returned her hug with a fierceness born of relief.

"They all seem to work pretty well together now that it's by choice and there's no threat of retribution from Tank and his guards," Rianthe said.

Kaiden nodded. "Let's call everyone together and ask them what they want to do."

"I like that. It sounds like no one here has had a choice in their lives until now. They have earned the right to decide for themselves."

It took less time to decide what to do than it did to get everyone in one place. All the adults wanted to stay, to help the children. Quite a few of the children, those sold by their relatives into servitude, opted to stay and make a life here. They would work the mine, but in a much more humane way. The humate would be given away or sold for a minimal amount. This fertilizer might well be the only thing standing between everyone and starvation. They all agreed that any payment realized from the work should go to improve their home and their lives. Rianthe could already see the pride in their faces. Each and every one stood a bit taller now. This was a good thing.

Some of the children, those kidnapped into a life of slavery, wanted to go home. The town, as a whole, agreed to begin the search to find their homes and get them back to their families. They would also be vigilant, to make sure no one else like Tank tried to take over. Kaiden promised he would be back to help as soon as he could.

By the time winter dusk had given way to full night, all was settled. Rianthe, Kaiden and Taschia could leave in the morning, to resume the search for Tevy.

Kaiden, unwilling to sleep in the barracks, had suggested they camp by the kitchen fires, which would help ward off the cold night. They set their bedrolls around the fire pit. Taschia joined them, stinking like a water-doused fire. She rubbed against Rianthe.

"Ack! Where have you been?" Rianthe asked her.

In the mines. I searched. Made certain all was clear.

"You're all wet."

"The mines drip."

"Well, you won't be sleeping anywhere near me until you dry."

I have found friends. I will be there.

"Good," Rianthe said as Taschia moved out of range, then shook off the excess water.

Thank you for moving away before doing that, she mind-spoke.

There was no need for both of us to be wet.

Taschia loped off in search of her new friends while Rianthe laughed at her sister-wolf. It felt good to laugh, something that had been missing of late. And there were still so many things to worry about, so much darkness still to come. She knew that.

Since there was nothing she could do about the future right then, Rianthe focused on the here and now. She needed to find her brother. To know he was safe. Rianthe laid down, head on arms, and looked across the fire at Kaiden. "Do you think he's all right?"

"Tevy?" Kaiden cocked his head. "If he wasn't, Taschia would get a whiff of it."

I do not sense my brother's passing, the wolf answered from afar.

Rianthe needed the reassurance. It had been a long time since he'd disappeared. "We still don't know who took him. If it was Taegar or someone else."

Kaiden flinched. "I don't even like hearing that name." He took a deep breath. "If Taegar had him, we'd have heard by now, wouldn't we? She would want to barter him for those runes you still have."

Rianthe nodded. "That makes sense. I guess the only way to know where to search is for me to seek him in a vision."

"Not tonight, though," Kaiden said. "Let's wait until morning. We've both been sorely used this day, and we need some sleep for a fresh outlook on things."

"Sounds good," Rianthe said. She pulled her pack over to use as a pillow, punching it until it fit her head just right. Laying there, as tired as she was, she found it hard to go to sleep. She kept reliving the day in her mind. She'd defeated Marta, at least for now. The Earth had bolstered her magic and Kaiden had added his strength, giving her what she needed to funnel the magic into stopping Marta. It still wasn't enough to convince her that she was the prophesied one. She'd needed help to defeat Marta, but there was a hint of promise there. For the first time, Rianthe was excited to get back to work with Roulf and to see where this magic would take her. Except…she punched her pillow again. She knew her destiny already.

"It will all work out as it will, Ri," Kaiden said. "Try to sleep."

His use of her nickname calmed Rianthe and made her smile. Pushing her qualms to the back of her mind, she closed her eyes, hoping that for once, they might have a good day tomorrow.

~~~

After breakfast the next morning, Rianthe walked out of Minor Town, Kaiden and Taschia by her side.

"We haven't seen or heard anything of Marta. Where do you think she went?" Rianthe asked.

"Straight to Taegar, just like Deakon," Kaiden said, frowning as he gazed off to the west.

And maybe straight to Tevy. Rianthe shuddered.

"I doubt we've seen the last of her," Kaiden said.

"I'm not looking forward to our next meeting, but that worry will have to get in line. Tevy is the priority right now."

"Agreed."

Sitting down in the brush just off the path, Rianthe
~~~

pulled her gloves off, focused on her little brother and reached for the Earth.

Where are you, Tevy?

She focused hard, reached out to him. Nothing happened. She felt Taschia's fur against her as the wolf joined her in the *ehwaz*.

I don't see him anywhere, Taschia.

I sense…something. My brother is…different. Something has changed him.

What?

I do not know. I cannot see. I do not like this.

The air around them swirled. Before escape was possible, a new scene unfolded.

Earth, in an epic battle for the awen, with Taegar. The white goodness of Earth slowly giving way to the increasing power of the Dark druid. Taegar turned toward Rianthe, her golden eyes dipping to where Rianthe had hidden the last three runes. Runes held back from the set before it was stolen and put in Taegar's hands.

Rianthe forced herself to stay still and not reach for the bag. Everything within her wanted to protect this priceless treasure from Taegar's greedy vision. She must not get these runes. If she did, Earth would perish, as would everyone on it.

"So," Taegar said. "The runes have returned to the descendant of Damian Royan. That boy no longer has them."

All the blood in Rianthe's body congealed in a leaden pool in her feet. Taegar knew who she was? Her heart raced. Her mind all but shut down. There would be no hiding now. Every nerve ending, every cell inside her knew that Taegar wouldn't stop until she was dead.

Rianthe didn't know what to do or how to answer.

"I will have the trinket you carry," Taegar said.

No. You won't. You'll never get them.

"You must come to me," Taegar said. "I am stronger than you. That will always be so, but I can make you more powerful. Your father never understood that. I would have added to his power, not detracted. He would have been stronger had he gone with me."

Stronger? Maybe, but not for long. Earth needed to survive in order for that strength to be realized.

"Together, we can accomplish things you cannot even imagine."

Rianthe could imagine a lot, and nothing Taegar had in store for her would be good. She shook her head.

"If you will not come willingly, you will come by force. I will find you and bend you to my will. Your death will be drawn out and so much more painful. For now, let this be a reminder that you have no choice in this matter because I am the most powerful. I will always be."

White light shot from Taegar's hands, hitting Rianthe in the chest with such force it threw her up into the air. She landed hard, pain shooting through her arm, her head, her back. Rianthe squeezed her eyes shut against it. The pressure around her neck, the bag lifting…

As quickly as the vision had come, it disappeared. Rianthe gasped, struggling to catch her breath. She clutched at the bag around her neck. *It's safe. The runes are safe with me.* Relief flooded her. When she opened her eyes, she saw Kaiden and Taschia rushing toward her. How did they end up so far away? They'd been right beside her.

Rianthe looked around and found herself not in the narrow glade where they'd begun, but across the trail in a copse of trees, many lengths from where she'd been.

Taegar.

Once again, Rianthe was reminded that these visions of hers had real-life consequences. She might get injured, or disappear like that tree-embedded rock. Or die.

"Are you all right?" Kaiden asked as he dropped to her side. He helped her to an easier position, then checked her arms, legs, and head. Anywhere he could touch to make sure she was okay.

"Ouch!" Rianthe said as he found the spot where she'd connected with a tree.

"I don't think anything's broken, but you're bleeding from the back of your head." He pulled out a piece of cloth and pressed it against the wound.

That hurt. Rianthe tried to pull away, but he stayed with her.

"You hold this," he said. "Try to apply pressure so the bleeding will stop, all right?"

Rianthe reached for the cloth. Their hands touched, skin-on-skin, and the change was immediate. Just like before, warmth flowed through her. Power-infused warmth. She felt it, wanted to wrap herself around it and never let go. Her pain disappeared and everything that was Kaiden became part of her.

She looked at him, saw his eyes reflect the same emotion. Overwhelming peace, togetherness, love. And, buried beneath it all, the darkness to which he'd been enslaved, thankfully for a short time. Bleakness without hope. And deeper still, confusion — a tendril of ancestral concern Rianthe wanted to know more about.

Kaiden dropped his hand and backed away quickly.

"Kaiden," Rianthe said, awash in the emotions of his turmoil.

"Not now," Kaiden said, waving his hand. "For now, we must focus on you. On Tevy. After that, we can sort out the rest of this."

Her nod was slow. She wanted to throw her arms around him, to tell him he was not the darkness she'd seen, he was stronger than it. He'd burst through, back to the light, and in time to help her defeat Marta.

"My head feels better," she said.

"Pull the cloth away and let me look."

When he got a good look at it, Kaiden whistled. "It's almost healed." His voice was full of wonder.

It is the gebo, *the bond between you that pulls your powers together for goodness*, Taschia mind-spoke.

"Bond?" Rianthe remembered back at the lake, when they'd touched for the first time without her gloves since her True-Naming. Something had passed between them. Ever since, she'd had a better idea of who the real Kaiden was.

Each time you touch, the bond grows stronger.

Kaiden had been privy to Taschia's statement, if the shuttering of his eyes gave any indication. He quickly handed her the gloves he'd brought with him. Even when the truth was embedded in his mind, he resisted.

"Can you walk?" Kaiden looked up at the overcast sky. "We should get on our way. It looks like rain is coming. We need to walk as far as we can during the daylight hours."

Rianthe nodded, pulling on her gloves and taking the hand he held out. "We've said our goodbyes. I'm ready."

Kaiden glanced back at Minor Town one last time. Rianthe saw the mask drop and raw emotion hit him. Fear, hope, longing, and darkness. All wrapped up in a very complicated man. Then the mask was back in place.

The Kaiden who tried to be unemotional, who always protected, who tried never to love, turned and walked away.

Their journey back had begun.

CHAPTER TWENTY-TWO

Leaving Minor Town turned out to be harder than Kaiden expected. He trusted the people there and knew they'd do right by the children, but it still didn't feel right, leaving them. He'd helped to free them. The responsibility for their well-being fell squarely on his shoulders.

"We'll go back," Ri had told him. "As soon as we can."

They could leave by the road. Kaiden knew now that it circled around and brought them close to their route back to the Rushmore Woods. Since they didn't know where Tevy was, they'd decided to go home, to see if any news of him had reached New Hope. But Kaiden had one more thing to do before they left, so they'd climbed the hill where he'd first seen Minor Town and walked until he found the spot. They stood now in front of the ashed remains of a funeral pyre.

"Who was he?" Rianthe asked.

"A boy. Just a boy. The first one I spoke with when I got here. The one…" He cleared his throat. "The one I couldn't save."

Rianthe put an arm around Kaiden's waist. He settled his arm around her shoulder. Taschia joined them, leaning against Kaiden's leg. Their support meant a lot to him. Their honor for this boy they had not known. It humbled him.

"I never even knew his name." Kaiden couldn't help the break in his voice. He would never get past this one child he hadn't been able to save.

He was brave, Taschia mind-spoke.

"Very brave. Never a word out of him while he was being beaten, even when it led to his death."

Then I will call him Valor.

Valor. Kaiden liked that. A lot. The smile on his face felt foreign. It had been too long. He patted Taschia's head. *Thank you.*

The brave should be honored.

"When things settle down, we should talk to the people of New Hope about naming something after this child," Rianthe said. "Maybe the lake?"

Kaiden's smile broadened. He looked down at the ashen Earth. "He won't be forgotten."

"Never."

Never.

The lingering darkness in Kaiden's heart dissipated, at least for now. Everything was in place and as it should be. He let go of Rianthe, looking northwest. Towards home. "We can go now. I'm ready."

"And I'm more than ready."

With a beautiful smile, she turned her face toward

home and they started off.

~~~

An icy rain found them by midday. Kaiden couldn't believe how hard it poured. Even with cloaks, by nightfall they were completely soaked. Civilization had never reached this area, so they couldn't find even a broken down structure to offer them respite from the relentless pounding. They hunkered down in a thick copse of trees that afforded little protection. Kaiden rigged a tarp from their blankets and some brush and tree limbs to keep the worst of the water off them. No fire would be lit tonight. Thankfully, the town had gifted them with bread and cheese. They ate huddled together and offered some to Taschia.

I will hunt.

"In the rain?" Rianthe asked.

Hunting is good when the water falls.

Kaiden smiled, more at Rianthe's laughter than anything. He'd always loved her laugh. Deep, rumbly, and full of life. Her heart still held joy in it. He wasn't so certain of his own. Too much had happened. He fought it, but found it hard not to give in to despair. If Rianthe was meant to save the world, and he was meant to protect her and help her, the world was indeed in dire straits.

Although, when they'd touched while fighting Marta, something had happened. He'd seen her magic, felt his joining hers. Was this the way this struggle was meant to be? Did it mean that, working together, they could hold the darkness at bay and bring happiness back to their friends and family? To heal Earth and give everyone a chance for a better life?

He wanted that more than anything, what he'd trained for since his youth. It was his destiny, and
~~~

whether he thought he was up to the task or not, he would do whatever he must to keep Rianthe safe, to help her in what she must do. If need be, he would die in the attempt.

"You learned a few things in Minor Town. I…caught a glimpse, you know, when we touched."

Kaiden pushed at their lean-to cover and water gushed off the side. He settled in next to Rianthe. It was time. He was ready to talk, and she needed to know his ancestry. That apparently, there was a dark streak bred within him. That he didn't know if he could control it. Kaiden took a deep breath, deciding to start with the easy part. "I found out about my parents."

"Oh, Kaiden," Rianthe said, grabbing his arm. "You've wanted so badly to know. I always hoped you'd find out. And that the news would be good." These last words were quiet, as if she knew something wasn't right.

"About my parents? Yes, the news about them was good, except that they're dead."

Rianthe clutched his arm a little tighter. "I'm sorry."

"I pretty much knew that already. But, Ri, they loved me." He basked in Rianthe's smile when she recognized his happiness. "There was no food and they were starving. When they figured out my mother was pregnant with me, my father gave her most of their food, keeping little for himself. After…after I was born, he gave her all the food so she'd be able to feed me.

"Ri, they sacrificed everything to keep me alive. They died of starvation trying to feed me." He saw the tears in her eyes. Rianthe reached up to cup his face, and he held her hand there, against the wetness that held more salt than rain.

"I want to take my gloves off," she said.

"Not now," he said, shaking his head. "I need to

claim this history, to talk about it. Not…feel it."

She nodded, snuggling closer to him. "I'm sad they're gone, but I knew, deep in my soul, that you were loved. How could anyone not love you?"

She ducked her head, but Kaiden used his free hand to lift her face. He needed to see her while he told her this next part. To know her reaction. He tried to talk, but the words stuck in his throat. Her face, scratched and bruised from battle and muddy from traveling, still remained the loveliest face he'd ever seen. He wanted to stay just like this, together, for forever.

Rianthe tried to avert her face. "I'm filthy," she said.

He held her there for another moment, enough time to give her some long-delayed truth. "You're beautiful."

Her eyebrows rose and her eyes rounded. Kaiden smiled. It wasn't often he caught Rianthe Royan off guard. He liked the look on her. He'd have to attempt that more often.

This time, when she pulled away, he let her go. There was still more to tell, and it may well break the bubble of peace between them. "Look at me," he said. "Please."

Rianthe did, visibly trying to still her emotions.

"I found out more. My heritage is dark. Bad blood courses through me."

Kaiden put up a hand to stop Rianthe when she opened her mouth to speak. "Let me finish. My ancestor, my great-grandfather, was involved in the Great Magic War."

"He had magic?"

"No. Worse. He coveted it."

Rianthe nodded.

They'd been taught about the discontent among those

unable to tap into Earth's *awen* and that those people had been very jealous of anyone with magical ability.

"Apparently, my great-grandfather became friends with the druids, attempting to get as close as he could to the magic. Still not satisfied, he whispered in the ear of a druid, one he thought might be susceptible to his ideas. He convinced her the magic should be used for selfish reasons, to make their own positions more comfortable."

He paused. So far, there'd been no sign from Rianthe about her feelings. Before he could finish, her eyebrows shot up again.

"Taegar?"

Kaiden nodded.

"Your ancestor is the reason Taegar broke from the Guardian druids?"

"Yes. That is the darkness of my past."

Rianthe stared at the ground for a long time. Kaiden didn't know if she was about to toss him out of their shelter or kill him with the knife she had tucked in the belt of her tunic. "I'm sorry," he said and shifted away from her.

Her head whipped up. "Sorry? Why?"

"My family caused the war that destroyed everything."

Rianthe scoffed, shaking her head with vigor and without hesitation. That surprised Kaiden.

"Your family did not cause that war. One man made suggestions. Taegar made her own decisions and took them to a whole new height. That war," she spat out, "was her fault. No one else's."

The tightness in Kaiden's heart eased. "But that's the blood that courses through me. I might turn…dark. Again. I…I almost didn't pull out of it back there." He nodded in the direction of Minor Town. "If you hadn't come and rescued me, Ri, I'm not sure what I would have done."

Rianthe knelt and got up close and personal, stabbing Kaiden in the chest with her finger. "Listen to me. I'm only saying this once. I didn't save you from anything. You. Saved. Yourself." She poked him with each final word. "Everything that happened in that town, and the information you learned, affected you deeply. Marta fed that, amplified it through powerful, Taegar-enhanced magic. Yes, it sank you to a dark place, but only for a while. You fought back from the brink. You brought yourself back. And *you* saved that town. You saved those children." With a shrug and a final stab of her finger, she sat back. "Well, you did have a little help there at the end."

Kaiden chuckled. With each word from Rianthe, the darkness within him lightened and the pain of his past dripped away. Rianthe joined him in laughter. When Taschia returned, she looked at them like they were crazy, then settled down between them with her soaked fur.

It is time to sleep.

For some reason, that increased their laughter. It was a long while before they quieted enough to sleep in their wet shelter that night.

~~~

Hunkered down under a large boulder, trying unsuccessfully to stay out of the rain, Marta shivered against the cold. She'd tried everything to get Kaiden to come with her. Every wile she had, or that had been gifted to her. None had worked.

Kaiden's ability to evade her charms had been
~~~

strong. Too strong. But it wasn't Marta's fault. She'd done everything possible. That Dark druid hadn't given her enough power. She should have known Kaiden's magic was strong.

Every bone and muscle in her body ached, like she'd been working in the fields for days on end without rest. She hurt all over. Glaring out at the storm that matched the dark fury inside her, Marta scooted back against the rock as much as she could, but there wasn't enough room to dodge the downpour. Her clothes were soaked, her hands wrinkled. Marta rubbed them together, trying to warm them. She looked closer at the pruned skin. Blue veins now close to the surface lent her hands an old, worn-out look. Water didn't do that, did it?

With rising panic, Marta touched her face. She felt dry, papery, drooping skin. She held out a wet strand of hair. The blond was different. Dirtier. Grayer. What was happening to her? Fear goaded her forward to lean over a puddle under the rock, undercover and undisturbed, and look for her reflection.

An old, ugly, hook-nosed hag looked back at her. Who was she? Marta's eyes widened and the reflection's eyes mimicked the movement. This was her?

She screamed. She dug at her magic, begging it to return the beauty she'd had scant moments ago. Nothing changed in her reflection though she tried repeatedly to change back. Marta scratched at her face, trying to dislodge what must be a mask. Bloody trails covered her cheeks and forehead.

Finally, she slumped back against the rock, anguished as the truth hit her. Her magic was gone. This was her destiny, to live out the rest of her life in a form no one would pay attention to, except to ridicule. She screamed again, sharp and piercing, over and over, until she finally subsided into hoarse croaks. She curled into the rock, an aching, aged woman who no longer had anything to live for.

CHAPTER TWENTY-THREE

Even though half of the fall season remained, winter fought to make an early appearance. Rain and wind forced them to travel slowly and find shelter early, so it took them longer than they wanted to get back home. By the time they reached New Hope, they were cold, bedraggled, soaked, and muddy. Miraculously, as they walked into town, it stopped raining.

"Nice homecoming gift," Rianthe said as she pulled her sopping wet cloak off her rain-saturated body.

Not much had changed. More huts were under construction, and they'd closed in the dining longhouse again. How many times had that been rebuilt now? Smoke rose from the ovens, making Rianthe's mouth water. She'd missed home. Missed the people. Missed the food. Anniah had developed an oven-baked noodle with seasoned, crushed tomato that Rianthe loved. Her stomach grumbled just thinking about it. It would be nice to have something other than snared food and water again.

Raisa saw them first and rushed over to embrace them all, even Taschia. Jonah joined them, his arms open for hugs. Word spread quickly and soon the entire village surrounded them with welcoming arms. No one seemed to mind that they were filthy.

Roulf dug his way through the throng, stopping in front of them. "Well, other than a little dirt, you don't look much worse for your journey."

Rianthe laughed. "We aren't." She glanced at Kaiden. "Mostly, anyhow."

"We are fine," Kaiden said.

"The smile on your faces verifies that," Roulf agreed, looking closely at them. "But you have stories to tell."

They nodded.

"We do," Rianthe said. "Later." Right now, she needed to hear about the one person not present. Tevy had always been among the first to welcome her home, his ready smile and boundless energy the token she sought.

"Tevy?" she asked, looking at Jonah.

He shook his head. "Nothing yet. We'd hoped he was with you."

Rianthe's stomach churned. *Tevy.* It had been weeks with no word. Where was he? And who had him? Oh, dram. It was so hard to stay positive, to not give in to the fear that something had happened to him. She would never forgive herself if Tevy had come to harm. Never.

"Could Taegar have him?" Raisa asked, clutching her husband's arm.

"I ran into our friend, Taegar, in one of my visions," Rianthe said. "I got no indication that Tevy was with her.

I think she'd have used that information against me if he had been." She'd been working hard to convince herself of that.

"And I found no trail, other than the false one Marta laid for me," Kaiden said, disgust mixed with worry in his voice. "I either was too far behind the wolves to hear them or Marta muted our ability to mind-speak. I'm not sure which, but I lost touch with them after about half a day."

"Marta?" Jonah asked.

Kaiden nodded. "There's a lot to explain, Father. Right now, we need to figure out how to find Tevy."

"Would he have gone off on his own?" Roulf asked.

Rianthe shook her head. "He's never done that before."

"It's not in his nature, unless his wolves call him," Jonah agreed.

His wolves. *Taschia.* Rianthe reached out with her mind.

I have sensed nothing in days. Not even a greeting from my brothers. I worry. They are not usually so quiet.

Rianthe crouched down and pulled off her gloves. "I need to locate him the only way I know how. Or at least try again to do that." Without giving herself time to think other than to focus on Tevy, Rianthe reached for Earth's soils.

Tevy! Where are you?

For the first time since Tevy had disappeared, Rianthe got a faint response. Not from Tevy, but from Hark, the eldest of his wolf pack.

We come. We bring our brother home.

Rianthe had not known this level of relief since she'd first fallen into Kaiden's arms all those years ago. She sat down, hard, on the ground. Tevy was coming home. Her heart sped up and tears wet her cheeks. Tevy was coming home. She whispered the words over and over. *Is he all right?* she asked Hark.

He is…changed. But he is all right.

Thank goodness. I am so glad you are with him, she mind-spoke.

We will always follow our brother.

Grinning to rival the sun that had so recently appeared, Rianthe knew the truth of that statement. It was hard to pull Tevy from his wolves and vice versa. Where had he been all this time? And why hadn't the wolves let them know they'd found him? There were too many unanswered questions for Rianthe to be fully at ease. For now, she would have to be content that Tevy would soon be home.

She broke the contact with Earth. Kaiden helped her up, careful once again not to touch her ungloved hands. Rianthe noticed, but couldn't care right then, not with her little brother on the way. "Tevy's on his way home. The wolves are bringing him."

I sense them now, Taschia mind-spoke to Rianthe. *They have never been this far away, but they grow closer with each moment.*

Everyone crowded around them began asking questions, all at the same time.

"Is he all right?" Raisa asked.

"When will they be here?" Mokie said.

Kathra joined them. "Are they hungry? Will they need food?"

Jonah held up his hand, giving Rianthe a chance to answer.

"I don't know where he's been, what happened, or

anything. Hark only said that he was all right. And that he'd changed."

Murmurs of renewed concern wormed through the group. Tevy was New Hope's son. Everyone had helped raise him. Everyone loved him. Everyone worried.

"Well, there's nothing else we can know until they arrive," Jonah said. "I suggest we get you warmed up"—he eyed them up and down—"and cleaned up, until that time comes."

I will wait by the forest, Taschia said.

Rianthe smiled at her friend's anxiousness to see her brothers. "Let us know when they're close, will you?"

I will.

After most of the group had dispersed, Rianthe, who never really worried about her appearance, turned to Kaiden. "You look like you've been dragged through a mud bog."

"You don't look much better yourself." He picked up a strand of her shoulder-length hair.

Rianthe laughed, smoothing her still too-short hair, wishing it would grow faster. She was ready to have the hair Kaiden loved again, but it would be a while yet before there was any real length to it. "I bet I do look as bad. Dibs on the bathing hut."

Kaiden laughed. "All right. You go first. Why don't we meet in the dining house after we're both clean?"

After the travelers had cleaned themselves, Jonah, Raisa, Roulf, Kaiden, and Rianthe gathered with coffee and some of the best stew Rianthe could remember. "Kathra, thank you. This tastes wonderful."

"I agree," Kaiden said, uncharacteristically speaking with food in his mouth.

They were both hungrier than they'd thought.

Rianthe took another big spoonful, relishing the rich sauce and heady flavors. Kathra blushed, nodding her head in gratitude at the compliment. "You deserve it, after what you've been through. Can I get you more?"

Kaiden vigorously nodded his head while Rianthe chose to stop with the one bowl.

"Now might be a good time to catch us up on what happened to you," Jonah said.

"Yes." Roulf quipped. "I, too, am interested in what transpired after you and I parted."

"Where's the book?" Rianthe asked, panic filling her.

"I set the book back in its alcove and the wall shimmered back into place when I stepped out. No one will gain entrance to that book's hiding spot until you return."

"What book?" Jonah asked.

"One that my parents left for me."

"I'd like to see that."

"Then you must travel to Origin Cave," Roulf said. "The book will not leave that place. We tried."

"You mean I tried," Rianthe said.

Roulf nodded. "It is somehow bound to the cave." He turned to Rianthe. "After making certain there was nothing in the tunnels, I came back here and awaited your return."

"I'm sorry I left you," Rianthe said.

"No need to apologize, child. You were following your instincts."

"And her instincts saved me yet again," Kaiden said.

Rianthe shook her head. "You saved yourself."

Slowly, taking turns, they told their story. When Kaiden got to the part where he found out about his family, and that Bhren had known all along, Jonah interrupted.

"None of us ever knew any of that, my son. I'm sorry. I wish we had known, but at least you learned that your parents loved you."

Kaiden reached across the table to grasp his father's forearm. "You've given me the love of a father. And Raisa, a mother's love. I didn't lack for anything. I realize that now."

"You are our son," said Raisa, who sat beside her husband. She settled her hand over Kaiden's. Jonah topped hers, the tower of love complete.

Jealousy stabbed at Rianthe. Kaiden had known a family's love since infancy and still had parents to love him. She'd lost that too soon.

Kaiden settled his free arm around her shoulders as if he knew her thoughts. It warmed her, that even in this moment that was rightfully his, he thought of her.

"I'm loved," he said. "I know that. Still, it was difficult to be ignorant of my past. I wish Bhren had trusted me enough to tell me. Although it's a moot point, it grates on me. I'm trying to focus on the positive, that doubts have been laid to rest. I had a mother and father who died trying to keep me alive, and an uncle to whom I was nothing more than a bargaining chip." He tightened the grip on his father's arm. "Unfortunate circumstances became fortuitous when they brought me to New Hope. Home. To my family."

His arm around Rianthe's shoulders tightened for an eternity's second and Rianthe smiled. This was the Kaiden she'd wanted to be beside. One who wasn't afraid to show his emotions. She prayed that would extend beyond this conversation.

"Where did Marta end up?" Roulf asked.

Rianthe frowned. "I wish we knew. She disappeared without a trace. We searched. There were no tracks to follow. It was as if she left without a single footprint."

"Well, let's hope she's good and gone," Jonah said. "She's caused enough trouble for one lifetime."

Everyone nodded their agreement.

"So what will happen to the children of Minor Town?" Raisa asked.

"The people there have vowed to search for their families," Kaiden said. "And those whose families can't be found, or who don't want to return to their families, may remain in Minor Town carving out a new life with their communal family. We did offer a third option, though."

Kaiden glanced at Jonah and Raisa, and Rianthe was surprised to see him blush.

"I helped them to escape a horrible life of slavery. I feel responsible for them. So I—"

"We," Rianthe interjected.

Kaiden nodded. "We, um, told them all that if they chose to abandon a town that had brought them so much pain, we would welcome them here."

"Here?" Jonah's eyebrows raised.

"How many?" Raisa asked.

"Even if a quarter of them migrate here, it could be fifty or so, mostly children. Some teens, some as young as six."

Jonah gulped and took his wife's hand. For several seconds, they held an unspoken conversation with their eyes. When they turned back to the group, Raisa answered Kaiden's concern. "We have always welcomed children here. We will not stop now, or ever. They will be wanted. And loved.”

“Thank you,” Kaiden said. Rianthe heard the humility and the relief in his voice.

“So all’s well that ends well,” Roulf said, beaming.

Rianthe wished that were so. Earth and its inhabitants remained in grave danger from Taegar’s growing powers.

“There’s one more thing,” she said.

“Taegar,” Roulf surmised.

Rianthe nodded. “Taegar.”

“Have you seen her? In visions?”

“Once, after we’d freed Minor Town.”

“What happened?” Jonah leaned forward.

“It’s not good. She knows I’m the daughter of Damian Royan.”

The whole table sat quietly.

“That paints an even bigger target on your head.”

Rianthe nodded, unable to stop a small shudder. Kaiden tightened his grip on her shoulder. “We’ll keep you safe.”

“I know you will.” At least, as much as he could. “She also knows I hold the remaining runes for the talisman.”

Roulf groaned. “This is not good,” he whispered to himself. “Not good at all.”

“I shouldn’t have even gone into the *ehwaz*.”

“It’s not your fault,” Kaiden said. “You were trying to find Tevy.”

“Kaiden is right,” Roulf said. “Our enemy was bound to find out both of those things eventually. Now, we must make plans.”

“To fortify New Hope,” Jonah said.

“To permanently remove the danger presented by

Taegar," Roulf said.

"To keep Rianthe safe," Kaiden finished.

They sat quietly, digesting the information. With a final squeeze of Rianthe's shoulders, Kaiden pulled his arm away and clasped his hands together on the table, his head bowed almost as if in prayer.

The others followed suit, deep in thought, staring at the table.

Finally, Jonah lifted his head. "Is there any indication that an attack from Taegar or anyone else is imminent?"

Both Kaiden and Rianthe shook their heads.

"Then there is time to do this the right way. We won't get much done sitting here being morose. Let's all rest and consider our options, then gather tomorrow after the noon meal to formulate a plan."

Everyone mumbled agreement and stood.

~~~

They come!

"They're close," Rianthe said, not waiting for anyone's response. She rushed out of the dining house to the commons. Taschia had disappeared. *Where are you?*

I run to meet my brothers. I have found them. They are here. All my brothers.

Before Rianthe could ask another question, the wolf pack burst through the trees and through the town to the center, where Rianthe, Kaiden, and others nearby were gathering.

The wolves ran around the commons, howling their glee. Sarsa joined them, showing more excitement than her old bones had allowed in some time.

My pups are home, Sarsa said, as she sat on her haunches, panting, her teeth showing in a wolfish smile.
~~~

They are happy to be home. I am happy, Taschia said.

The wolves kept running around and around. Continued howling. But where was Tevy?

"Why are there more wolves than there should be?" Kaiden asked.. "Look, there, a tan and gray wolf I've never seen before."

Rianthe saw the wolf then. He trotted over to her and stopped at her feet, looking up with big blue eyes. Looking familiar.

The air shimmered around the wolf. Everything blurred for several moments. When it cleared, Tevy stood there, naked and grinning wider than Rianthe had ever seen.

"Tevy!" she cried, clutching him to her. She said his name, over and over again, until his muffled protests got through to her.

"I'm all right, Sis. Geesh, I'm all right. Let go."

Rianthe held him back from her, looking him up and down. She turned him around, this way and that, until he yanked himself away from her.

"Sis. Really. I'm fine."

"Where have you been, Tevy? And what was…that?" She waved where, seconds ago, a tan and gray wolf had stood.

"That," he said with a grin, "was me!"

"You?"

The wolves howling quieted, but there was so much chaos Rianthe couldn't think straight. Raisa thrust a pair of pants and a shirt into Tevy's hands. Once he pulled them on, Rianthe herded Tevy into the dining hall and sat him down on a bench. She sat opposite him. The rest of the town filed in and circled around them.

Rianthe took a deep breath. "How about we start from the beginning?"

"Well," Tevy said. "On the day I was born—"

"Not that far back."

"But that's where the story begins. Just let me finish, Sis. Geesh, you're impatient."

"You've been gone for weeks. We didn't know where you were, if someone had taken you. We didn't—" Her voice broke. "We didn't even know if you were alive."

Tevy teared up. "I'm sorry for that, Sis. Really, I am. I've got to tell the story from the beginning so you'll understand."

"Okay," Rianthe said. She nodded and ratcheted down her impatience.

"Our mother died at the moment I was born," Tevy started. "I know now that something happened at that moment. Something special."

How could anything special have come from the horror of that day except for Tevy? He was the only blessing.

"You know how you went through your True-Naming and were supposed to come into your power then?"

She nodded.

"Well, when Mom died during my birth, some of her powers passed to me."

This was news to Rianthe. "How do you know that?"

Roulf sat beside Tevy. "I've heard of this. A long, long time ago, back before the Great Magic War, it was said that if someone imbued with magic passed in the process of birthing, some of that power transferred to the newling."

Tevy's head bobbed up and down. "I'm still six years from my True-Naming. Six years! Yet, I've come into my powers now."

Rianthe heard the awe in his voice. Her own mind was filled with wonder. Her Tevy had come into his power organically?

"I can shift-change, Sis."

"What?" Rianthe wanted to dispute what Tevy had said, but since she'd seen it with her own eyes, she merely shook her head.

"I can change into a wolf. Want to see?"

He yanked off his clothes and, once again, the air around him shimmered. There, before her, was the same tan and gray wolf she'd seen earlier. He trotted over to her and nudged her knee with his nose until she ran her hands along his fur. Tevy the wolf leaned into her, a happy, tongue-lolling grin on his muzzle.

Rianthe couldn't wrap her head around it. "This makes no sense. How can you change like this? I've never heard of this happening." She looked at Roulf. "Is this what you do?"

He shook his head. "No, child. I can only mimic, apply a façade to fool people. This"—he reached over to scratch Tevy's ears—"is the real deal. It's new to me, also. You never know how Earth's magic will affect someone. It's always been thought that it enhanced a natural ability or tendency."

Tevy shimmered back to himself, redressed, and sat by Rianthe, returning her hug as she pulled him in tight. "Are you disappointed in me, Sis?"

"Disappointed? How could you ever think that? I've never once felt that way about you. Not now, not ever." She searched the faces of the people around them who'd listened to Tevy's story. Saw the happiness on their faces. The acceptance. When she turned back to Tevy, he looked worried. "Look around," she said. "Everyone accepts you. You have become who you were meant to be, little brother. We are all happy for you. Me, especially." She rubbed the top of his head.

Tevy ducked down. "Ah, Sis." He sat back down across from her.

"So you ran off to go through this…metamorphosis by yourself?"

He nodded. "I was crazy out of my head."

"That does explain some things. You were pretty down and uncommunicative before you left."

"I didn't know what was happening. All these feelings were inside me. And pain. I hurt all over. I had to get away, to figure this out. I needed to be somewhere where I wouldn't hurt anybody."

"You thought you might hurt someone?"

"I only knew that I was changing somehow. Until I figured out what was happening, I needed to follow that road by myself."

"You couldn't have told me you were going?"

"You wouldn't have let me go," he said.

He was absolutely correct. She'd have tied him down if that's what it took to keep him in New Hope. "You're right. I wouldn't have."

"See? So I ran. And ran and ran. I don't even know where I ended up. By then, the pain had become almost unbearable."

"I hate that you went through that by yourself."

"I wasn't alone. At least, not for long." Tevy smiled. "My brothers found me. They seemed to know more than I did. They huddled around me, kept me warm and safe until my transition was complete."

Rianthe crossed the space between the benches to grasp Tevy's hands. "I'm glad they were there for you."

We are his family, Taschia mind-spoke.

We are all his family, Rianthe answered.

Yes. You are all my family, Tevy said.

"It was so cool, when I first changed. Well, not at first. It was still painful. It took a while before shifting didn't hurt anymore. I can't believe how much farther I can see, how much better I can hear! You'd be amazed at wolves' senses. As a wolf, I'm happy. I feel like I really belong now."

"I thought you were happy as a human, Tevy."

"I was. I am! I have the best of both worlds. I can be with you and with the wolves. It's awesome!"

A chuckle rumbled through the gathering. Rianthe looked at all the smiling faces and saw the same joy in them that Tevy felt. That she felt.

She stood, bringing Tevy with her, squeezing him tight. "I'm glad you're all right. I'm glad you've found your *awen*. But most of all, little brother, I'm glad your family has grown."

"Me, too, Sis."

"However—"

Rianthe almost laughed at the concern on his face.

"No shifting willy-nilly. No running off with your brethren without telling anyone. And, you still have human chores to get through each day, as well as Studies with Anniah. And you will eat human food."

Tevy nodded his head so vehemently, Rianthe was afraid it would nod right off. Outside, the other wolves howled their happiness.

New Hope had always been *wunjo*, a magic-accepting town where they lived in harmony. Bhren had designed it that way, supposedly to help Rianthe bring back the full power of the *awen* and heal Earth.

Maybe, he just hadn't realized how accepting they'd become. Or had he? Rianthe remembered all the afternoons she'd spent in his tower room, pouring through tomes, learning to read, write, and to understand history.

Beyond the books and the table in the middle, the room had been devoid of embellishment or art. Except... Rianthe tried to remember. There had been one thing. A painting. No, a carved skin, like the ones Tevy made. Right by the top of the stairs.

Of a wolf.

~~~

Kaiden found her later that day in their spot. The promontory overlooking the lake. It was so good to be home. To be back in New Hope. With her. And free of the dark thoughts that had invaded his mind for too long.

He climbed the rock wall and joined her as she stood looking out over the water, her gloved hands holding her cloak tightly closed.

"It's good to be home," she said.

"It's good to be here with you."

Rianthe smiled up at him, a genuine smile with no hidden agenda. Kaiden beamed back, pulling her to his side.

Together, they watched the water ripple as a fish jumped.

Together, they made a silent vow to bring this peace to the world. To find a way to be with each other.

Together.

The End
~~~

Thank you for reading **Enlightenment**, the second book of the Earth Legacy series. **Birthright**, the final story, is the culmination of everything Rianthe and Kaiden have learned in order to take on Taegar, the Dark druid bent on binding Earth's magic to her will. If you enjoyed this book, please consider leaving a review wherever you prefer, and know that it would be greatly appreciated.

For new release information and news about Laurie Ryan, please join her newsletter. More information can be found at laurieryanauthor.com

AUTHOR'S NOTE AND ACKNOWLEDGEMENTS

Middle books are not easy to write, and this one was no exception. In order for Kaiden to recognize his worth, he had to go to a very dark place. I have to say, parts of this story weren't fun to write. I can only hope that I paid homage to Valor, as he was pivotal in helping Kaiden Darcy become the man he was meant to be.

As always, it took a village to get this book to print. Lavada, Faye, thank you so much for your unwavering assistance, critiquing, letting me cry on your shoulders, and supporting me throughout. To my editor, Libby, you're the best! Thank you, thank you, thank you! To my beta readers, Kathy and Alaina, and to my fans, thank you for your support and for giving me a reason to write.

I strove to pay homage to druid beliefs in this story because of their unfailing respect for nature. While most of the terms in this story are runic in nature, I chose the druid term *awen* to represent Earth's magic. It translates as something like flowing spirit or inspiration and felt completely right for this series, which is all about listening to the earth as it tries to help us all to survive.

I believe we are near the point where drastic changes will be needed to ensure the continued existence of future generations. This story, this series, comes out of that belief. I hope you enjoyed it.

Thank you.

BOOKLIST

Contemporary romance stories by Laurie Ryan

Fantasy by Laurie Ryan

Survival
Enlightenment
Birthright

Tropical Persuasions Series
Stolen Treasures
Pirate's Promise
Dare To Love

Standalone

Northern Lights
Healing Love
(also part of the Holiday Magic anthology)
Lost and Found

Women's Fiction by Laurie Ryan

Show Me

ABOUT THE AUTHOR

Laurie Ryan writes fantasy and contemporary romance. Growing up a devoted reader, Laurie Ryan immersed herself in the diverse works of authors like Tolkien and Woodiwiss. She is passionate about every aspect of a book: beginning, middle, and end. She can't arrive to a movie five minutes late, has never been able to read the end of a book before the beginning, and is a strong believer in reading the book before seeing the movie.

Laurie lives in the beautiful Pacific Northwest, in the shadow of Mt. Rainier and a short drive to beach-walking next to the Pacific Ocean, with her handsome, he-can-fix-anything husband and their gray, seventeen-pound cat, Dude.

www.laurieryanauthor.com

Turn the page for a sneak peek at the final story in the Earth Legacy series.

BIRTHRIGHT

Earth Legacy Book 3

Prologue

Taegar thrust her hands into the stream of light that emanated from the floor. Power infused her. Strong, heady power. This was what she wanted. This was her destiny. Boundless power. She swelled with it, let it lift her from the ground as she consumed it like sacred sustenance. She floated there, almost incorporeal, awash in Earth's *awen*, the magic she coveted beyond anything else.

Regretfully, Taegar removed her hand. While stronger than the magic in her cave, the magic here seemed stifled as well. Until she possessed the complete rune set, she must remain patient. That talisman, designed to keep her from magic rightfully hers, must be found. Her golden eyes brightened as she glared at the stones. So many, yet so few. Several were missing, held by her enemy, Rianthe Royan. Daughter to those who'd scorned her all those years ago.

The overland trip to this cave, her first travel of any kind in many, many years, had depleted most of her power. So little remained of her body—the one she'd been born with more than one hundred and twenty years ago—that she could only move with the aid of magic. But the risk had worked in her favor, for she was born anew in this place that Damian and Valena Royan thought to hide from her. There could be no hiding. As soon as she ripped the remaining runes from that girl's lifeless body and released the limitless magic Earth had hidden away, she would bind it to herself for all time. She would be unbeatable. She was nearly that now.

And it felt very, very good.

"I am Taegar," she said to the empty cave. "I am the *isa*, that which provides clarity to the world and bends it to my righteous path. I am *thurisaz*, creator of chaos, and *tiwaz*, ruler of all. I *am* the Dark circle."

Things were coming to a head. Soon, she would confront the one who stood between her and her destiny. Soon, she would have what she needed to complete her metamorphosis from Dark druid to immortal god. She would have everything she'd waited for all these years.

Very, very soon.

* 9 7 8 0 9 9 9 9 5 9 7 7 4 3 *